More Praise for *Shipwrecks*

The people of the worlds Jerry D. Mathes creates inhabit the roughest edges of the American dream, understanding more than most that "no matter how hard a person worked or loved, failure had its own ways." This collection carries us through the heartrending realities of those rough edges, from the slick deck of the fishing trawler, to the repo man on the streets of LA, to the isolated hunter kneeling on the deep green floor of the spruce and pine woods in rural Idaho, even into the learn-it-early heartbreak and hope of the boy who sees, once again, that his name is not there, no matter how he searches the Little League roster. These are people who know and understand intimately both the beauty and brutality of bad weather. These lives, fraught with longing and loss, poverty and adultery, death and disappointment, in Mathes' gifted hands, become testaments to the persistence of the human heart, even as we are constantly tossed on relentless waves, spiraling between grief and transcendence, so beautifully detailed in the title story, with "every day dawning as unpredictable as lightning." Mathes' lyric and carefully crafted prose balances both his characters and us as readers perfectly between the poetry and pain of living hard lives in hard times. But always, like that faint light in the distance that shows us all the way home, there is hope, the hope that lets us never give up on each other, or on this miraculous life. Jerry Mathes is a visionary chronicler of wounded souls, people who know that "blood and seawater tasted the same," of those for whom surviving daily with their dreams intact is the greatest victory, of the human trek from rock bottom to redemption as the truest nobility. This collection will haunt you, follow you, call to you from the ash-gray wind, like the distant voice of the fisherman, who, even while drawing in empty net after empty net, somehow finds a way to keep on singing.

—Mary Carroll-Hackett, Author of
The Night I Heard Everything, and *A Little Blood, A Little Rain*

"Jerry Mathes II is a writer from the immersion school of fiction. This story collection was not assembled in a writing workshop or fine arts program, but crafted by a wordsmith who traveled the nation with a steady pen in hand and a keen eye on the human condition. Winners, losers, unlikely heroes and tragic dreamers populate his stories like figures woven into an epic tapestry. His characters are the people we fear in real life because they remind us too much of ourselves. Mathes' fiction shows us that even the lowliest serfs possess a nobility that vanquish the most regal of kings."

—Tom Reynolds, Author of *Wild Ride: How Outlaw Motorcycle Myth Conquered America.*

Shipwrecks and Other Stories is a point-on evocation of the American West as it slides from the twentieth century into the twenty-first. From the Alaskan fishing harvest to the Sonoran desert to the glitz of Las Vegas, Jerry Mathes depicts the violence, the anger, the heartbreak, and the beautiful compassion with which his men and women of the West live their lives.

—Mary Clearman Blew
Author of *All But the Waltz* and *Jackalope Dreams*

Shipwrecks and Other Stories is chock-full of rough lives and hard times, yet these stories are laced with hope and threaded through with moments of grace. With his intimate knowledge of the natural world, from the desert to the sea, Mathes creates vivid settings, sometimes malevolent, sometimes benign, but always a presence to be reckoned with. Like Stephen Crane and Raymond Carver before him, Mathes shines the harsh light of realism on the daily conflicts, large and small, that define his characters' fears and desires and, often, determine their very survival.

—Kim Barnes
Author of *In the Kingdom of Men* and *In the Wilderness*

SHIPWRECKS
AND OTHER STORIES

SHIPWRECKS
AND OTHER STORIES

JERRY D. MATHES II

Stephen F. Austin State University Press

For more information:
Stephen F. Austin State University Press
P.O. Box 13007 SFA Station
Nacogdoches, Texas 75962
sfapress@sfasu.edu
www.sfasu.edu/sfapress

Book design: Shaina Hawkins
Cover design: Shaina Hawkins
Distributed by Texas A&M Consortium
www.tamupress.com

LIBRARY OF CONGRESS CATALOGING-IN-PUBLICATION DATA
Mathes, Jerry D. II
Shipwrecks and Other Stories/Jerry D. Mathes II

ISBN: 978-1-62288-133-8

'As always, to the Girl Posse'

STORIES FIRST APPEARED

Still Life. Winner of the Meadow Novella Prize, 2015.

"Helpless in the Hands of Strangers." Finalist in Narrative Spring Story Contest, 2011.

"Repossession." Finalist in Narrative Winter Story Contest, 2011. (2011).

"Drinking Sangria in the Cold War: 1988." Finalist in *Narrative* Fall Story Contest, 2010. This story was developed into a short film by SFA Productions.

"Still Life." Narrative. Finalist in *Narrative* Spring Story Contest, 2010. (2010): Nominated for a Pushcart Prize.

"Birth of the Hippo." *Narrative*. Finalist in *Narrative* Fall Fiction Contest, 2009. (2010): Notable Story in the anthology *Best of the West* and Nominated for a Pushcart Prize.

"In the River's Mouth." *The Platte Valley Review*. (2010): Nominated for a Pushcart Prize.

"An Unusual Snow." *The Dos Passos Review*. (2009).

Red Flag Warning (novel excerpt). *Narrative*. Finalist in *Narrative* Fall Fiction Contest. (2008).

"A Hunter's Story." *Shenandoah*. (Fall 2008): Nominated for a Pushcart Prize. Finalist for the Obsidian Prize.

"Looking for the Mule." *Grist: The Journal for Writers*. (2008): Special Mention in *Pushcart Prize XXXIV*.

"Shipwrecks." *The Dos Passos Review*. (2005): Special Mention in *Pushcart Prize Anthology XXXI*.

"Between the Grass and the Dirt." *Talking River Review*. (2003).

TABLE OF CONTENTS

SHIPWRECKS

My wife always threatens me with homicide. Before
dinner, Rosalina dices some tomatoes and aims the twelve-
inch chef's knife at me. She exaggerates her Spanglish,
even though she is fluent in English and Spanish, as she
says, "Mira, Kurt, mi auntie killed her trouble making
husband muerto, con un knife también." The blade reflects
gold from the stove's flames, like the crucifix around her
neck. It is just as true that her grandmother had shot
a lover, not for cheating, but for drinking without her,
although he lived to limp about it. I laugh with her at the
benign threats; after all, for her, I found an onshore job
at Micron and quit the sea, except for Sea World and the
odd visits to a beach with the kids. I still love the ocean:
water breaking over the wheelhouse the color of a bad
thunderstorm, bright days with the ocean as flat as slate,
and dolphins running the bow wake. Every day dawning as
unpredictable as lightning.

* * * *

Five years before, a big storm had blown up the Gulf
of Alaska; gale force winds rolled forty-foot swells from
open water. Waves beat us. Each time we quartered up a
swell, the side-rail dipped into the sea, and as we crested,
the boat yawed, clearing the deck, before the opposite side
sliced the surface, like a rocking sluice box. I understood
batten down the hatches. Three deckhands and I rode out
most of the storm in our bunks, up front in the fo'c's'le,

two to a side, angled into the bow. The skipper piloted
the *Judith Marie* for Metlakatla. Our hold brimmed with
halibut and ice. We had done well and planned to run to
Bellingham, trying to be the first long-liner to the lower
Forty-eight. The fifty-foot boat had a rough time rounding
Dixon Entrance, past the southern tip of Prince of Wales
Island in Southeast Alaska. The Inside Passage was a
tough go, but easier than the open gulf.

After rounding the cape, mid-afternoon, we got a
mayday call, woman who said her bow-picker, the *Salmon
Chaser*, was taking on water, "in need of immediate
assistance." The skipper called us up from below, told us
to be ready. I rolled over in the top bunk as Malibu Carrie
and Liz pried themselves out of the bottom bunks, one
at a time, into the cramped area. The space between the
bunks had the floor space of a pup tent, allowing only one
person at a time to dress. Malibu Carrie's thin tan lines
reflected the dim light as she slipped into her sweats. Liz
had no tan lines, confident that her pale body, in the event
of shipwreck, could be useful as a rescue beacon. Malibu
Carrie played volleyball for Pepperdine, majoring in
political science and cocktail mixing. Whenever we docked
at a town, admirers never failed to crowd the cleats to help
tie us off. She knew the politics of beauty and suffered
for that knowledge. Fishermen and cannery workers
bought her drinks and she danced, but before closing
time she'd slip back to the boat alone, and drink Gatorade
while reading US News and World Report or a president's
biography. She had been working on one about Jefferson.

Liz discovered the sea after a ten-year marriage and
two-year divorce, which she lost. She walked out of the
Omaha courthouse and thumbed rides up the AL-CAN
Highway until she hit Homer. Her first summer she tended
bar at the *Salty Dog* on the spit in Homer and spent the
winter in the interior tending a trap-line, alone. Snowshoes

carried her miles along creeks and through spruce forests. The silence was as overwhelming as the cold. She learned the art of solitary talking and quieted the chatter of a modern childhood, a mind of constant background noise, while she scrapped hides. By spring break-up, when great sheaves of ice broke and slid down river and snowmelt left bogs and mires, she had revised the necessary elements of herself—found she had lost nothing in Omaha.

When they cleared out, Mitch—the women called him Mitch the Bitch because he was gay—climbed down from the starboard bunk, hairless, stretch marks and spidery veins etched his gut like a ship's rigging. He fished herring in the spring, and then made the run from San Francisco to Norton Sound, gillnetted Bristol Bay salmon until August, and long-lined for halibut in the late summer. He made enough money to stay stoned, play the mandolin, and write poetry all winter. Sometimes, he'd leave and fly to New York so he could play his mandolin in the subway. When I first walked the docks, asking about a job, I didn't realize I'd be asking to camp with total strangers. Last on the ladder of experience, I dressed and made my way up.

Close, we beat into the irons to the floundering boat's lat. and long. Wind and waves rocked us hard. We wedged ourselves in the wheelhouse with our slickers on, gathered like monks in orange, leaning together in a cell. I dozed and woke, trying to keep upright. We sweated, confined in rain gear next to the oil stove, moist and hot like a jungle. The rugged island bobbed out the window a league and a half away, as if we were the island, and it a ship with its forest of masts hung with the heavy canvas of clouds and fog.

The skipper called down when he sighted her, and we got onto deck and hung on. We spread down the portside with ropes and dropped the bumper buoys. The skipper motored alongside the *Salmon Chaser* as close as he could and tried to keep her in our lee. I could see the swamped thirty-footer; three people waded in the cockpit up to their thighs. We bobbed high and low next to each other on the swells and troughs. The wind roared against the back of my hood as the boat pitched. The tops of waves sheared off and shot-gunned us with pellets of saltwater and rain.

Malibu Carrie yelled, "Treadwell, throw your fucking line when they pass close to us." I timed the swells, clenched and unclenched my hands, then heaved. The rope uncoiled and carried the line over the floundering boat. A deckhand grabbed the line and pulled. We crashed together. The aluminum of their boat bounced against the bumper buoys and screeched against our steel hull. The terrible racket rattled the wind like a thousand screaming gulls. The deckhand passed the line to another guy and he jumped onboard our boat. I couldn't hear when the last man turned and yelled at the woman, but she left the wheel, grabbed the line. He jumped onboard, turned, and thrust his hand out, expecting hers, but she was back at the wheel. She brushed brown hair out of her mouth; it caught the wind like streamers. Rain blew back over her colorless face. She mouthed the words, exaggerated in slow motion, like stretched videotape: I'M STAYING. I'M SAVING THE BOAT.

The man screamed. I couldn't make out his words. His arms thrust to her, but she had already heeled the vessel around. A wave smashed her, and its force combined with the weight of the water she carried, cracked the boat across the chime, the two halves sank. Fast. The man tried to throw himself over, but Mitch grabbed him around the waist and pinned him against the gun'le. We searched for hours, other boats joined us, and the Coast Guard flew their orange and white birds, divers ready to cast themselves into the sea. Some debris floated to the surface, but no sign of her. The storm ended.

After that season, I went to Boise to visit my brother,

a high school math teacher, and I met Rosalina and decided to stay awhile. I sat in a bar, talking to a skinny drunk. His nose arched over his pinched face like a bloodshot mound. As conversations went, he wanted to know what I did.

"I fish," I said. I hadn't made up my mind if I was going back out or not, but I didn't know how to do anything else except maybe wash dishes or deliver pizza.

He said, "I build boats." He talked about his great project in his backyard and wanted to show it to somebody who knew the sea.

I thought of the *Salmon Chaser*. I pictured the woman, brown hair flowing away from her face, still gripping the wheel, never relenting under the freight of heavy water. I knew the sea.

My then girlfriend, Rosalina, her heavy, black hair hung braided down to the small of her back, had a game of darts going with a bigheaded horse-shoer from the track. He led with his steak-fed belly, causing his darts to fly low. Rosalina was all strength and tits in a black tank top. A tattoo of a cutthroat trout chased a fly across the river of brown skin on her shoulder blade. She was hard from field labor, livestock, and wading spring runoff. Her brass darts streaked into the board, shining like pyrite in bar light. The shoer was twenty bucks down to her, and in ten points, it would be thirty. What the hell, I couldn't have thought of a better time to call last game.

I waved the bartender over, to buy a six-pack to go.

The strung-out Italian's eyes twitched. "You go to see the boat? That guy is a loony, you should no get involved."

"Don't worry, Lou, I don't want any part of a boat. They sink."

He blinked and rubbed his hands together as if they itched. "That's a right. Remember, watch out for that a woman you with. Senorita Margarita, she'll stab you. She's got the fire." Ill-defined muscles, covered with skin like crepe paper, were taut against his skeleton. "I mean it. I married me a Mexican wife, and she a cut me good. You want to see?"

"No thanks."

He pulled the snaps of his shirt anyway, revealing a long ragged scar that arced from his rib cage to his navel.

"Well, damn, Lou, that wound looks like Mexico. She did brand you as hers." I said, picking up the beer. "She left off Baja, though." Rosalina had asked me a couple of days before if I wanted to get married and I had said sure. I knew Lou exaggerated everything, but I figured if she was willing to stab me, then she must love me.

We walked through a light rain. The scent of sage and cheat grass rolled down the dark hills and silicate in the sand shined in the gutters like herring scales knocked loose on the deck. A misty night, drops speckling my face, reminded me of being onboard a boat—a long night haul, after a poor run, and the wheelhouse swayed, overheated, humid, and bitter coffee mixed with the smell of lost fish; no one talked, and I ducked out to stand in the cockpit in the rain and shiver, listening to the sea, realizing that if I fell into the luminous plankton, plowed up in the wake, no one would know until my watch came due.

He led us through a wooden gate and flicked on floodlights. On the grass sat a capsized, sixty-foot skeleton built of two inch steel tubing, about four feet across the beam. A heavy-duty jungle gym; a monumental work of angles, measurements and cuts, beads, grinding, and sweat in heavy leathers under a welding hood, and although I knew nothing about ship building, I knew a violation of displacement when I saw it, that ratio between space and mass keeping boats and ships floating on the water's surface. With so much steel, he had built an anchor with deck space. We each opened a beer.

I didn't know what to say to the guy: "Break it apart and make it bigger," or "It's a fine lawn ornament." He looked at us and licked his lips.

Rosalina walked around the end of it, skirting a large pile of scrap metal mixed with beer cans. "You do this all yourself?"

"Yeah."

"You have kids? I bet you, they love this."

He shrugged. "They love it, when they're here."

Rain beaded on the steel's oiled surface. "I want to stay at sea for years, put enough stuff on her for months. I'm building her to hit a reef and keep on going. You know, stout. Five-eighths steel plate on the exterior and quarter inch on the interior. Real stout."

I thought about 250-foot trawlers disappearing in the furious Bering, 100-foot tenders hitting the rocks, bleeding diesel and oil and 50-foot fishing vessels rolling against the shore like dying whales. The continent's edge is a hard place, and beyond, a vacuum of disappearing. I knew I couldn't tell him that unsinkable ships don't exist. "You been to sea?"

"No, but that don't matter none. I studied it in books, and I got the engineering down. I got faith she'll float. Hold on," he said and went into his house.

Rosalina said, "That little man's going to die on this thing."

I smiled and raised my can. "Salud, chica." The boat would never float. It'd slide off the trailer straight under the water or he would weld until nothing remained unfused and the whole of what he created would become clear—he'd die all right.

He returned carrying a coffee-table book, trying to open it and not spill his beer. "See, this is what I'm shooting for." The picture covered two pages, a Polynesian canoe with an outrigger. A thatch awning straddled

amidships, and the mast was stepped in the center of
it. Chickens huddled in the bow, and several islanders,
wearing grass and feathers, did chores. "Those boys sailed
all over in these. Mine's going to be steel and use tandem
diesels, and you can see that I still need to fabricate
the outrigger, but it's the same design. Been used for
thousands of years. It's all right here in the book."

I tilted my beer back, and then crumpled the can,
before pitching it into his scrap pile. The Oregon coast
lay five hundred or so miles to the west and over four
thousand feet down. All I could think of to say was,
"You're a long way from the ocean."

He said, "The ocean will come to me."

Dazed, I remembered the wicked scream of a
husband watching his wife yell her last windswept words,
a siren's voice, calling the lost, and the left behind— him
wrapped in the arms of another man holding him back.
A husband, who would forever love the myth of his
lost marriage, knowing that the risk of losing her was
the greatest risk he had taken and lost. Rosalina leaned
forward, peered into the wreck of iron. The darkness.
Her gold crucifix dangled away from her chest, swinging
between shadow and light. I thought about the skinny
welder standing in the rain, balancing his book and beer
and the fisherman struggling on a slick deck. Two men
with everything they had invested in the sea, and boats
that would never sail, muttering about misplaced faith,
waiting for the end and the long wasting of failure. And
I'd find myself tangled with them, all of us faithful to
death, searching blind for the sea.

* * * *

Rosalina's knife chitters against the cutting board's grain
as she dices peppers. I wonder what happened to my old
crew. We strangers came together, binding our fate to fish
and the sea, and learned each other's stories and what

we thought our futures would be and, finally, parting,
becoming the story. They would probably never believe I
had settled down, after making fun of my brother's settled
life—college, teaching, married, two-point something kids,
and debt. I am still the kind of guy who walks out into
bad weather, eyeing the lightning, but I don't skirt fringes
anymore, and not because Rosalina would stab my body
if it washed up somewhere. I had to risk loss like that
fisherman five years ago and invest my life in a wife and
children with all that can break it apart like rough surf—
the stable life is like waiting for a shipwreck, always a
sudden storm away and out of control. I fell for Rosalina,
and the night we met the boat-builder, I knew I'd have to
chance the sea wouldn't reach Boise.

BIRTH OF THE HIPPO

The first night Tracy Jane sneaked into the municipal
pool she feared being seen in her swimsuit. She felt it
looked like a spinnaker in a gale. The temperature hovered
in the nineties, and she was sweating. She winced at the
rattle of the chain on the gate, her great shadow cast
under the moonlight, and the splash as she lowered her
bulk into the dark water. The late travelers' thrum of
tires and car engines from the highway and the occasional
dog barking at imagined trespassers broke the stillness.
After she slid in, she went under, spun to the bottom,
and pushed her body up, a dried leaf on the current. She
twirled and rolled and felt ease slip into her burdened
joints, released from gravity's awkwardness into the cradle
of the water. She became transfigured into a swallow in
flight, or as she said to herself: a hippo in the rainy season.
On the National Geographic Channel she had
watched a documentary on the hippopotamus, and the
British narrator said the hippo shed its tedious bulk in
the water and became as graceful as any gazelle on land.
She sat up in her bed and turned up the volume, watching
the lumbering beasts walk along the bottom of a river
or lake as if they were skipping on the moon. After she
clicked off the television, she lay back into her pillows and
wondered at the feeling. How many people had called her
a hippo or a sea cow or a walrus? Too many to remember,
but none, she guessed, ever thought of the grace hidden

in each of those animals—or the danger, for that matter. It amazed her to learn that the hippo killed more people than any other animal in Africa. Among all those large predators and venomous snakes and flesh-eating insects, a fat herbivore was the killer elite. Probably, she reasoned, humans took her for granted because of her girth. Tracy Jane slept and dreamed of water.

The next afternoon before work she parked her Escort down the block and strolled by the local pool. It was at the edge of a residential neighborhood by the high school, and the back end faced out into the desert. The Complex, as the locals called it, was actually two pools: one with a water jungle gym, painted in bright primary colors, constructed of slides, spouting dolphins, and bars and platforms for little kids, and the other a large lap pool with high and low diving boards on one end. Lifeguards in red trunks or one-piece suits sat high on their perches or patrolled the edges of the pool with silver whistles clamped between their lips. Tracy Jane watched the children splashing and playing in the kid section with moms and dads reclining on the lounge chairs or wading close by. Some people lined up at the diving boards, each trying to outdo the last. In the far corner were some local college girls with boyfriends, reading, gossiping, and occasionally getting up and taking careful steps, wary of any sudden movement that might dislodge their slight bikinis. Tracy Jane remembered what it was like swimming as a kid and longed for it as she watched, but she didn't want to enter the crowded water. On the playa the penitentiary stood in the distance like a medieval walled city with one road in and a desolated kill zone around it.

That afternoon she went to work at the local pizzeria in the corner of the mall. It was a small place with a few tables for dining in, but they did a brisk evening business in takeout and delivery. Her station was in front next to the windows, where people could watch her shape, twirl, and sauce pizza dough from the sidewalk and from the customer waiting area that let out into the mall. Every day the boss, Andy, his grin creasing his round, flushed face, would squeeze her shoulder and say, "How's the slapper in chief?" A title she earned because she was the fastest in the region, with three large pepperonis in fifty-five seconds. She could toss the dough, keep it spinning in the air, and twirl it on her finger, but she couldn't do the acrobatics that the kids always wanted because she couldn't pass behind her back or between her legs. Practicing was out of the question in the public eye, so she kept her head down and kneaded, shaped, and slapped the dough in a spray of cornmeal as fast as she could. She tried not to look up when the cowbell on the door clanged. Every couple of evenings a high school boy stared at her through the window with his cheeks puffed out, his long greasy hair framing his acne-covered face. Sometimes he had a friend who mimicked waddling, then they'd laugh and point, run down the sidewalk, the concert dates on the backs of their T-shirts fading away. She wondered how long they waited before she noticed them.

The delivery drivers were high school and college kids who helped top the pizzas before rushing out with food, sodas, and hopes for tips. A mousy teenage girl took orders or leaned against the phone counter playing with her hair when it was slow. Usually by 10:00 p.m. it was only Andy, Tracy Jane, and a driver, who spent most of his time in the back cleaning and washing dishes for closing, folding boxes, or sneaking out back for a smoke.

Her clothes clung to her in the heat of the restaurant, and on her breaks she stepped out back, hoping for a desert breeze. At 11:00 p.m. a couple of nights a week two cops stopped by on their lunch and ordered a pizza. Enrique always said something nice to Tracy Jane. She found him attractive—dark hair and eyes, smooth skin, and it was obvious he worked out. He leaned against the Plexiglas. "You have the fastest hands I ever did see."

Tracy Jane blushed, and she lost her rhythm.

"Look now, I bet you could work magic with those hands. What's that called when the hand's faster than the eye?"

"Sleight of hand, Enrique," his partner, Wally, said. Wally was thinner and taller, with a shock of blond hair that came down to wire-rimmed glasses.

"Yeah, that's it. You ever see such fast hands, Wally?"

"Only on a cardsharp."

They both laughed and went to their table.

Andy sidled up to her. "I think the Mexican one likes you."

She wrinkled her nose. "He's just being nice. Not all cops act like dicks."

Andy was a larger man, and it made her uncomfortable when he leaned in close to her like he was sharing a secret. His breath smelled of the green peppers, jalapeños, and sausage that he ate on his pizzas. "Suit yourself, but I know an interested guy when I see one."

Later that night, when they were dropping the money in the night bank deposit, she saw Enrique and Wally parked in the Safeway parking lot. Enrique turned on his roller lights and shut them off as he waved out the window. She waved back.

Andy chuckled, "Yessiree, that's an interested boy. Mexican boys like the larger ladies, you know."

She didn't say anything. Just 'cause he was fat and doughy didn't mean he could talk about her weight, and she didn't like how he talked about Enrique or made Mexicans sound like taco pizzas. Tracy Jane thought about what Andy had said. Enrique seemed to be interested in her, but her experience had taught her that only desperate men had sex with her, and then they disappeared. Usually they wanted to do the kinkiest things right away, like she was a star in a porno flick, and she wondered at their raw need to possess her in that way. The desperation caught in their voices as if she were fulfilling a dying request. She didn't mind the wild and perverse sex because when the men heaved their last sigh it exhilarated her. But what she disliked was being alone again after the grabbing up of clothes accompanied by hurried excuses. One guy had said he needed to get on the road so he could visit his sick mother in Nogales. In the vacuum of their leaving she wondered what she needed to do to keep a man, a boyfriend. Over the past couple of years she had drifted away from men, preferring to be alone but still desiring the searching hands not her own.

The next evening Tracy Jane had her head down, kneading dough, when the cowbell clanged, followed by a cacophony of female voices.

"Oh, my gosh, that is fast."

Tracy Jane looked up and saw the swim team: some tall and svelte, some short and skinny, and some more like weight lifters, with broad shoulders and thick thighs. They all had the tops of their sweatpants rolled down below the twin pinnacles of their hip bones. The one who had spoken had her ponytail pulled back so tight each strand of hair on her head looked to be under high tension. After a few cursory glances at Tracy Jane's pizza making they went back to cell phones and chatting. Tracy Jane overheard one saying, "Can you believe Angie makes us dummy-lock the gate? Some kid stuffed gum down the padlock 'cause Liza left it out. You believe that?"

"No way. What good's that?" another asked.

"Appearances," she said. "That's all." Tracy Jane looked up and recognized her as one of the lifeguards.

A slam on the window caused her to jump and

silenced the swimmers. She looked up, and the kid with
the greasy hair and acne was blowing his cheeks out, his
right hand pressing a sticker onto the glass.

"That little bastard," Andy said as he made for the
door.

"How rude," one of the swimmers said while another
giggled.

Tracy Jane brushed her hands on her apron and
examined the sticker. It was a cartoon of a chubby woman
inside a red circle with a red slash across her and the words
No Fat Chicks in jagged letters at her feet. Tracy Jane went
into the back and sat in the bathroom. She couldn't figure
why someone would go to so much trouble to make her
feel worthless, like all those years in high school when
bands of kids scrawled cow on her locker or made mooing
sounds in the cafeteria or the parents pointed at her and
cautioned their skinny kids about overeating.

Andy knocked on the door. "We got orders."

Tracy Jane wiped the corners of her eyes and read the
Employees Must Wash Their Hands sign in English and
Spanish for the millionth time. Next to it was a laminated
poster informing her of her right to work in a harassment-
free environment. Staring out at her were three beautiful
and thin women in front of an American flag.

Andy tapped. "I scraped the sticker off."

She sighed and gathered herself to do what was
expected of her. When she had come home crying as a
girl, her mother always brushed her hair and said, "Blow it
off and move on."

That night after work she cruised by the pool. It was a
gloomy fortress with its chain-link fence and the concrete
pillboxes at the gate where people paid admission.
Moonlight glinted off the water, and Tracy Jane thought
it serene and peaceful after the chaos of the day. The light
over the deep end was burned out. Shadows from the

diving boards and the snack shack darkened the water.
The kids' jungle gym looked like a blackened skeleton of
a ship washed onto a beach. She eased up to the gate and
checked the lock. Sure enough, it was not latched. Out
by the foothills of the mountains the prison glowed. The
sodium lights surrounded by the dark space of the desert
made it look like it was floating free of the earth, a strange
galactic body.

She jumped when the headlights swept her as she
backed away from the gate. She pressed into the lightless
corner. It was a patrol car turning onto the street, and she
saw Enrique and Wally searching hedges with a spotlight.
They didn't notice her next to the admission booth and
drove on. She had parked her Escort a block away on a
side street.

She hurried to her car and slumped behind the wheel a
moment before starting it. She didn't have air-conditioning.
The sweat on her body made her feel sticky, and she wanted
to race home and shower. She wanted to be clean and lie
in her sheets with the soft light of the television bathing
the bed and its sound drowning out her inner monologue.
But before she pulled away from the curb, she looked back
over her shoulder toward the pool and thought of the cool
water, empty, dark and deep, and freeing.

The next morning Tracy Jane got up and went to
JCPenney in the mall and selected a swimsuit, the first
since she was a kid. She approached the racks at a slow
pace, eyeing everyone who wandered in her direction or
who looked at her as if she were approaching the adult
section in the video store. The colors were bright, and she
noticed when she finally thumbed through the sizes that
at a certain point they became one-pieces and grew larger
skirts. A clerk approached her, and Tracy Jane slipped
away and then back. She wasn't sure of the size and
thought she could buy one, take it home, and bring it back

if it didn't fit. She picked a plain brown suit and waited in line. The cashier chatted with everyone, and the more she chatted, the more Tracy Jane felt like bolting, but she hung in there, thinking of the near weightlessness of the water and how hippos shed dry weight and glided along the bottom of rivers, ponds, and lakes. She smiled at the thought of gliding.

Finally reaching the counter, she noticed the sign: NO Returns on Swimsuits.

The cashier asked, "Do you have a Penney's card, and if not, would you like one?"

Tracy Jane read the sign again but was afraid to make a scene, so she shook her head and gave the woman cash. When she tried on the suit at home it was too small. After looking at the size, she went out to a different store, dropping the new-old suit in the donation box at Goodwill.

The mall had a Ross, and she went in thinking maybe she'd find a cheaper suit so that if she again got the wrong size it wouldn't cost as much money. She couldn't bear to ask to try on a suit. The thought of undressing, dressing, undressing, and redressing in a cubicle the size of a Porta Potty made her cringe. She imagined bumping into the walls and the other women in dressing rooms rolling their eyes and wrinkling their noses at the disturbance. No, better to try it on at home and give it away.

It was after 1:00 a.m. before Enrique and Wally walked in. Tracy Jane thought they might not be coming in that night, but she looked up at the clang and saw Enrique's big smile and the sparkle of his badge and name tag. "A large double meat and a couple of Cokes," he said.

Wally drew his riot baton and sat at a table. "I'll be burping grease all night."

At the register Andy rang up a phone order. He hung up and said, "You guys running a little late. Gave you up for MIA. Missing in Antonio's." He laughed, and they grinned back.

"Their pizza maker is no match for your girl," Enrique said.

"We had a call to take care of," Wally said. "Some wannabe gangsters."

"Some white high schoolers fighting with some Latinos," Enrique said. "Bunch of jackasses in this small town causing big-city trouble."

"We don't even qualify as a little city do we?" Andy asked. "I mean, what's it take to be considered a city and then to have an inner city for that kind of problem?"

"Our inner city is the four blocks that make up Main Street," Wally said.

"My parents grew up in a village in Mexico, and there were factions," Enrique said. "There were no white people to hate, so everyone hated anyone who left for America and came back acting like big spenders, and, worst of all, everyone hated those who never came back."

Andy laughed so loud that Tracy Jane jumped. "Yessiree," he said, "that's a fine thing."

Wally looked puzzled and asked, "Do they hate the people that stayed behind now?"

"No," Enrique said, "they hate white people. It would be a sin to hate those that didn't make it. It's not humble."

Wally and Andy chuckled.

"I moved from Phoenix to get away from gang crime," Wally said. "These punks around here live in a fantasy. No idea how tough those streets really are."

"You'd think with the prison over there, it might make them think twice," Andy said.

Wally shifted in the seat and adjusted his utility belt. "Some of them kids are here because their dads are in there. No sense in it all."

When the pizza was ready, Tracy Jane cut it and took

it to the officers' table. She turned to leave, when Enrique
stopped her. "You don't say much. Maybe some night
when I'm off we can go out to dinner and a movie."

She smiled and glanced away but didn't know what to
say. She felt the words catch in the bottom of her throat,
and she shrugged. She wasn't even sure she heard him
right. Must be some joke, she thought. Why would a good-
looking, athletic man want to be seen with her? Imagining
being with him at the local multiplex thrilled her. Zit
Face wouldn't dare mess with Enrique, too afraid to take
a beating in a public place. She smiled. That would be
all right, she thought. She was about to say, "What for?"
when Andy yelled out, "We got an order for twelve pies."
She mouthed instead, "Maybe," and walked back toward
the waiting dough.

In the water Tracy Jane hid under the shadows of
the diving boards when she heard a noise in the desert
beyond the fence. A few cars and a motorcycle went by,
and she thought about people traveling at that time of the
morning. People working at all-night diners, at gas stations
and mini-marts, graveyard at the prison, the bartenders,
and soon the newspaper trucks would be rolling—the
whole culture that never saw the day like everyone else.
She'd been working swing for four years, and when her
sister or brother talked about prime-time television, she
had nothing to offer. She felt out of tune with what it was
to lead a normal life.

A week ago she had sneaked into the pool, and she'd
been back every night. The first couple of days she had
worn her suit under her work clothes, but it trapped the
heat next to her body, and the straps and elastic cut into
flesh. By the fifth night she carried the suit in her purse
and put it on under her work clothes in the bathroom
before quitting time. And by the sixth night she left the
suit at home. Beside a hedge where the pool employees

stacked the lounge chairs, tables, and umbrellas, she stripped and slid into the water naked, and even as she felt exposed and vulnerable, she also discovered a surge of adrenaline at the danger of being spotted.

Floating felt good, and her mind wandered away from the noise. She was about to come out from underneath the shadow when she noticed someone standing in the desert by the fence smoking. She felt the urge to sink and fought to keep from gasping or panicking and flailing in the water. She wondered if the person saw her, but whoever it was seemed oblivious. Maybe he was passing by or a teen hanging out away from the prying eyes of the neighborhood adults. A few minutes went by, when another person showed up. The smoker tossed down his cigarette and crushed it. Their voices whispered, and with water in her ears, Tracy Jane couldn't make out what they were saying. She recognized the silhouette of Zit Face, the sharp ridge of his nose jutting at a severe downward angle, duck wings of hair curling away from his ears and his sunken chest. At first she wasn't sure, but when he turned his face, the light glinted off his hair, and his profile was etched against the far glow of the prison lights. The two figures exchanged something and then split off in different directions.

On the way home she shivered and thought the right thing to do would be to tell Enrique and Wally, but then she'd have to explain how she had witnessed the exchange. She wondered how often those two met behind the pool. Once a week? A month?

The next night she didn't go to the pool. She went home and lay in bed, leaving the television off. In the dark she felt heavy, her sheets suffocating until she kicked them off, and then the mattress like a giant mouth closed about her.

She fluffed her pillows and lay back. Her back was sore and her hands ached. She had slapped out pizza after pizza, a busy night, but that was good because it made the time go fast. She recoiled, shivering from her tailbone to her scalp. The sourness in her stomach made her sit up, and she climbed out of bed. In the kitchen she drank some warm milk. What a sad life I have, to wish it to pass faster to death, she thought. She wished she had gone to the pool. It made her feel good and free, and she could count on one hand the number of times she had felt so good. Her life was winding through to middle age, and all she could show for it was a regional pizza record and a not-very-happy life where pieces of shit ridiculed her every other day. A waste, she thought, just to mark miserable time until you died. Who grieves the fat bachelorette when she dies at the end of an empty life? Made the time go fast until she was upon her dying day wishing it had moved a bit slower. Like a town's whole economy based on a prison, where the only product for all the dollars sucked into it was convicts.

She woke up on the floor, slumped against the couch, thirsty and sore. Emptiness, worse than the physical ache of hunger, wrenched her guts, and even as she took the antacid tablets, she knew the pain would linger. She showered and readied for work. She visualized asking Enrique out on a date and how it'd make Andy's jaw drop.

Tracy Jane floated free of the wall, gazing up into the sky. Her body undulated with the water. The new-moon night let the stars shine their brightest. Enrique and Wally hadn't come by that night. Every time the cowbell clanged she looked up from the dough or the sauce or the toppings in the stainless steel bins. Sometimes the clang caused her to lose rhythm, and she'd tear the dough or slop sauce on the counter. She considered that they didn't come by every night but hoped her anticipation at seeing him might have charged the air and brought him to her. Andy had the night off, and it struck her that she didn't even know what he did outside of work. Maybe he was taken for granted as a bookworm or video-game geek, but instead he closed down the bars hustling chumps on the pool table and stumbled home with the last woman standing. Maybe he lived an alter life as a swinger and had group sex with wild fetishes, or maybe he spent his weekends in the city getting high with hookers. She liked the idea that he had some sinister secret below his putz exterior.

Tracy Jane moved her hands in small circles at her sides. Water sloshed around her face and muffled her hearing, which made her feel sealed off. She watched her breasts, belly, and toes breaking the surface and drifted into the shallow end by the steps in the corner. The water was warm and the air still. The lip of the pool blocked her view of the desert, but the prison glowed like a fire over the horizon. Through the water she felt a vibration of a muscle car on the street. The faint smell of cigarette smoke caused her to put her feet down. The concrete bottom was rough, and even with her displaced weight the burden of her size pressured her joints. Before she started sneaking into the pool she had no idea how much pain her body caused her.

She wondered whether, if she peeped over the edge of the pool, the hedge would hide her. She smiled at the thought of the two conducting their dark business and catching the sight of her naked body floating in the pool. It might even be fun to slip up the steps, rising out of the water, screaming like the hippo she saw charge out of the water hole on television. They'd crap themselves. Two small-town punks pretending they were streetwise thugs. Serve them right. The crunching of rocks under feet stopped, and the two started whispering.

Tracy Jane crept closer to the steps. The pulse rose in her neck and beat in her temple. The metal rail was cold in her grip, and her stomach gurgled. She was going to do it but wanted to wait for a few more seconds. The smell of chlorine swirled over the water's surface. In the distance were the sounds of cars and semis motoring along the highway, covering the soft slap of water. Her flesh tightened. She braced her feet, and gravity exerted its force along the superstructure of her body. She prepared to haul herself up by the safety rail, when the night was broken by the shout of "Police! Everyone stay where you are." A second voice: "Freeze."

The sounds of running and the clattering of equipment hanging from belts followed. Tracy Jane pulled her hand back and shrank against the wall. She recognized Enrique shouting. Someone was climbing the chain-link fence. "Get the runner."

Above her she saw Zit Face on the fence and the arms of Enrique pulling his legs.

"Let go, spic."

Enrique's hand went to his belt and came up with a stun gun. He jammed it into the kid's hamstring, and the kid screamed and fell from the fence.

"Spic, huh? Spic this."

Tracy Jane heard the crackle and the kid scream again. She smiled. She remembered him blowing out his cheeks and bulging out his eyes and laughing, and she thought, Laugh now, Zit Face.

"You want to be a tough guy." Zzzzzz. The smoke of scorched cloth and skin drifted over the pool.

"Ahhhhh. You fucking spic. Beaner with a badge."

A sickening thump and the whoosh of air forced out of a body. "How about we talk about your attitude, you white piece of shit?" A series of rapid blows mixed with the groans and sucking of air. "Quit resisting arrest."

In the water Tracy Jane became rigid and cold. It felt like the beating would never end, and horror mixed with her delight, as it was hard to feel sorry for a punk after she had wished him so much harm. With each strike, she saw the waddling and heard the laughter, and the sticker on the window flared in her mind. In some way she felt that he was taking a beating for all those who had made her life miserable, but she started to feel ill at the sounds of Zit Face begging for mercy, all his bravado gone. With the sound of each kick and punch, she imagined Enrique's smile when he had asked her out.

She lay awake for hours after dawn, wrestling with her delight at Zit Face's beating and the guilt she knew she should feel. The whir of her air conditioner finally lulled her into a troubled sleep.

The next night when the cowbell clanged, Tracy Jane looked up. Enrique and Wally came in. One of the things that had been nagging at her was if she'd be able to look at him and how she'd react to seeing him. She smiled, and she felt lighter afoot. Wally's belt clattered as he sat at a table. "Let's get a Hawaiian," he said.

Andy emerged from the back, carrying his clipboard. "How's the local boys in tan?"

"Another night of sweeping up scumbags," Wally said.

"Yessiree, they got it coming," Andy said.

Enrique leaned against the Plexiglas. "You never said if you'd like to go out with me. Well, would you?"

Tracy Jane looked at him as she continued to shape the dough and nodded. Sure, she thought, he's hot. She even found that the more she reflected on the incident at the pool, the more she was attracted to his dangerous side, what was hidden in him and people didn't see in daylight. She noticed Andy looking out the corners of his eyes at her.

In the night after their first date she took him home. At dinner she had had a couple of glasses of wine and now was light-headed.

"I have beer, milk, and water. If you'd like a nightcap."

"A beer, sure."

They sat on her couch, and as he shifted his weight he leaned close to her. She turned her face to him and saw the desire and kissed him.

She expected him to be rough, but he wasn't. He was gentle and caressed and kissed her in a long foreplay, and in a bigger surprise, after they were finished when he got up, it wasn't to grab his pants and head for the door but to get her a warm washcloth. They lay in the loose sheets and pillows not saying anything. He stroked her hair. This was what it was like not wanting a moment to end. She wanted to stretch it out as long as possible, stave off the loneliness that she now felt keenly.

Tracy Jane ran her hand over his chest and down his muscled abs. Along the street a car idled, the sound punctuated by the newspaper hitting the front door like a loose backhand. She wanted to bring him to meet her mother on holidays and have her look him up and down with her crooked smile. She wanted to have Enrique stand next to her sister's gangly, hawk-nosed, pasty-faced husband. More than one holiday, she wanted a lifetime of holidays with him faithful by her side. All the desire of her girlish dreams of marriage and men rose up, and she felt the loss of something she had never had. As her head on his chest rose and fell with his breathing, she felt him falling asleep. She kissed his cheek and whispered, "I saw you at the pool."

He raised up and fixed her with a puzzled gaze. "I can lose my badge."

"Don't worry," she said. "It'll be our secret. All couples have secrets." She laid her head on his chest, lightly.

"I guess that's true." He lay back on the pillow, his heart ticking over, as she thought of the water, the slap it made against her body and how it had held her above the weighted earth.

REPOSSESSION

We had parked in a corner to get a view of all the
incoming traffic to the employee area. I wore black
slacks, a white shirt, and a black tie, so that I looked like
a Mormon missionary or a Nazi, with my close-cropped
blond hair, and not a repo man. My driver and wing-
woman, Carla, had feathered blonde hair and wore jeans
and a loose blouse she could pull up to flash her boobs
and throw people off. Whenever she did it everyone
looked and everyone stopped, even women, because she
had three nipples—two on one boob, which made it look
like a sock puppet with bugged-out, googly eyes. I have to
admit that I did want to know what it was like to feel them.

The dealership owners we worked for, who called
themselves Persians, which meant Iranian in the late
eighties, had us cut the keys from a code and gave us the
paperwork to track down the vehicles. For this truck we
knew the guy would be showing up here for his shift, and
after he'd gone into work I'd sidle up with my key and off
I'd be. I hadn't been selling many vehicles, so it was nice
to make some money getting them back. Carla sold a lot
of cars but came with me for the extra cash and for some
excitement. She said she kind of missed having some
action in her life after getting out of the army.

Carla turned on the radio to a pop station. "You ever
think they don't know why their car's missing?"

"They know, all right. Like that guy that parked two

26

blocks away at a friend's house."

"I suppose," she said.

"There he is." I pointed at the truck pulling into the lot. It slammed to a stop and a man with a flattop jumped out, literally, as his chest only came up to the bottom of the door, and rushed into the store.

Carla looked at her watch. "He's late. It's after two."

"Overdue, is more like it." Carla pulled up next to the truck and in seconds we were driving for the dealership. An easy five hundred bucks.

At home I got into bed next to Iris after picking my way around the piles of clothes and stacks of books strewn about the bedroom floor. We'd been living together a year and a half but had known each other for about ten years. She rolled over, and in a sleep-sludged voice said, "Yikes, a stranger in my bed."

"Sorry, the last guy worked the graveyard shift."

"Is your girlfriend okay?" She often referred to Carla like that.

"Fine. Did you call the landlord?"

"I forgot."

"We got to get it fixed. I don't want some fence jumper wandering in here." The back door to the patio had a broken lock. A privacy fence blocked it off, but anyone could climb it to test the door. This was LA.

"You can do it too, you know."

"I know, but you said—"

"Okay, fine."

"You could give me a chance to finish."

"Why? I know what you're going to say."

We lay there a few minutes. Water dripped in the bathroom. Sound carried in this apartment in strange ways. She said, "My nephew Paul is going to be in town this weekend. You'll like him."

"Cool." I had a great relationship with all my nieces

and nephews, and people often asked why I didn't have kids if I got along so well with them. "What did you do tonight?"

"Stayed at the library until they threw me out."

"You weren't home?"

"Group project is due on Friday, and Bob can only meet after ten."

She'd been talking about this *group* project for a month, and it seemed like only Bob's name came up. "What time does it close? I mean, it seems if this is such a big deal he'd make time earlier in the day and not worry about when the library closes."

"He has a job. I guess I could always bring him home with me."

I chuckled. I felt I was getting a little ridiculous, so I snuggled into her back. "Sorry." Her hair smelled of cigarettes and French fries. Usually, she showered. I ran my hand under her armpit, under her breasts, down the escarpment of her stomach, and into her underwear, where I caressed her pubic hair.

"I'm on my period."

"I thought you were on your period last week."

"It's only been three days. Go to sleep."

I kept my hand where it rested, feeling the warmth and pulse of her body. Under my palm her stomach gurgled. Her breathing slowed as she drifted back to sleep, and I lay listening to the drip, drip of water, thinking it had been at least eight days.

In the morning Carla drove us over to the east side. A light truck this time. The houses were run-down 1920s-style bungalows. On some of the porches sat groups of Mexicans, hanging out chatting. Carla crept up the street until we saw the address.

"Supposed to be red," she said. "That's the address."

Some of the guys on the steps started to stare at

us. "Let's go around the block and see if it's on another street." As I said this, a red truck loaded with newspapers that rose above the cab turned onto the street and stopped. An old Mexican got out. He wore a yellow straw hat and a button-up cowboy shirt.

"That's the one," Carla said.

He left the door open and as I got out, I heard the truck's engine still running. The old man was at the tailgate, shouting up to the guys on the porch, and they all shared a laugh. They looked at me with that *if I have to see one more brochure about the word of God I'm going to scream* look. The old man was laughing, no doubt mocking me in their neighborhood, as I slid into the driver's seat and sped away. In the side-view mirror, he stood gawking after me, his arms outstretched and the bright sun making his cowboy hat into a halo. Behind him, Carla turned onto a different avenue. I braked at the stop sign. Some of the guys had leaped from the porch and were running for me. I popped the clutch, and the top two rows of papers slid into the street. On the main drag, I stopped at a light. The guys had stopped running at the pile of newspapers and started collecting them. Next to me an old woman in a Land Rover was motioning for me to roll down the passenger window. I leaned across and as soon as it was down she yelled, "You lost some papers. Some Mexicans are stealing them."

The light turned green. I waved at her, popped the clutch, dumping more papers as I hit the ramp for the 710 and out of all their lives, which is what I liked. The mess was now somebody else's.

I parked the truck in the service area and went to see Faheed, the finance manager. The dealership sprawled over several blocks and sold seven different makes of cars, and part of the showroom was dedicated to pimped-out, garish collector cars: a gull-wing turquoise Mercedes; a plaid Cobra with gleaming side pipes; a Ferrari, red, of course; a green-and-yellow-striped Lamborghini; a red-and-white Stingray; a pearlescent Porsche Carrera; and my favorite, a stock 1936 Rolls-Royce Phantom. Over his runner's build, Faheed usually wore lightweight, cream-colored suits. Perched on his nose, thick horn-rimmed glasses dominated his narrow face. He looked like he should be teaching philosophy or theology and not punching through the paperwork on a Jetta.

"Matt, how good to see you," he said as he moved around his desk. He fiddled with the knot of his tie before sticking out his hand.

"We got the Ford this morning. What else you got for us?"

"Only one."

Well, that'd suck for me, I thought. I'd have to go back to the sales floor if there weren't any more cars to go after. That bothered me a lot. I didn't make any money selling cars. I didn't have the killer closer's mentality that put me at odds with the buyers while I pretended to be on their side. I knew my commission was based on how much I could get the other guy to pay, but when the customer asked if there was anything else I could do, I knew there was. Some of the other salespeople had a way of keeping people from leaving the lot, and getting the potential buyer trapped in the cubicle and convincing them the car they just test-drove was the car for them, and getting them to pay full sticker price. To me they seemed like desperate streetwalkers fighting for a corner. Junkies for the dollar. I'd only been going after cars a week and half, and I knew there would be others to go after sooner or later. Two kinds of consumers in the world of car sales: those who made the payments and those who didn't.

"What car?" I asked.

Faheed handed me a folder from his desk. "An Eclipse."

I looked over the paperwork. Faheed asked me what was so funny when I laughed. "This is the first car I ever sold. Now I got to get it back." I had netted almost a grand on its sale and it was all beginner's luck, and the sales manager. I hadn't made as much in the past six weeks.

I picked up Carla and we rolled through the guy's apartment complex and then through the mall parking lot in Covina, where we had record of him working at an electronics store. After driving a couple of laps through the lot we cruised some of the neighboring strip malls, but we found nothing.

I looked at my watch. "It's only one. Let's try back this evening."

Carla nodded. "You want to get some pizza?"

In the pizza joint, the dark wood paneling and wrought-iron chandeliers with flame-shaped lightbulbs hanging over the bench seating made me feel like I was in a medieval cafeteria. We sat across from each other at the end of one of the tables. We ordered a large sausage-and-mushroom from the waitress, who was wearing a flouncy dress that pushed her boobs up and out in an imitation of a bar wench. Carla said, "Let's get a pitcher. We're not on anybody's clock."

"Sure," I said.

We ended up drinking two more pitchers of beer and walked to a bar.

She ordered a vodka tonic and I got another beer.

Carla swirled the ice in her drink. "Want to go to the movies?"

"What's playing?"

"*Who Framed Roger Rabbit* is what I want to see."

I checked my watch; only four o'clock. Iris had been talking about seeing the movie too, but summer school and that *group* project took all her time. I shouldn't have, but at that moment I started to get angry with her for spending so much time with Bob. I'd never met the guy but heard enough about him. I'd asked Iris every week for the past four to go to the movies, and it was always she had to meet with Bob because of his schedule. Then forgetting to call about the patio door aggravated me. That was part of our deal: she called for maintenance on the apartment, and I took care of the car. We shared the labor, and we were supposed to be sharing time. Not to mention I was supporting her while she went to school. She could make a little time for me. One thought piled into another like a chain-reaction accident until I said to myself, what the fuck. Why should I wait and maybe miss the movie in the theater? I drank my beer and the coldness made my skin tighten. "Sure."

We walked to a theater. It crossed my mind to cruise by the mall to look for the Eclipse, but I shook it off. I was too wasted to drive. I smiled at the thought of repo-ing my first sale. When I had started in sales I had no idea how many vehicles came back, and I certainly never expected this. The guy I'd sold it to looked like a reliable person. He was a young Taiwanese, just out of college and going to work for one of the defense contractors in the fall. Eric Chang. The job in the mall was supposed to be a temporary gig, working for one of his uncles, or so he told me. Faheed certainly thought he was legit after a couple of reference calls. Maybe his uncle cut his job. I didn't figure the guy for a deadbeat. Oh, well, I thought, shit happens, you still have to pay up or lose the car, even if it ain't your fault.

On our way over, Carla staggered into me several times, and once we were in the darkness of the theater, she grabbed my hand and dragged me to where she wanted to sit. I almost spilled my popcorn. I admit I thought she might've been coming on to me a little. A little physical flirtation, but I didn't want to read more into it than was there. The third nipple crossed my mind, and as I looked down out of the corner of my eye, she turned to me.

At first I thought she had busted me staring at her tits, but she said, "I love the theater. It reminds me of going to the movies with my dad before he died."

"I'm sorry about your father." The words in my mouth felt like dried dough. The beer swirled in my head and I kept thinking of her nipples.

"It's okay. It's been a while. Thanks for hanging out."

Her eyes reflected the projector light and shadows flitted over her face. I turned back to the screen. "Not a problem. Anytime."

As I raised popcorn to my mouth, she reached around my shoulder and pulled my cheek to her lips. "Thanks." Her voice was low and quiet.

I brushed the popcorn I had dropped off my lap. Normally she carried herself with an aloofness that some guys might have taken for frigidness, but she always laughed and kidded with me, so I figured her for shy and not the kind to flirt or be open with a lot of people. The kiss and teary eyes threw me a little. I didn't expect that in the least. Along with her aloofness, she also put up a tough front. She talked about her time in the army, playing rugby, and fighting with her older brothers, but later after we started driving around together she talked about playing in a jazz band and being a theater geek. Maybe she felt like an outsider and needed a little time to get to know you.

The film started and we both laughed the whole way through. I felt my beer buzz fading as the final credits began to roll. We made our way out, and the late-afternoon sun made me squint. The heat lingered and the air was thick. A group of kids walked in front of us, miming the movie's characters and imitating the crazy voices. Some couples held hands and peeled away from the crowd into the parking lot. I wondered what it'd be like to be with Carla. Not just a one-night fuck, but what it would be like to live with her. I wondered what she wanted out of life and what kind of couple we'd make. Did she like to get up early on her days off or loll about in bed? Did she watch a lot of television or did she read, and what did she like to read or watch? I wondered about her family and her dead father and what it would be like to be inside that kind of family dynamic. It dizzied me a moment. How did other couples live? Iris was only the second girlfriend I had ever lived with and while at first it excited me, the drabness of day-to-day living with both women shadowed me. It couldn't be that way for all couples.

"Want to get another drink?" I asked.

"No. I'm tired. Think I'll go on home. Let's look for that car tomorrow."

"Sure."

We walked back to her car and then we drove back to the dealership. The whole time I wondered if she'd reach for my hand or slip her arm around me like she had earlier. She stared into the stop-and-go traffic and didn't talk. The AC whirred from the dash. I thought about putting my hand on her thigh or caressing her shoulder, but stopped short, my hand trembling. I hoped she didn't notice.

After she dropped me off, I drove my Volkswagen Fox to the mall. Normally I'd never use my car to look for a repo, but I was bugged that it might be there. It was a tricked-out car. One of those models the boys in the service department do some work to: racing wheels, tinted windows, some engine modifications to pull a few more horses out of it, and a customized interior with a Bose stereo system and thumping speakers. It priced out at ten grand more than the factory model. I didn't question it then, but I had no idea why they let that guy drive that car off the lot. The promised wages of a better future? That ain't paying the bills now.

By the time I got back to the mall the sun had flamed the smog red, and dusk brought out the shoppers. The parking lot was jammed like bumper cars at the carnival. I went in and cruised by the store. I shuffled through knots of people. In front of the store, I found a bench where I could easily see the counter. I didn't want to go in and draw attention to myself. Shoppers wandered by with bags, and some just walked along eating a corn dog or swilling a soda as they stopped and stared into windows. I didn't often come to the mall alone. Some weekends, when she didn't have a bunch of homework, or between semesters, Iris liked to come and walk in circles and people-watch. I wondered what other people-watchers made of us. To me it was a waste of a perfectly good afternoon. Maybe that too was a sign of our growing apart. At first I didn't mind it, but as I sat there, I realized how much I hated spending my time in the mall. I only did it because I wanted to be with her more than I didn't want to be in the mall. Funny how I clammed up and went along after she'd say no to my suggestion of a trip to the beach or the botanical garden. I bet Carla liked to go to the beach.

Satisfied Eric Chang wasn't in, I wandered off to my car and drove by his address. The space at his apartment was empty. I backed into a visitor space and shut the motor off. The streetlights glazed the cars and grass around the complex. The noise of traffic filtered through the cooling air, and the sprinklers came on. My eyes burned from the smog and my body became sluggish as the beer wore completely off. I eased back into the seat and stretched my legs, trying to relax. My weight sank into the seat. I closed my eyes for a moment.

When I woke up, my mouth tasted like straw. I shook my head and rubbed my eyes. A Chevy pickup occupied the parking space. I started my car to go. It was one in the morning.

Iris, curled under the blankets, rolled over when I staggered into bed. "Take your shoes off and stay awhile."

I collapsed onto the bed. "Maybe you should take off your shoes and shower instead," she said.

The hot water felt good beating over my body. I rinsed my mouth out and spit before peeing into the drain. Eric Chang had a lot going for him. I was sure he had relatives who would float him until he got on his feet. That business of his uncle's made me wonder what his parents did for work, and the other aunts and uncles. I thought they would be tight-knit. But I couldn't say. Maybe he had shamed the family somehow, and in one of those dramatic moments where he became dead to them, he sank on his own. Maybe he had too much pride to ask for help. Some people would rather die than ask. When I had seen him on the dealership lot, picking his way through the rows of cars, I thought that he looked solid, one of those guys who thinks superficial things like fancy cars and clothes are where it's at and miss the under-lying truth. Well, he'd be getting an education in reality now.

When I climbed back into bed, Iris snored softly. I always liked the sound of her sleeping, long breaths undulating from her chest as she dreamed of God knew what.

Carla picked me up at the dealership. We drove over to the mall. I walked into the store. The guy I figured to be his uncle smiled. "Can we help you?"

"Nah." I looked over the car stereos. "Wait, maybe you can. There was a young guy working in here. He knew a lot about these." I motioned to the stereos. "He around?"

"My nephew. No he gone. Northrop, they hire him. We so proud of him."

"Thanks," I said. His smile didn't diminish. "Is he still in LA or did he have to move?"

"Hawthorne."

"His family must be happy he's still close."

"Yes, family very important."

I left, wondering, what the fuck.

Back in the parking lot, I climbed into the Golf and said to Carla, "Nothing. You know, his uncle said he got that fat job at Northrop."

"Crazy." Carla started the car. We cruised by his apartment again, and nothing. Carla wanted to work the floor for a while when we got back to the dealership, so I figured I might as well too. I did have on my best black tie.

I made no sales in three hours. It really wasn't that busy and nothing but a bunch of browsers anyways. Carla scored a couple of quick kills and she was slugging me on the shoulder and grinning at me after each car rolled off the lot. Once the customer cleared the sidewalk, the sale was final and they couldn't return the car. Believe me, it had happened. Buyer's remorse, where they come cruising back, bitching they didn't really like the car. Not what they wanted or expected: blah, slammed, blah, dunked, blah. Of course the salesperson was always on their side: "If there was anything I could do I would, but you see, you signed the contract, which is legally binding, and you, my friend, drove off the lot. You are now the proud owner. Here, let me call service and I'll set you up with a free first oil change." Whatfuckingever.

When Carla's fourth sale pulled away I suggested we get a late lunch. Afterward we could go and see if our boy had made any appearances. I figured I could maybe find out from his uncle where he might be.

She smiled at me. "You going to try and get me all drunk and teary again?"

I put my hands to my face in mock shock and in a Scarlett O'Hara Southern drawl said, "Why, Miss Carla, I do declare it was you who were trying to inebriate me."

"Maybe I was."

We found this pub close to the mall with dartboards along the wall and a real snooker table. A picture of the queen hung behind the bar and a Union Jack on a pole stood in the corner. A few old boys in flat caps sat on stools with pipes clenched in their teeth, mumbling to each other. Their accents were thick, but one of the old fellows was telling a story of flying a bomber over Germany. I thought it interesting that Faheed's accent was similar to theirs. I had the fish and chips and a stout, and Carla had chicken strips and a lager.

Carla cracked her knuckles as the food arrived. "What a good day."

"It'll be good if we can find that car."

"That'd just be a little extra for me." She ate a strip and after swallowing asked, "Why do you stick with sales? You aren't very good at it. You seem to hate it."

I sat back. "I guess I don't have anything else going for me." I wondered for a minute about what real job options I had. Nothing, really. I wanted to go back to school, but Iris had to finish first and then I would. Even then, I wasn't certain what I wanted to study. I liked geology, but I also had an interest in psychology, figuring out what made people tick and do the things they do, but that was a whole lot of school and a whole lot of debt. Then I thought about Iris and what we had going on. She could leave me and all that I had invested in our future would be shot. I even thought about the thoughts I'd been having about Carla. There she was, sitting across from me on a summer's day. I had spent more time with her than with Iris, and Iris had spent more time with Bob than with me. I wondered if Iris and Bob went out for dinner and drinks to discuss their project. I knew Bob wanted to run his hand up Iris's leg as far as he could. He was a guy and she was damn beautiful, but whether he did or not, and whether she let him, was the thing.

"That's how I felt when I got out of the army. I was a military cop and thought I wanted to be a sheriff, but somewhere along the way I lost the enthusiasm for it. The next thing you know I was selling cars and driving you around."

"At least you're good at it."

"Yeah, but who knew?"

"What are you up to this evening? Want to go out?"

"My girlfriend is coming back from Germany later tonight, so I'm off to the airport."

Indeed, I thought. Who knew. "Sounds like a good plan."

She smiled. "I got a secret. You want to know it?"

I knew we were in new territory. "Yes."

"My third nipple isn't a nipple."

I was leaning forward to catch her words and now felt suspended over a cliff. "You're fucking kidding me."

"No. It's a pasty."

I laughed and rocked back in my chair. "Of course it is. How funny." I wondered if she was lying to me, trying to make me quit desiring her.

"It's fun to flash people and see the change in their expression."

"Well, it has helped us get away a little quicker with a car."

"It's all about acting—the fast lie that'll bail you out of trouble." She looked about with a conspiratorial grin and reached into her blouse. When she pulled her hand out, pinched between her thumb and forefinger was her nipple pasty.

I raised my drink. "Here's to your fake nipple and your fast flash." And we drank.

After lunch we went by the mall, and still nothing. At the dealership I was shocked to see the Eclipse, and Eric

Chang standing face-to-face with Faheed. I thought, what the shit? Spit flew from Eric's mouth as he yelled. Faheed remained calm faced, like the knot of his thin tie. I walked up ready for Eric to start swinging. As a repo guy you had to be ready to bob and weave.

"Be reasonable," Faheed said.

Eric recognized me. "You let me drive off. You should've known."

"Fuck, man, how was I supposed to know you were a deadbeat?"

"Deadbeat?" Eric slipped into the car and raced the motor and popped the clutch. The tires smoked and the car lurched backward and spun a tight circle in the blue-black cloud. Salespeople and some guys from service scrambled between the rows of parked cars. Faheed stood his ground with his arms crossed. The car's rear end was still moving sideways when the car jumped forward, the tires squealing. The undercarriage showered sparks of steel and concrete as the car shot over the curb and plowed into the grass, where the engine died. The door kicked open. Eric stormed over to Faheed with clenched fists. I thought he was going to swing and stepped between them.

I put my hands up. "Wait, now."

Eric stopped, gritting his teeth. "You are nothing but a bunch of crooks." He turned and walked off the lot and down the street.

"That was crazy," I said. "He looked so mild mannered when we sold him the car."

Faheed just nodded. "That's the last of them."

"Oh, I'm sure there'll be others," I said.

Faheed smiled. "Nonpayment repossessions, sure." He told me that all the cars Carla and I had brought back weren't for nonpayment but for a bad bank deal. The dealership had approved the car loans and sent the paperwork to a bank that someone in the owners' extended family had started, but it had gone tits up. That left the dealership with worthless contracts and no money for their "inventory" out driving around town. The people they let have the cars didn't qualify through a regular bank, so they sent me and Carla out.

"That's just shitty," I said.

"You sold him the car."

"But how was I to know he wasn't qualified?"

"That's your excuse? You didn't know?"

"You're the one that approved them."

He pushed his glasses up with his index finger. "Yes, but I'm not acting like this is a moral outrage. I'm a businessman and this is business. Shitty or not, this is the way it is. We didn't force them to sign. Surely you must have wondered how that young man was able to drive away with such an expensive car." He cleared his throat. "Also, we have decided to let you go. You're not producing any sales."

"What the fuck? I was ready to take a punch for you."

"Be that as it may, you are taking up space in the sales staff."

"That's bullshit," I said. "I can still go after cars." Crap, I thought. This was not the time for me to be looking for another job, if there were any decent ones to be had.

"No," he said. "We don't think so. We have a real repossession company that handles all the others."

"You could've given me some warning," I said, but he was already walking away. I stood there for a moment like it hadn't really happened, some mistake of my hearing. Salespeople were milling around the front doors, and others made their way to buyers on the lot. A tow truck rolled out of the service area, its chains rattling from the boom. I shrugged. They might be coming for my car next month. I went to say good-bye to Carla, but she was already gone, to get her girlfriend.

The drive across town to the apartment was a jam of accidents and heat. I sweated my way through the stench of exhaust breathing out of hundreds of cars. I laid on the horn a few times, flipped some people off. In the rearview I saw some guy racing along the emergency lane, so I turned the nose of my car into it, making him slam on the brakes. I laughed as he yelled. Fuck him. That's what you get for thinking you can get over on everyone. I didn't care. This day was shit.

My shirt stuck to my back with sweat as I got out of the car. I just wanted a cold beer and to veg out in front of the TV. I'd figure out a plan in the morning. It surprised me when I opened the door at the apartment and found a man sitting on my couch. Bob, I thought. That just figured. They weren't expecting me home in the afternoon. Library, my ass. A tall, good-looking guy with wavy brown hair and a tan stood up. His white polo shirt was tucked into his creased khaki slacks, and no perspiration stained his shirt or beaded on his forehead. He'd been here awhile. I could hear the shower from where I stood. "Fucking Bob."

"I'm—"

"I'm what? A Bible salesman waiting for my girlfriend to get out of the shower?"

"No, I—"

"Get the fuck out before I bust your head." I couldn't believe the nerve of this guy. I lose my job and then come home to this. Iris and I were going to have a short talk.

"Listen—"

"Last chance, asshole. When I come back, be gone." I walked into the bedroom and banged on the bathroom door.

The water turned off. "What?" She sounded pissed.

"What's the meaning of bringing Bob over here?"

The door popped open. Steam rolled out and

condensed in the apartment air, making me realize how cool it was inside the apartment. She stood holding a towel in front of her like a magician's cape before a trick. Her black hair hung around her shoulders. "What did you say?"

"I told Bob to get the fuck out. I had a shitty day, just wanted to come home and drink a beer, relax, but instead that guy's on my couch with you in the shower." For a second I thought about Carla waiting in the airport. What would she do if her girl didn't get off the plane? We always figure things will happen like we think they will, but the world has a way of taking what you have when you're too busy to pay attention.

"Bob?" As she said the name, the puzzled look left her face. Her jaw tightened. "You idiot, that's my nephew, Paul. The one I told you was coming."

I snapped my mouth shut at the surprise of the news. In my mind I had raced ahead in the argument and thought that I had every conceivable comeback to anything she could possibly say, except, of course, that I was wrong. My brain was a clutter of syllables and half-formed words trying to make sentences. The only thing I could think of to say was, "But he's not a kid." I knew it was already a lame defense because why wouldn't he be Paul, but sometimes even when we know the truth, we still have to ask for confirmation and she gave it to me.

"No shit. There's only two years between us. My parents had me when my sister was already in college."

I knew that. "Fuck, I'm sorry."

"Get out." Her face reddened and she pressed the towel harder against her body, rumpling it up in her fist. "You thought I was cheating on you. Just get out." She slammed the door.

I stood there a moment like a traveler turned away from the town gate. In the living room Paul still stood. "I'm sorry," I said.

He nodded but never made eye contact with me.

"I lost my job today," I said as if that justified me acting like such a prick.

He nodded again, still looking down at the coffee table, and I walked outside into the heat.

Later that night I sat in my car at a sports complex, drinking a beer. I'd watched a softball game, but now the place was deserted. The humidity had shot up. Sometimes to cope with a head full of problems, I just forget them and have a few drinks until I can start making sense of the world. I looked in the rearview mirror and loosened my tie. I felt a little ridiculous still wearing it. It made sense to let her cool down. I started the car and headed back. I figured to let myself in and lie next to her, run my hands under her breasts and down her body, past her navel to the edge of her panties. She'd wake and I'd beg forgiveness, try to regain what I had lost. She'd either do it or not. I parked a little up the street so my lights wouldn't shine into the window from my parking space.

The door chain was hooked at the front door, so I climbed the fence and let myself in the back door. The air conditioner whirred, and the kitchen floor was cold. I kicked off my shoes, tiptoed across carpet, and opened the bedroom door just enough to slip in. Streetlamps streaked the room through the venetian blind. As I picked my way around the clothes, some dishes, and books to the edge of the bed, I saw the white polo shirt and the khakis heaped in a stripe of light. I looked closer and saw two forms spliced together like commas under the sheets of my bed. Well, fuck, I thought. Fucking Bob. That nephew story was some quick acting. I had no energy left for chasing after something I wasn't sure about anymore. Had I ever been sure of anything? Before sneaking out I considered leaving with his clothes, just for fun, but they didn't need to know I had busted them.

Outside the night air tasted gritty. Sprinklers sprayed water evenly over the pavement and the grass. I stared at my empty parking spot, thinking for a second my car had been stolen, but I'd only forgotten where I'd parked.

LOOKING FOR THE MULE

We stood at the edge of the shaft, then started down the ladder, my grandfather, his partner Charlie Donner, and I. I was fifteen, working my first summer in their goldmine, the *Purgatory*. The three of us waited before switching on our headlamps, feeling our way down each rung, as the light of the mineshaft's mouth receded like falling away from the sun. Whenever I descended into the *Purgatory Mine*, I felt the void crush in around me. The black was absolute until we switched on our headlamps. As I worked, I strained between hammer blows, listening for creaking timbers or the slow grind of shifting rock. I kept breathing, but it was as if fluid half-filled my lungs. I envisioned a crumbling arabesque of granite, lichen, and moss, forcing air out of the earth with a giant whoosh—a sigh for the dying. Grit and sweat encased me in a mineral husk. At noon, we trekked back to the ladder and switched off our headlamps. As I looked up the ladder, I shivered and lost my balance trying to stand still in the mine's dark, goldless bottom.

Charlie Donner whistled a tune I didn't know. He said to me, "If this life don't suck a fellow's balls up, Wes, nothing will."

I thought I was special, living like I was in the Old West. No one mined like this in the late seventies, as far as I knew. Hundreds of abandoned shafts pocked the American southwest, but most operations were huge like

the Kaiser iron pit mine at Eagle Mountain, California in
the eastern Mojave Desert, where my father drove massive
dump trucks that spent work shifts spiraling down into the
open pit mine and back up to dump ore. It was about an
hour and half overland from the *Purgatory* and sometimes
we could hear its blast siren on the wind. My small high
school sat in the shadow of the mine's tailings heap.

I followed Charlie up the ladder, Grandfather last. We
climbed for the speck of light, and I tried not to climb too
fast and bump Charlie. I grabbed each rung as if I were a
hundred feet above the earth. My hands always weakened,
and the arches of my feet cramped, as I climbed out and
tried not to slip off the path leading away from the shaft.
I wanted to collapse, away from the hole. The slightest
breeze drew goose pimples out of my skin. I felt the
atmosphere move—the earth's slow spin.

We weren't guaranteed to find any more gold, but I
felt freer than my father locked into his cycle of driving
trucks hours a day then watching television and drinking
beer, waiting for those canned vacations once a year or
the other high school kids working as dishwashers or
clerks or whatever crappy summer job they managed to
scrape up. My father felt his dad was wasting his time out
in the desert, and that I needed to earn an hourly wage
to learn what being in the workforce was like. At times I
felt torn. It was my mother who convinced him to let me
spend time out here to get to know Grandfather better
and to quit moping around the house. "Wes loves staying
out there and needs to stretch himself against the desert
before adult life takes hold. Besides," she said, "Charlie
likes the change in conversation."

Grandfather and Charlie were both lean and scraggly
like the Joshua trees scattered around the mine. They
wore sweat-stained cowboy hats. Charlie had a jutting
chin that he pointed with when his hands were full, and

my grandfather's wild eyebrows collected dirt, until they looked like mountain ledges. As a kid, I thought those two old men never aged. In 1942, they had dropped out of high school in Bristol, Tennessee and joined the army together. I loved those early photos of them: cocky hillbillies in their army uniforms. I thought about them only a couple of years older than me, going off to war.

I hiked down the ridge to check on Molly, their mule, although she really belonged to Charlie. She was like a long legged dog, and I looked forward to feeding her. At eighteen years old, she had hauled a lot of supplies, and my mother had a photo of me on her back when I was four. When she saw me, she switched her tail, walked once around the pen, and then came to me, pitching her head. I went into the corral and as I scratched her ears, she leaned against me. I laughed. "Geez, Molly, stand on your own four legs." She turned her head to me and chuffed. I patted and rubbed her ribs.

When I came back up, Charlie sat on a rock, rolling a smoke; a book about Jedediah Smith lay next to him. He crossed his legs and smiled when he saw me, and thumbed over the ridge. I climbed past Charlie after he let me have a drag, and I saw Grandfather talking to two hikers. The college aged man and woman wore shorts, khaki shirts, and lightweight hiking boots. Carabineers, rock anchors, helmets, and rope hung from their packs. Grandfather grew agitated when he saw hikers, thinking they might be environmentalists bucking to expand Joshua Tree National Monument and shutdown his operation, but he looked relaxed. As I got closer, I heard their conversation.

The man said, "We're from Irvine. A friend told us there was some gnarly rock climbing out this way."

"Yeah," the woman said. "Like, we saw the oilrig and thought it'd be cool to check out."

I couldn't see Grandfather's face, but knew he was

smiling when he rubbed the back of his head. He pointed to the derrick and saw me when he looked back. "That head frame's for hoisting ore." He winked.

I waved and said, "Wouldn't get so lucky as to hit oil. It'd ruin our lifestyle."

Grandfather stayed to talk with the climbers and they asked him about any rock faces around. I went back up to where Charlie sat. He looked up and said, "That old man will tell them stories until the coyotes start yipping. How's Molly?"

"Lazy."

"Me too." He handed me the cigarette.

"How's the book?"

"Good. I had me a funny thought when I saw them folks down yonder." He patted the book. "Folks like old Jedediah here came scouting around, looking to open a country. Now we got people who only want to wander around and climb rocks like they was on a playground."

"Recreation nation," I said.

"All less than a hundred years or there abouts. There was hardly nobody out here when we trained up for the War." He pointed west with his cigarette. "Right over there."

I looked at the horizon.

He drew in a drag, blew a stream of smoke and said, "I been out here a long time."

"Would you like me to rustle some lunch up?"

He nodded, dropped his butt and crushed it under his boot. "No one lives off the desert anymore."

Just these two old men, I thought.

Grandfather rarely left the mine after Grandmother had left him for Africa the year before. By the time I finished my first year of high school she'd be dead. A week after the news, I got a postcard from her: *I saw the gorillas. Made the trip worth taking. Love, Grandma Ev.* The smell of frying eggs or Estée Lauder powder always made me think of her.

Her leaving shocked us kids, but my parents later admitted they were surprised she stayed so long. I was hurt that she had taken off and at the news of her death I searched for all the wrong relatives to blame, but finally understood it was her. It was who she was, just as digging in the earth was Grandfather.

The rift between my father and grandfather widened after her death. It started when Grandfather refused to help his son after an argument about going to the Colorado River with friends during a Spring Break instead of working in the *Purgatory*. Grandfather told him, "Money and your mother have spoiled you, what you need is hard work." Dad dropped out of college and went to work for the company mine in Eagle Mountain, and anytime they were in the same room it made my stomach hurt and throat tight, especially after Grandmother left.

What made Grandmother as unswerving as a train for all those years and what finally caused her derailment? Did she get up one morning in a house bought from a mine that kept her husband and say to herself, "I've crocheted my last doily," and called the Peace Corps? I only knew that Grandfather and Charlie had struck a vein of gold that could've retired them both, but they kept digging and blasting, even after the vein pinched off, confident they'd strike the metal seam again.

After lunch we descended into the earth and worked the afternoon. We gathered at camp as sunset colored the Palen Mountains pink in the east. The wind picked up and switched to the southeast. I sat by the campfire, embers flying up as mesquite burned. I massaged my feet and hands from holding a six foot long rod of steel, the rock bit, or the sledgehammer and hauling the ore cars up the shaft, drank coffee and smoked a cigarette Charlie rolled. It could've been 1879 under the darkening sky. I had finished my first year in high school and understood more about busting rocks with explosives than how the school sports program fared or any of my class subjects, with the exception of history.

Charlie poured more coffee into our cups and said, "I'll never forget when we first came out West. I never did see so much sky or land without trees." He pulled thread from his ragged pant cuff. I loved this story, but had only heard him tell it four or five times like those definitive family stories we tell occasionally. "Me and your granddad said then, that after the war, we're done with Tennessee."

He pointed down the long arroyo. "We tracked the gold from down yonder."

Grandfather said, "We were a couple of greenhorns digging around, fresh from riding around Europe in those suffocating Sherman tanks."

Charlie said, "It did take a few years to wear all the green off, and then a few more to find old *Purgatory*. We made some finds, nothing but a taste though. Enough to keep us at it."

"Finding gold is like finding critters out here, you really got to look, all this empty space hiding things. Fact is we almost walked over this deposit. It was rusty gold and looked more like iron than gold, but gold she was," Grandfather said. "Right after that I wrote for your grandmother to come out and wired her more money than her family had ever seen."

I thought of them wandering, loaded for prospecting: rucksacks, rock hammers, shovels, canvas water bags, tins of food, magnifying glasses, mercury, nitric acid, carbide lamps, magnets, and gold pans—two men wearing new jeans, old army boots and determined smiles, clattering at playa's edges, shoveling the dirt and rock. Seeking something precious.

The night cooled. I started to cook some canned meat and canned vegetables in a cast iron skillet. Charlie cracked open his bottle of Yukon Jack, sipped out the neck and passed it to me. I swallowed the syrupy fire and handed the bottle to Grandfather. They laughed as I gulped air and sipped at my coffee. The terrain darkened and became featureless. I could see the horizon against the paler night sky with stars like scattered silver flakes on black sand. Our fire floated on a black disk as if we crouched on a sable plain and if I wanted, I could walk over the valleys— on air.

The next afternoon, I held a rock bit, and Charlie swung the sledge. It was heavy and with each swing it felt longer and my hand numbed. The hammer rang. I twisted the drill's shaft and made sure it was set in the hole we were drilling. He hit it again. They only used old equipment that could be used without compressors, or generators because they had started that way and figured why invest in more than they needed and haul more equipment up to the claim than was necessary. We bored holes to pack with dynamite to blow a crosscut. He hit the bit again, and I twisted it, shards of rock flew like pieces of glass in my headlamp's beam, a small puff of sparkling dust. He hit again and my hands slipped. The hammer caught the edge of the bit. It careened up, wrenching the drill down and crushing my hands into the rock. Charlie yelled back for Grandfather. Charlie said to me, "Don't worry, I don't think it's fatal. I suspect you'll be fine enough for cards tonight." I held my hands close to my body as if they were cut gems. I'd never been hurt so bad, but I kept it to myself. He was right. I understood as a child that men didn't make much of their injuries and went back to work as soon as they could. Even my father at the company mine, who had Worker's Comp and insurance, wouldn't use it unless the supervisor told him to. I'd flex and unflex my hands through the pain over the following days, willing them to heal. What else was there for me with those two old men working without a gripe?

We quit work, walked to the ladder and returned to the surface.

A thunderstorm rolled in out of the southeast. Cumulus clouds sparked and fired the afternoon. We sat on the edge of the ridge and watched as the clouds built up, at first low over a distant mountain range like dust from a distant cavalry troop. Dark streaks of rain looked like a black pedestal holding the clouds as they billowed and spun across the blue sky. I liked watching squall lines. It advanced over the desert; the black rain cast a shadow of water and when the wind started gusting, we lowered our heads against the sand and the first fat drops fell. It felt like being supercharged within the static of the cell.

We retreated to the shack and drank and smoked Bull Durham and played rummy until we had to light the kerosene lamp, while the squall beat the shack's sides and pinged rain off the tin roof, lightning filling the shadows, and thunder so close it was like sitting next to a string of sonic booms, causing me to flinch.

Grandfather and Charlie got a glassy look and they smiled at each other. Charlie dealt the cards over an old army blanket that covered the table. He wouldn't play unless he could deal over the wool and say, "We got to have some kind of standards in this place."

I had turned Molly loose to graze earlier. In the morning, she'd be standing in the corral waiting for a can of oats and a scratch on the withers or behind the ears, to lean against me. This ritual was what I imagined other kids saw in ball games or school dances. Outside I could hear the alien sound water rushing down the arroyos, filling the playas and natural cisterns where animals would drink for months. It was like a wet wind blowing through the high desert peaks.

The squall line passed over. Wind still blew and each gust slung rain a little harder. Grandfather only let me have a couple of snorts off the scotch, but it was enough. I scooped the cards off the table when the glasses and ashtrays shifted and shook when a dull rumble came from down the ridge. Rocks clattered, and then only the wind remained.

"Sounds like a small slide," Charlie said. "I hope old Molly weren't in the way." He sipped his scotch.

In the morning, Molly waited for her feed and used me for a post as I scratched her ears. After, I followed Grandfather and Charlie and walked down the trail. We found the slide, sun shining on the uncovered rocks blocking the trail on the edge of the arroyo. A huge granite boulder sat in the center.

Charlie knelt down and said, "We'll have to blow this thing down the hill. Good thing I didn't want to go into Indio for a burger and a date shake." He laughed as he took off his cowboy hat and dusted it against his thigh.

Grandfather edged close to the rock, placed his hand on it and pushed on it a little. He turned and started back toward the mine. "I guess we'd better get some dynamite," he said.

Charlie and I stood and Charlie slipped a small bottle from his pocket, took a sip and handed it to me. The Yukon Jack burned my throat. "That's it, not too quick. A fellow don't want to rush down a good drink," Charlie said.

We climbed back down with several sticks of dynamite, some fuses and blasting caps.

"I reckon we ought to put the charge under that side and roll her into the ravine over there," Charlie said.

"Suppose that'd be the best one," Grandfather said. He pointed at me. "You go on and get up the hillside on the other side of that small bluff."

I looked a quarter mile to where he pointed. "What? I'm not man enough anymore?"

"Now, Boy, I think your parents would stretch me like

a hide if I got you killed. Charlie here will tell you, even an experienced hand can kill himself."

"I help set charges in the mine."

Charlie smiled and said, "This is a different set of rules. Things won't fall out of the sky in the shaft. Once, in France these engineers rigged a set of dragons' teeth to blow and after the blast, pieces of concrete and earth dropped on them. I tell you, I laughed so hard when they got up rubbing where the chunks hit them."

"Let me help with something."

Grandfather said, "I suppose you can clear out a place to set the charge, while we get it ready."

Charlie measured out two arm lengths of fuse, clipped it, and set a cap onto it. He put it into his mouth and crimped the cap, so it would not slide off. He had lost the crimping tool six years before and started crimping blasting caps onto the fuses with his teeth. He had said, "I just feel the edge, come back a tooth's width and bite."

I moved some rocks and created a pocket for the dynamite, then found a couple slabs to lay over it to help direct the blast. "I'll head up the hill," I said as they started to insert the cap and fuse into the stick of dynamite.

Down the ridge and out into the flats, the desert air hung with coolness and the rain invigorated the greens among the browns, whites and yellows of the earth. The small leaves of the bitter brush, mesquite and sage and small clumps of grasses scattered about like star bursts. In a couple of months most everything would be brown again, except for the spikes of yuccas, Joshua trees and the cacti. The shadows still held dampness, but under the sun the land was dried. I looked down the ridge. Charlie bit on another cap and handed it to Granddad.

I sat and waited for them.

Charlie let out what he called a Rebel Yell, and it sounded like a shriek of a cat hit by a car and made me jump a little, even from that distance. He and Granddad had lit the fuses and walked up the trail toward me.

They squatted by me, and we waited. The smoke from the fuse drifted downhill as it burned under the rock. I braced for the explosion. The faint sounds of dirt bikes traced through the air. I turned my head trying to place where the noise was coming from or see a trail of dust. Nothing. Smoke had quit coming from the rock. It sat in the trail. I kept trying to anticipate the explosion, the dull thump, staring until I had to blink my eyes. The sound of the dirt bikes faded. Charlie said, "I reckon we'll give it a few minutes and I'll go on down and check on it."

Grandfather said, "We can wait longer than that."

Charlie said, "Hell, it ain't blown in five minutes, it ain't going to blow in five hours. Fuse must've gotten damp. We'll just have ourselves a smoke first."

He rolled three cigarettes, passed them out and lit them with a match. After he fired his, he shook out the flame, flicking the stick into the brush. I continued to stare at the rock. No smoke floated or hovered around its base. I tried to keep on alert. I didn't want the charge to blow when I wasn't ready.

Charlie stood and started down. "I'll be back directly," he said.

He reached the boulder and knelt next to it. He shaded his eyes, peering into the seam between the boulder and the ground. From where I sat, his back was to me. I watched as he moved rocks away from the boulder. He eased out the first charge, then the second. He extracted the fuses, tossing them down the hill. After placing the dynamite on the ground he stood and waved to us. We waved back like he was some outfielder who had just caught the last out. Measuring the fuse, he cut it, and then he fished a blasting cap from the box in his shirt pocket. He seated it on the fuse's end and bit down on it.

I saw his head snap back and an eruption of blood as the blast erupted from the bottom of his jaw. He collapsed.

I ran, stumbled, down the ridge. Grandfather followed me. When I got to him, I couldn't believe the blood splattered everywhere. The blast knocked Charlie unconscious, but he was still breathing. Burned and torn flesh bled. Bone and teeth had spackled down the front of him. I tore off my shirt, dropped to my knees and tried to stop the bleeding. My thin shirt was useless. I slid my arms under him. My hands and legs ached, but lifted him, knowing his only chance was to get him to town. I stumbled and tripped, but never fell and rocks jammed my feet and the thorns of brush and cactus caught my clothing. My breath came hard. My body reacted, and I was divorced from it. I didn't look at the man in my arms. I focused down the ridge. I knew I had to get there. All I saw was the truck and willed myself toward it step by step, because it was the only way out of the desert for Charlie, and I was the only one who could get him out. I heard Grandfather was still high on the hillside, yelling for me to keep going to the truck, "Don't wait for me, go. Get on down to the hospital."

Charlie bled to death halfway down the mountain. I wasn't sure until I got to the bottom by the truck, but I felt less of the weight of him. I've heard people talk of dead weight and always thought that meant heavier. I stretched him out in the bed of the truck while I waited on grandfather to reach us. I gasped for breath and my head full of the sticky iron smell of blood. With my shirt I tried to clean the blood and bone shards from his face and chest, but the blood soaked shirt couldn't absorb anymore, and I ended up smearing it around, doing nothing. Far away to the south, I could see dust from dirt bikes and birds soaring on thermals. Jumping from the truck's bed, I threw up and tried not to cry. Charlie had always joked,

"If I die, don't feel obliged to eat me—on account of my namesakes and all." And that was all I could think about.

* * * *

After Charlie's funeral, my father banned me from going back to the mine. We sat in the kitchen of our prefab company house: Grandfather, Father, Mother, and I. An argument broke out, brief and vicious like a street fight. Grandfather asked if I could go back up and take care of Molly and close up the mine so he could go visit friends from the war he and Charlie had had down in San Diego.

My father said, "Absolutely not. You have to be crazy, old man."

Grandfather said, "Of course you don't want to teach the boy how to finish a job, just how to quit."

"My boy is going to start learning how to operate in the modern world. Banging on rocks, hoping to strike gold is a worthless dream."

I blurted in, "What would you know? You copped out and took the safe route."

My mother said, "Let it go, all of you. Please, let it go."

His eyes never left me. He looked like he was chewing rocks then said, "You're no man. Someday you'll get it, maybe, maybe not."

Grandfather said to me, "Now, don't be disrespectful to your father. I'll take care of it myself." He left the house, and all I heard was the sound of the rough engine, fading away.

* * * *

School had been in session less than a couple of weeks. When I got home from class, my mother mentioned that a friend of Grandfather's had called from San Diego. Apparently, he hadn't shown up yet. She mixed margaritas, and I walked out the door and into the desert. I climbed a ridge to watch the sunset. As I sat down, what my mother had said registered with me. I got up and ran home. In the kitchen, I told Mom that I needed to ride my dirt bike up to the mine to see if Grandfather was up there and if Molly had been looked after. She looked at me and said, "Your father doesn't want you up there."

I had to go. But she was adamant. "You can wait and talk about it with your father. That old man has been up there since the Forties, he's fine."

Another few hours could matter. I knew she would never change her mind. Retreating to my room, I stuffed a pack with some gear and waited until I knew she was watching television and strode out.

* * * *

I hadn't been in the desert for a couple of weeks and it had been a week since I left home. When I got to the mine, it was still in disarray, and Grandfather's old red Dodge was gone. I thought about Molly. Down at the corral, hoof prints led out of the open gate. I figured Grandfather probably found Molly missing and went for help to round her up. I knew I had to follow the mule's tracks. I couldn't leave Molly out here to be ravaged by coyotes. Charlie wouldn't have wanted that. It hurt that Grandfather didn't come to me for help, but after thinking about the argument with father, I understood.

I picked my steps with care. The stones slipped. Hot morning air convected the fragrance of pinion pine and mesquite up arroyos. My lungs filled with air like incense. Cholla, prickly pear, ocotillo, and barrel cacti were scattered among the Joshua trees and yucca plants—in the desert, everything was swathed in spikes or thorns. A dust devil on the playa leaned with the wind and smog blown inland from Los Angeles streaked the southern sky. I shifted my bush hat back and scouted the trail for rattlesnakes or tourists with six-guns, pretending to be cowboys.

The desert felt like prehistoric space to me. I could fix

a spot to navigate by and by midday feel like I had made
no mileage toward it. I thought of the immigrants, who
wandered into this desert like Charlie and I used to talk
about. I wondered if they thought their life so bad back
east that they figured this wasteland worth crossing. Charlie
and I also talked about the people not fitting into the world
of cities and towns. I was only looking for a mule.

Molly's tracks pocked the trail, and I followed them.
I imagined Molly waited at the corral for days before
wandering off. The mine had looked untouched. The first
day I struck out on foot. Taking off like I did, I didn't stop
to check the fuel, and I'd be lucky to make it back home
on what was left.

Ahead of me, the trail ran into a base of a butte and
angled up the steep slope. I labored and sweated up the
slope and at the top looked over the desert of folded and
broken rock. The tracks faded, blown away by the ridge-
top winds. With my binoculars, I scanned the landscape. I
saw a place in a bend of a wash at the base of small cliff
where the brush was denser and greener. I knew I could
find more water there. I also knew that where I found
water, I might find Molly. Grandfather told me how he
and Charlie found all the springs and used them as camps
before striking gold. I wondered how he was.

I scrambled down, kicking dust and stones, to the
base of the hillside and worked my way along the sandy
bottom of the dry wash. It was a narrow channel. The
brush had been scoured from the banks, leaving reddish
and gray stones. I wasn't worried about flashfloods
because when I was on the top, I saw no clouds, except for
the smog.

In the bend of the wash, the cut bank was ten feet
high and the rock face extended another thirty feet higher.
Just above the high water mark a petroglyph was carved
into the granite: a bighorn sheep. The water wasn't on the

surface, so I knelt in the sand and scooped it away from the shaded bend. Damp, the fine grains stuck to my hands, and as I scooped, water started seeping in. I dug until the hole was deep enough for me to take a long drink. Sometimes at springs, cisterns, or defendable buttes, I'd find pottery shards, stone tools, or arrowheads. I thought of how in a hundred years someone might come across the *Purgatory* and try to piece together the culture of hard rock miners.

In the shade, I ate a can of beans, and then drank from the hole. The only tracks in the wash were lizards, pack rats, rabbits and the occasional snake. I hoisted my pack onto my back. My body was stiff. The long days exhausted me, then sleeping on the cold ground, in an old, wool army blanket, waiting and not waiting for scorpions or snakes looking for warmth, the rocks rising up after my body pushed through the sand. My body ached from the hours of climbing and walking. Grit and grime chafed my feet, armpits and crotch. Sand lived in my mouth.

I heard a small plane. I knew the fire fighter at Lake Tamarisk had his own plane and sometimes flew around and knew someone could be looking for me. I moved into the bend next to some brush and sat. Every time I heard dirt bikes or aircraft, I hid. For the same reason, I never lit a fire, even during the day for fear of sending smoke. I didn't want to be found and forced home before I found Molly.

When the sound droned off, I got up and climbed up the ridge. I looked for a reasonably flat area about a third of the way down, a spot out of the flood area and off the windswept ridges and out of sight. If I were lucky, I'd hit a thermal belt where it'd be ten degrees, or better, warmer. I found a nice flat area that had a small screen of brush. The sun started to go down, and I was in the shadow of the ridge. The morning sun would hit me as it cleared the horizon. The warm wind moved down slope.

I ate some Spam and beans with a tortilla. The food
was warm from being carried in the pack next to my
back. I sat in a dried shallow depression rimmed with
mesquite and ironwood. Locoweed rattled when the
wind gusted a little. Across the arroyo, on the ridge top,
the sun illuminated a low stonewall. A natural formation
that someone who didn't know better might think was
built by pioneers or Indians. The light caught its edges
and deepened the shadows in the cracks between the
rocks. I watched it until it disappeared into the darkness
and fell asleep wondering how far off Molly was and
how Grandfather was doing. I also thought of my
parents, although I knew they would be more pissed than
concerned.

In the morning, I started a grid search to the south
and around noon sat under the shade of mesquite just
looking at the playas. I napped a little. I was tired. At the
top of a mountain, I saw I-10 to the south, the artery of
commerce between L.A. and Phoenix. Semis, cars, buses,
groups of motorcycles, RVs, and trucks towing boats to
the Colorado River or Lake Havasu. It must have been
Friday. A train smoked and cut across the desert like a
Chinese dragon. It seemed to float above the ground. I
thought about the troop trains Charlie and Grandfather
talked about riding on. They had been out here before
the interstate. Back then the highway was two rough lanes
and rutted roads and mule trails were the only way to get
around. So much had changed in the desert.

I shook my head and pinched the bridge of my
nose, massaging it. At the edge of a playa, I spotted what
looked like a vehicle. With my binoculars, I saw it had the
same faded red color as my grandfather's truck. Excited,
I started down ridge. I had to get down there to help
Grandfather. I didn't know if the truck got stuck or if
he had parked and taken off over the desert on Molly's

trail. Rocks and dust scattered ahead of me. The slope was steeper than I thought. I kept my eyes on the truck as my speed built up. I grabbed at a bush and leaned back to slow down. Thorns dug into my palm, and I let go. I slid further. My foot grazed a rock, twisting my ankle. I cursed.

A sharp pain shot into my calf as I slid into the wash. I sat and took several deep breaths. My ankle throbbed. The laces on my boots had loosened, so I cinched them up to keep the swelling down. I stood. "Stupid son-of-a-bitch," I said as I flexed my ankle and grimaced. A loss of focus had killed better men than me. I could still walk. I had to walk, and I limped down the wash that cut out onto the playa.

After a mile, my ankle numbed. I made it to the truck, and it was my grandfather's. The rear right tire had been spun off the rim in the sand, and the axle was wedged on the ground. Walking around the truck, I found Molly's tracks leading out onto the playa and next to them, Grandfather's boot prints. I shaded my eyes and looked across to the other mountains. Nothing moved. High up in the sky turkey vultures drifted on the haze. I followed the boot tracks.

The dirt on my body itched. I stumbled on the small ripples of earth left where the water had evaporated. The flatness made walking easier, but I felt a little delirious on the stark white dirt under the sun. I squinted and fell into the steady step after step like a being rocked in a cradle. I lost consciousness of everything except where I put each foot and the heat swallowing my body as my mouth dried. I walked during the dangerous part of the day when I should've been under the shade of a rock or bush, glassing the desert for movement. A time when heat stroke could knock you down before you ever knew you were struck. My mouth thickened with mucus. The sun drew an arc over me until its rays shone in my eyes whenever I looked up. Dizzy, I stopped and took a drink.

I followed on, hoof and boot tracks one after another and me on the flat plain crossing an occasional slash a motorcycle had cut. Sometimes the footprints stumbled, or left drag marks where the heel or toe didn't get lifted all of the way. A speck on the dried lake bottom, I thought of the broke down truck and that maybe I should've turned back for more help, but knew there was no time. The time for turning back for help was done, and I knew if anything was to be done, it had to be done, now. In my mind I could hear Grandfather and Charlie laughing, telling me, "You took that drink, now swallow it." I had to follow those tracks, to the coast if needed—modern world or not, I still had to walk in the old way, the tracker and the tracked.

I stopped close to the old shoreline of the dead lake. After a couple of minutes and another long drink, I clambered up to a flat spot and saw Molly's head above some mesquite. I laughed, did a little foot shuffle, but restrained myself from yelling, so as not to spook her. Not that I could've yelled very loud anyway with my parched throat.

I walked to her. Standing still, she tilted her ears toward me. I smiled. I thought she might come up and lean on me. As I cleared the last bush, my stomach went sour and as the smell hit me, I turned and vomited. My legs cramped. Grandfather lay dead in the sand. His old canteen, canvas rucksack were strapped on his body, and it looked like he died in the act of crawling, moving forward. My legs wobbled, and I fell to my knees. I sobbed, but found the desert had dried the tears in me—only sweat came out of my body.

The months of the summer and fall collapsed onto me. My gut hurt. I sweated as an evening breeze picked up and cooled my skin. I knew the times of Charlie and Grandfather kicking around the desert to make a living were all gone. It wasn't 1879 or 1949—it was 1979. I would never live like those two old men. Nothing left but ruins, artifacts and the bones of ghosts under the burning sun. It was ridiculous to think what they held onto could've helped me anymore than what my father had. His ways were fracturing too, except he wouldn't have a piece of desert to isolate himself on to ignore the world, only a lay-off notice and the unemployment line.

Molly pawed the ground and snorted. I had lost track of time. I stood and rubbed my eyes. The sweat burned. The sun began to set. Taking out my water bottle, I rinsed my mouth with the warm water, and then poured some in my hat for Molly to drink. She pushed my hand down as she slurped then lifted her head and chuffed at me. Water sprayed me. I wiped my face and then scratched her between the ears as she pawed the ground. I winced into the sky, said, "It'll get cool soon." My voice cracked. Bile soured in my throat as I looked at Grandfather's body in the sand. I took out my wool blanket and covered him.

I knelt by him. I didn't know any of the rituals of prayer or funerals, so I mumbled, "God rest his soul." It felt false and cheap. I stood and looked around wondering which direction to take. The highway lay to the south out of sight. I stretched and decided not to go anywhere for a while. The sunburned smog traced a red scar above the mountains, while the western sky erupted with the color of bloodied oranges. The ancient lake tinted yellow and faded to dark as I gathered brush for a signal fire.

A HUNTER'S STORY

"The wilderness is a tonic."
Henry David Thoreau

In the morning it rained. A cold front drove over the
Clearwater Mountains. Jock sat in the tree line close to a
game trail, waiting for elk. Fireweed blazed along the old
road bank where slash piles had been burned. The white
pines were only about five feet tall, but the alder choked
the old skid roads. The brush, saplings, and deadfall made
moving through the tall timber difficult, except for the
game trail. As the rain started, Jock slipped under an old
red cedar, taking care not thump his recurve bow against
the tree limbs. The fronds and branches had woven a
thick roof. It would be dry under the boughs until winter.
The scent on the wind filled with water. Jock rested his
lean body against the trunk. He had grown up in these
mountains and had lived nowhere else except on his
grandfather's ranch and, when it was gone, in the small
town along the Clearwater River. He cocked his head,
listening for animal sounds between the raindrops and
creaking trees. If the storms blew away before evening,
and the wind calmed, he could still hunt. He smoothed
water off the bowstring.

Jock loved the bow he built: the smell and feel of
the wood, and the dust in his hands, filling up the whorls
of his fingerprints and how each thin slip of wood had
been fitted on the other and glued together. He tillered

and sanded, shaping each limb until they were mirrored likenesses affixed to the riser he had made. The finished wood gleamed, and the wood grain waved through the laminated layers like distant hills. He didn't want the die cast aluminum compound bows strung with wheels and pulleys. He looked for the sweeping line that looked like his wife's waist and hip and as she grew with child, her belly swelling like a bow being drawn over seven months. The practical beauty of a tool at its simplest fit his hand.

Thunder rumbled, and the wind rushed down the drainage on the backside of the ridge. Jock clipped away a few branches of alder, huckleberry brush and three white fir saplings to open a shooting lane. He felt the breeze moving down hill and raised his nose into the wind for the musk of rutting bulls. The last time he had hunted this ridge was with his brother, Kip, who had left the county three years ago. Within the month Jock was leaving too.

Jock didn't want to move to the desert, to a mining town in Nevada where the only tie to the land was blasting gaping pits out of it. When he had driven down to apply and interview for the job, the heat taxed his breath and the open land made him dizzy. After he returned to Idaho, he smoldered with the uneasy feeling that when he and Ellen left for the waterless country of bitter brush and ranges of barren rocks, it'd be the last time they'd live in these mountains where they had both grown up. She wrinkled her nose and asked why he couldn't find a good job someplace green. He knew she'd grow tired of looking at the browns and grays of the desert and herds of trailer homes strewn across the basins of dried lakes. He feared she'd get tired of living in the desert and then him.

The wind came over the ridge and roared in the treetops. Branches rubbed together, and the occasional falling limb punctuated the creak of swaying trunks. Jock breathed in the pine, fir, cedar and the urgent smell of stormy air. He loved bad weather. A sharp crack of thunder rumbled as the wind gusted harder. The shadows darkened under the timber as the clouds thickened. He felt the whole land swaying under the storm, and he heard the water filling the draws and the streams rushing down to the rivers and reservoirs.

The rain let up, and the temperature rose. Water dripped from the boughs, pelting the brim of his hat. No elk came down the ridge. Jock heard a bull bugle in the distance, but it was a long way off. He looked into the sky and measured how far the sun needed to touch the horizon with his hand. He got up and started down the trail.

Jock made his way through a stand of larger pines, pausing every few feet, cocking his ear and sniffing the air. He jumped a small creek and went up a draw until a small meadow opened ahead. It was forty yards across, further than he felt comfortable shooting. He knelt next to a six-foot white fir. He noticed some of the brush had been broken and rubbed by a bull, exposing the pale inner bark. Scattered bones from a winter kill poked out of the grass. The breeze came at a forty-five degree angle. Unless the elk came up from behind, they wouldn't wind him. He held up his bow and sighted down the arrow, feeling the wind on his cheek, and shifted for his point of aim. He relaxed his arms. The white fir blistered with sap on its smooth gray bark. Jock squished a blister and rubbed the pungent sap on his shirt.

For three days Jock had left before sunup and came back to camp after dark amid sounds of four-wheelers and trucks running over gravel roads. On the second day, cirrus clouds gathered high in the west, then a cold front had moved in the night of the third and a cold rain made Jock move his bedroll into his tent. It had been hot — high 80s low 90s — but this morning he saw his breath as he fried potatoes in the drizzle. The cooler weather would make the bulls more active and send them into the full rut. Jock rubbed beeswax on his bow's limbs to protect the long, clear grain and then strung his bow. He hefted it each morning, nocked an arrow, drew the string to the corner of his mouth, enjoying the tension along his arms deep into the muscles of his back, and shot the arrow into a stump.

Jock scanned the meadow. His family had grazed their herd here. He and his brother chased cattle up these ravines and driven them down to the meadows and loaded them on trucks for either the ranch or auction. They had kept equipment running, even manufacturing parts in the shop or jerry-rigging equipment like pump motors until someone got into town. Jock liked to work leather and apply saddle soap and work oil into harnesses, saddles, headstalls, and all the rigging of running horses. The smells of earth, cut hay, and livestock saturated his clothes, his skin and hair. At the end of the week, Sunday, he took comfort that his work could be held in the hand or looked at in the field. When Grandma had sold the ranch after Grandpa died, Kip went logging and then left for steady work in a south Idaho mobile home factory, and Jock went into town to sort nuts, bolts, washers, and plumbing fixtures, and answer home improvement questions. Whenever he pushed his timecard into the clock it was like the snap of a closing lock. After waiting a half-hour, Jock got up and crossed the meadow into the trees.

Jock hiked up a two-track that had been rutted and scooped out by large tires. Kids had driven up in the spring and gone crazy mudding. The ridges bristled with conifer trees, which caught the breezes like wooden wind chimes. Tracks of elk, deer, and a few coyotes pocked the trail. He spotted bear scat by a patch of huckleberry bush. The afternoon shadows deepened, and Jock stopped. He knelt as still as he could. Aside from the occasional distant rumble of logging trucks, pick-ups, and the four-wheelers, he listened to magpies, sparrows, and squirrels. Ravens dove and circled, most likely over something dead, a hunter's gut pile or a predator's kill.

Jock listened to some elk in the brush and trees down the ridge in a meadow where they were feeding. He took his pruning shears and clipped some spruce boughs to clear his shooting lane. He loved the smell of fresh cut wood. A squirrel chattered. The elk started up the trail to a bed down area. They moved at an easy pace, grazing and looking for predators. Two calves moved into the shooting lane twenty-five yards away, picking their steps, sniffing the air. Jock held his bow with an arrow nocked. He didn't move. Several cow elk walked past, then Jock saw a bull coming up the trail through the branches. It was as big as a quarter horse. The antlers shone dully. The bull stopped with only its head exposed. Jock's heart pounded. The bull shook its head and looked back. The antlers swished the air. Its ears twitched. In two steps, Jock would have a clear shot. A woodpecker's staccato knock echoed in the woods.

Beads formed on his upper lip and his brow. The air did not move. Jock focused on the neck of the bull. He needed a clear shot at its chest, the heart and lungs. The bull pawed the ground, kicking up clods in the trail. It kept looking over its back, ears canted downhill.

Jock flexed his fingers. Elk lower on the hill started galloping as the bull bolted forward. Jock saw only the blurs of the animals as they crashed through the brush and small trees. They cleared the ridge top and were gone. Uncoiling his legs, he sat with them stretched out in front. He pulled his bag around and took out a granola bar. As he wondered what had spooked the animals, he heard the faint rumble of a four-wheeler.

The noise continued up the ridge, powering up and down the insistent revving of the engine. Jock caught glimpses through the forest as it worked its way up the trail. The rider wore camouflage and a compound bow rested in the handlebar-mounted rack. Exhaust swirled around and it stank. The rider leaned over, scanning the ground. The four-wheeler lurched into the shooting lane, paused. Jock sat, glared and spat. The man slid and spun his tires, powering up the hillside. Jock rose. The damp duff muffled his footsteps as he walked through the trees and onto the ridge. A trail followed the ridgeline and Jock walked uphill. After a mile he came to the top where the land opened to small bowl. Two does and a yearling grazed, lifting their heads every few bites to look around.

On a knob, Jock knelt at the edge of the clearing. Water soaked his knees. The dampness and coolness would keep his scent down. He wiped off his bow and string with a bandana and nocked an arrow. He heard the breaking of branches over the ridge. The deer loped away.

The rain stopped, leaving the sound of it dripping from the trees and brush. The breeze blew into Jock's face, and he smelled the pungent elk. He put in his mouth-reed and brought the plastic tube to his lips and blew the sound of a bellowing elk. It started low, but ended with a higher pitch and a series of barks from deep in the chest. Brush cracked and popped. Jock felt strong as the cool air filled his lungs. The bull bugled. It was urgent and made Jock shift a little. The tops of trees vibrated as the elk knocked its antlers against them. Jock made another quick call and dropped his tube and made a series of cow chirps with his mouth reed.

Antlers four feet in length and spread a yard apart emerged above the brush, each tine arced and curved up like bone scimitars. The bull stepped into the clearing. Steam rolled off its body. The elk was over fifty yards away Jock estimated and hoped the lust would carry it twenty more yards into his killing range. The bull shook

its head and water sprayed. Its nostrils opened and closed
on clouds of breath. Jock felt as taut as the bowstring he
gripped. He breathed deep into his gut to calm his hands
and slow his breathing. He smelt his own musk of fir and
pine pitch, dirt, and wood smoke. The animal could charge
and trample or gore him. He thought about another cow
call, but only if the bull looked away. The sun broke
through the low-flying stratus cloud and the bull's hair
shone copper and blonde. The leaves and pine needles
hung with crystal drops. The elk stepped into the clearing
and bugled. Jock blinked, breathed deep. Water and sweat
ran down his neck. He was always surprised that the
sharp-eared animals couldn't hear the torrent of blood.

The bull, full in the clearing, lowered its antlers and
thrashed a snowberry bush and came up with vines and
mud. It turned its head and bellowed again. Its erection
thumped up and down along its belly. It pissed. It looked
over its shoulder. Jock lifted his bow, and mewed a soft
cow call. The bull lurched forward. Its neck outstretched.
Jock waited for it to lift its head or turn, so he could shoot
into the chest cavity. Jock focused on the snout fuming
puffs of steam and waited. The bull stopped fifteen yards
away, lifted its head and looked south. Its loud and guttural
call echoed down the ravine.

Jock sighted on a swatch of tawny hair the sun grazed
and aimed at it. He pulled back on the string and all the
muscles in his upper body flexed, and he heard the creak
and pop of the bow's lamination separating. He released
the arrow as the bull spun. It scattered water and clods of
mud. The arrow struck in the center of its body, behind
the heart and lungs. The elk disappeared almost from
where it entered the clearing. Jock inspected his bow.
Along the edge of the upper limb, above the handle, rough
cracks formed along the smooth lines where the glue
didn't hold the layers of wood together.

Jock laid the bow in some wild roses and stood. The sounds of elk stampeding disappeared into the draw. All the energy drained out of him. He wiped his face then looked at his hands — sweat, grime and calluses, the deep lines and scars, hands with which he would caress his wife's swollen belly for two more months. A cold breeze picked up and the rain misted. Fall had blown into the mountains. Winter would be early, and he wasn't ready for the change. He stared at his palms and fingers for a minute, thinking how no matter how hard a person worked or loved, failure had its own ways. Geese honking caused him to turn skyward and see the flock flying in a ragged V under the thick clouds. They wobbled in the wind. Jock moved his feet as the mud sucked at the soles of his boots. He watched the geese fly south.

Jock hiked down to camp, carrying his fractured, beautiful bow. He started a fire as darkness closed. With a stick he stirred the coals and placed a potato in them. He emptied a can of corned beef hash in a cast iron skillet and set it next to his coffee pot. He lit his lantern. After eating, he boiled out his skillet and washed his dishes in the stream at a spot that had been flattened and widened by his family's cattle years ago. The fire popped and crackled as he banked it for the night. He stood into the smoke to dampen his scent in his clothes and on his body. The fire settled and smoldered. The night quieted.

The broken bow lay on his sleeping bag. Good with his hands, he was not used to the things he built failing, and as a hunter, he had never lost an animal. It stung to think his last hunt before leaving the mountains would be a bust. He stared into the glowing coals, inhaled the smoke and felt the cold at his back. He stood.

From his truck Jock took out some duct tape, pliers and a coil of copper wire. By lantern light he dried the bow and wrapped tape over the fractures creasing the edge of the limb. He clipped eighteen inches of wire. Jock began binding the limb. With his left hand he held the first coil and pushed each turn and exerted pressure, keeping the wire taut with each wrap. He made sure the coils didn't overlap or create any gaps. He fed the six-inch tail through the loop and doubled back over the coils gleaming like Ellen's hair. He bent the wire ends together and twisted them into a braid with the pliers, creating a pressure bandage over the broken limb.

Jock straightened his back and twisted to loosen his muscles. All he needed was one shot to finish off the wounded bull. He decided to get a few hours sleep and hike up to the bowl to begin tracking at first light. He didn't want to spook the wounded bull out of its bed in the dark. The fire glowed and pulsed as he turned off the lantern. Clouds lowered and the rain stopped. Jock kicked off his boots, stripped his clothes. Before sliding into his tent, he stood in his underwear staring into the impenetrable blackness of the surrounding trees as if he expected to see something. He squeezed his eyes closed, blinked and then turned to go to sleep.

Light grayed the mountains, and Jock stooped over the tracks the bull had gouged out of the earth. He stood and scanned the trees down the ravine. By his foot, a blood splatter discolored the grass. He had searched for the arrow, but had not found it and figured it was still in the bull. The morning air was calm. Jock followed the trail, taking care not to slip in the wet grass. The tracks were spread six to ten feet apart with the occasional leaps of twenty feet. Jock waded through some huckleberry bushes, his pants dampened by the water shed from the leaves. On the other side of the copse, he found one set of tracks, but nothing further down. He doubled back to the last one and circled out to find the direction the elk had taken. The bull had zagged back up the hill tracing a check mark in the brush.

The bull's tracks merged with a herd a hundred yards up the hill and they had galloped along the contour. Jock got down on his knees to sort out the prints. Bull hooves were larger and splayed more dramatically than the cows. The bull he wanted had a front right hoof that curved out and a slit ran crossways on the right rear. He sorted one of these two out of the mud pixilated by the herd and kept going. For the rest of the day he followed the tracks, except to eat. He heard them sometimes crunching in deeper timber. Toward sunset the four-wheelers raced around as hunters rushed against the failing light.

Darkness forced Jock to fish out his headlamp, and he continued as the herd circled back around to the bowl where he had shot the elk. He heard a group of elk on the ridge and stopped, so as not to spook the animals. Jock backed into the trees and gathered some deadfall, tore the heart out of punky log with a hatchet and started a small fire. He took his Carhart jacket from under the top panel of his pack and removed a can of beans. After heating the can, he rigged a space blanket so that the silver side faced the fire and he lay down between the fire and shelter. Before dawn he awoke cold and shivering, his breath as gray as ash. He sat up and gathered his legs and arms close to him and rocked for a few moments before he worked his way to his feet and gathered more wood and parts of the log. In the darkness, he heard a generator running from down in the main drainage. The sky was clear and the stars glistened.

In the firelight he looked at his elk tag. The plastic coated paper shone. It was creased and wrinkled from being carried, folded, in his pocket. He planned to tag the bull even if he tracked it to a bloated corpse picked at by ravens and flies. Some hunters he had known in the past would give up and look for another elk, not wanting to use their tag on spoiled meat.

For three more nights he spiked out away from his camp, following the elk through the forest, skirting clear-cuts, and deep into the mountains, past the place of his last round-up, the draw where he was bucked off a horse and broke his leg, by the butte where he had roped a rank cow to drag her from the brush, through a meadow where he and his brother got drunk and had shot bottles off each other's heads, and all of his past and all that he had known. The last of the batteries for his headlamp had died, and he hadn't eaten in a day. He marked the trail with a length of flagging, took note of the landmarks, and hiked back to his camp.

When he walked down the skid trail, a white sheriff's truck was parked at his camp. The deputy squatted next to the fire, with the coffee pot on the grate. The coffee smell hung thick in the air. As Jock approached, the deputy stood and faced him and stuck out his hand. He was thin with large glasses and a bristle brush moustache.

"Ellen's been worried," he said.

Jock took his hand. "How you doing, Charlie?" Jock's voice cracked, and it surprised him. He hadn't spoken in days.

"Finer than you look."

"Chasing a wounded bull." Jock cleared his throat.

"A nice one?"

"Pretty fair. Ellen called?"

"You're a couple days late."

"Couldn't leave a wounded bull."

"Understandable, but she's in a way."

Jock looked into the mountains he had hunted.

"That bull'll die or wolves will bring it down," Charlie said. "Either way, it'll get ate. You need to get on home."

Jock nodded. "Reckon you're right." The clear sky deepened toward night and bats, out early, swung wildly over the meadow like kids playing tag. The most important thing, Jock knew, was to get back to his wife, and his coming child and make their future work out no matter where they had to go. He unstrung his bow and laid it on the fire. From his pocket, he pulled out his tag and tossed it into the flames. The copper windings glowed and deformed. The glue flared blue, the wax dripped and the laminates popped and cracked. Charlie handed him a cup of coffee, and Jock drank it as he watched the wood burn.

IN THE RIVER'S MOUTH

Blood and seawater tasted the same. Saxon had slipped when the boat yawed and hit his jaw on the side rail as he scrambled to get away from the net racing into the Bering Sea. Brandon braced himself on the opposite side of the deck, and all around them the boats battled to set out nets in the pitching sea. Fishermen in bright orange and yellow and dark green scrambled as the sea churned, and the din of engines crashed the air.

Before leaving Los Angeles, Saxon had envisioned himself on a lone vessel on the open sea, but was shocked by the mass of boats that looked like an industrial peninsula jutting from the coast. Smoke rose from the sea and planes circled overhead. Skippers paid the pilots, who could easily spot schools of fish swimming for the North Line. The flashes of aluminum hulls contrasted with the boats of faded paint and scuffed fiberglass. Buoys and old tires hung from the boats' sides, offering some protection as they rammed each other, trying to squeeze ahead. Nets got crossed or wrapped in propellers in the confusion, while jet boats drawing six inches of water glided over gear. The *Lucinda Lee* was a wooden boat, bought for Drake, the skipper, by his father when Drake had come back from Vietnam. The boat was old then, and Drake said he'd move up into a newer boat later, but every season, Drake checked the hull and repainted it.

They thumped into a trough as the vessel shuddered

along its thirty-two feet of waterline. A wave splashed over
Saxon, running off his slicker hood and into his reddish-
blond beard. Saxon was still finding his legs and every day
discovered how slight the sea found him.

"Goddamn, that looked like it hurt." Brandon's voice
rose above the clatter of diesel motors and Drake's tenor
voice from the flying bridge, singing opera. To Saxon it
was a confusion of syllables, a mixing of sound where
meaning was lost.

Saxon pointed. "The net." An hourglass shape was
twisted into its center. He braced himself as the boat
rocked.

"Ho, Skip, stop," Brandon yelled. He was nineteen,
lean and tall, clean cut except for a smudge of a soul
patch. Even with his multiple earrings, Saxon thought he
looked like a military poster of a muscled recruit.

Drake glanced back and idled the engine down. He
was taller than both Saxon and Brandon and his light hair
and beard were smeared with gray. When he stood on
the flying bridge pointing and hollering he looked like a
prophet in the pulpit.

Saxon and Brandon hauled the net in cadence and
pulled the boat backward against the sea as they balanced
against the pitch. The day before Saxon had pulled a
muscle in his right forearm and with every grab and pull, it
throbbed.

He was glad he hadn't busted any teeth or bones
against the railing. His wife, Guadalupe, was back home
in So Cal with a stack of bills and high blood pressure.
Sometimes he looked at a photo of her he kept in his
wallet. It helped to stay focused. He had gotten laid
off from manufacturing dial faces for gauges, lost the
insurance and the income they had set their debt to. She
had hurt her back on a landscaping job and couldn't work.
They sold their little Bayliner, camper, two four-wheelers

and the dirt bike. They didn't want to lose the house.
He looked for better work, but nothing paid what they
needed. He started delivering pizza at night and driving
a produce truck in the morning. He heard about fishing
when he was watching the Lakers with a friend at home.
Jake had brought his girlfriend over and the couples grilled
steaks on the hibachi.

"You can make bank up there. Guys get enough they
kick it all winter and travel," Jake said. "You ever see me
with another job since that sorry-assed construction job
two years ago?"

Saxon thought about that conversation and how after
it, he couldn't think of anything else. They emptied their
bank account for airfare to King Salmon and in May he
flew out, leaving Guadalupe with three weeks worth of
groceries.

Saxon had already been on different fishing boats,
different fisheries, for three months and each one a bust.
In Norton Sound, after fishing for herring, the permit
holder disappeared into the interior without paying him.
Then there was the boat that hit the rocks when the
skipper misjudged the tide rounding some cape, and now
this boat with its minor equipment failures. Only a month
and a half more. He knew he could make it.

The lacquered sea swelled, holding the boat under the
gray sky. With the net back onboard, Drake maneuvered
to reset. The drone of the engine increased. They trailed
diesel smoke and spray. Clouds furred the sky. Brandon
and Sax leaned against the transom.

"This sucks, fucking up the first set, Sax, with fish
rolling just ahead of us."

"There's more fish." Saxon didn't want to hear about
another fouled-up situation and how good the fish were
running.

"It's never as good as the first set." Brandon wiped

his nose with the back of his rubber-gloved hand.

"We'll have to make do."

"Making do won't get me new rims and tires for my ride."

"All right you two," Drake yelled down, "let's see if you can get it right this time."

Saxon flung the buoy through the horns of the fairlead and the boat's motor pulled the sea apart. The two deckhands stood back while the net went out. Other crews were already bringing in the first sets and were busy picking the fish.

Drake slowed the boat when Saxon called that he was almost to the end of the net. "Keep her on the boat, boys," Drake said. "We'll let her soak a bit." He climbed down the ladder, starboard to the exhaust stack and mast. Portside of the stack was the entrance to the wheelhouse.

"What the *hell* happened to you?" Drake pointed at Saxon's jaw with his middle finger.

"I slipped."

Drake nodded and then lifted his chin toward Brandon coiling a rope. "Second season. He can plug in all those damned earrings, but he still can't tie a bowline." Drake spat over the side. "Don't know what his dad was thinking. It's going to take more than going to sea to make him a man."

Saxon smiled as he worked his jaw. Only two days aboard the *Lucinda Lee*, he didn't know either of the men well enough to judge them against each other.

Drake packed a new wad of leaf tobacco into his mouth. "He lifted weights all winter and now he's big and full of nothing."

Saxon glanced at Brandon who stared out at the horizon. The coastal mountains looked as if they were built of pitted iron, folded and clawed, with long streaks etched with colors of pewter, bruise green, and dried blood. The arc-scorched blue ice glowed on overcast days,

towering over moraines, the rubble-strewn paths of the
last ice age.

Getting ready for lunch, they stripped off their
slickers and hung them on hooks outside the wheelhouse.
An action Drake demanded to keep the fish slime out. The
wheelhouse was small, the size of Saxon's old camper. It
held the galley, table with benches, and the captain's chair
and wheel to pilot the boat.

The oil stove constantly burned under a coffeepot.
Wet sweats and tee shirts hung from wires, steaming into
the moist air. Magazines—*RC Aircraft, Smithsonian, Playboy,
National Geographic*—and sea worn novels—*Dubliners,
Adrift, The Hagakure, M is for Murder, To the Lighthouse, War
and Peace*—were crammed into racks. Vapor clung to the
windows and rivulets ran streaks of light down the glass.
The smell of salt, sweat, and burnt coffee was so strong
that it was hard for Saxon to remember the perfume his
wife dabbed behind her knees and at her throat. Drake
shouldered in and poured coffee over a shot of scotch.
Brandon sat in the small dining booth looking through
Muscle and Fitness. Breakfast dishes curdled in the sink.

Saxon rinsed a cup and got some coffee. He looked
out the window over the table and sipped. The swells
emerged from a fuzzy horizon. Saxon liked the feel of
the sea, the rocking of the boat, and in a big sea, he liked
how it felt impossible that the boat could ever escape
the storm. The dishes clacked and Brandon turned the
page of the magazine. Saxon saw the two page spread
of a woman and man pumped up and flexing. Brandon's
eyes flitted over the photograph, his mouth open. Drake
nudged Saxon from in front of the sink and picked up
the dish strainer. He hefted it in his hand as if judging the
balance of a knife. He pitched it at Brandon. He flinched
as it skittered on the table crumpling the pages and
wrinkling the body builders.

"Clean dishes go there after they've been washed."

Brandon picked up his magazine and smoothed the picture before getting up. Saxon brushed against Drake to give Brandon enough room to get by him.

Drake turned and Saxon almost thought he was sorry. Drake's face mellowed, and he sipped his coffee. "Me and his dad ate the same red clay at Khe Sanh."

Saxon nodded. He knew Khe Sanh was in Vietnam. He didn't know anything about it and felt like he should know more, but figured it better to keep quiet and not open too many wounds. Keep the boat steady and keep to his work.

Brandon shoved the dishes around. The electric pump thumped as he ran the hot water and poured soap over the dishes.

Drake pushed by Saxon and walked out onto the deck. He pulled the five-gallon bucket with a rope tied to the handle from the side deck and pitched it in the ocean. Saxon turned away from the door before Drake hauled up the seawater. Saxon didn't like crapping in a bucket much less watching another man do it.

Brandon scrubbed each dish and dropped it in the sink. He flexed his arms and looked at Saxon. "I could tear him in half if I wanted." He rinsed the dishes, put them in the strainer and sat down. Saxon poured a little more coffee on what remained in his cup and drank it as he braced himself against the boat's roll on a swell.

Drake looked in the wheelhouse. "Get ready to haul the gear." He climbed the ladder.

Over the last couple of days Saxon had tried to figure out Drake. He was friendly when he wasn't pissed off, but it didn't take much for him to get pissed. Saxon understood that when the crew screwed up, it cost him. But there was something else driving him. Something other than fouled nets and dirty dishes in the sink. Saxon understood anger and rage. He had gone off in the past, flipping off a jackass in traffic and even punched a pitcher who threw a fastball to close to his head. No big deal. No one was hurt very much.

Saxon went out on deck and left Brandon flipping through his magazine in the wheelhouse. Drake stomped his foot on the flying bridge deck. The pounding reverberated and Sax could see Brandon giving the middle finger to the roof of the wheelhouse.

Drake hollered at Saxon, "Go and drag his worthless ass out here."

Saxon leaned into the wheelhouse. "Come on out. Fuck him. We'll get through this together." Brandon stared. His mouth was drawn tight like a pursed net. Saxon wanted to keep out of their personal fight. He only wanted things to go smooth and keep working. Brandon blinked and let a long flow of air escape from his mouth, but he nodded and followed Saxon out into to the cockpit.

They set the gear. In an hour they started hauling it back in. Drake sang along with cassettes to the *Hallelujah Chorus* and Beethoven's *Ode to Joy* as Saxon and Brandon worked. The end of the net came on board with the last buoy and they paused to catch their breath before clearing the fish.

"One hell of a voice, huh," Brandon said as they picked the fish.

"I don't know much about opera, but I bet he could make some money at it."

"He could have. My dad says Drake had a scholarship to Julliard. Got the boot because he refused to sing for some president. Protesting Vietnam or something. Lost his deferment, got drafted."

Saxon thought about when he registered with the Selective Service and how he never connected it to the draft. It was only later as he watched a program about the

Chicago Seven when he realized that he had never been forced to choose sides between going to war and killing or burning his draft card and heading to Canada. He tried to imagine being a soldier, but didn't think he could kill. He was glad he never had to make the choice. At least Drake still sang from the bridge of a fishing boat.

Brandon pulled a hatch cover off and wedged it along the side where it wouldn't fall. He pushed fish in with his feet so he didn't have to bend over, and a few fish fell between the brailler bags and the bulkhead of the hold. Saxon grabbed the other cover and laid it over the nets. Drake yelled, "Don't put that upside down. It's bad luck. And get it off my nets." Drake began to sing again.

Saxon flipped it over and slid it up the side. It wobbled, clattering against the wheelhouse as a swell slapped the boat. He picked up fish and tossed them in as fast as he could. The silver bodies slipped and Saxon was careful not to step on them as he waded through them. After the last fish, Saxon and Brandon flaked out the empty net on deck. As they motored to a tender to unload, they looked at the fish sloshing in the hold.

The sun crept toward the horizon in volcanic colors. They would unload after dark and wait for the announcement of the next opener.

"How does your girlfriend like you being gone all summer?" Saxon asked Brandon.

"Don't have a girlfriend. I don't know what's with women. I was going to take women's studies in school to help my chances, but my advisor said that was the most pathetic thing she'd ever heard."

Sax smiled and thought, what a pup.

They waited behind a dozen other boats to unload at a tender anchored in the channel. The boats were tied bow to stern, like goslings strung out behind an iron mother, so the skippers didn't have to mind the wheels. The smaller boats rose and fell on the swells running up the enormous black hull. When Drake idled alongside, a crane swung over and a hook was lowered to Saxon, who captured it, so that it wouldn't swing into the wheelhouse or get caught in the lines as the boats tossed about. Brandon gathered the loops of a brailler bag, and Saxon hooked them. Saxon waved his hand at the crane operator. The winch whirred and the cable tightened, and hesitated before the bag jerked loose. Each bag was hauled out of the hold and the fish were dumped into a tank on the tender and weighed. Drake watched the scale, writing down the numbers.

After unloading they anchored in the river entrance. Drake got them each a can of Pabst and then sat in the pilot's seat, reading *The Tempest*. Saxon braced himself between the counter and the table, opened the box of macaroni and cheese and emptied the noodles into boiling water. Brandon sat at the table, leaning into the bulkhead. He gazed out the small window at the gray sea sky. Saxon had kept a salmon and gutted it on deck and rinsed it with seawater. He looked through the store of herbs Drake kept in plastic bags.

"Which of these do I use?" Saxon had found it funny at first that a guy like Drake was a gourmet, but realized he too liked to cook.

"Marjoram, dill, basil and the parsley. I wish we had olives." Drake rested the book on his lap. "You'll have to use the lemon juice too."

"Is that what lemon zest is?"

"No, that's fine-gratings of the peel."

Saxon stuffed the fish, tied it closed with string, and coated it with olive oil before sliding it into the oven. After dinner and another beer they descended into the bow of the boat and wedged themselves into the narrow bunks. Saxon fell asleep, his jaw aching.

Two and a half hours later, Saxon's eyes opened. He

sucked muggy air. He couldn't sit up, the bunk above only ten inches away. The wooden edge was wet from his palm's sweat when he levered himself onto the floor. He heard only quiet breathing and the low slap of the tide changing against the hull. They started their slow, clinking swing on the anchor. Saxon made his way onto the deck. He needed to stretch his legs, get out of the cramped quarters below deck.

Reflected light surrounded the boat. The stars were not so distant from the calm water. Saxon tucked his hands in his armpits, shivering in sweat. He never knew what he dreamed, only that it wasn't good. His chest hurt from his heart pounding.

The sound of another guy pissing into the sea carried across the water. Sound was hard to judge, the boat could be a quarter of a mile away. Like how the lights of Egegik up river sometimes seemed farther than the constellations across space. Saxon's heartbeat slowed as he contemplated distance.

Saxon remembered a couple of days before he left, the scent of Guadalupe's skin dripping from the shower, the color of creamed mocha. She had a small scar on her right jaw from a fall as a kid. Her skin was like nothing he had ever smelled, and he loved to inhale as he kissed her between her neck and shoulder. In one breath he became suspended, her terry cloth robe soft against his chest. She turned and her robe slipped down, hanging from her elbows. He stooped, kissing her, as if he were already gone—missing her—she took his hand and led him into bed where they made love. He finished short. She locked his hips with her heels and tickled him until he squirmed out of her and onto the floor.

"You're getting weaker, sailor," she said. She rolled off the bed and onto him and they grappled on the carpet. Guadalupe always talked and giggled when they made love. She said, "It'll be better next time." He didn't like to

think about it, but they had never been apart so long, and
he harbored fears he'd come back forgotten or that even
in six months she would change and become a stranger.
Many men, and even a woman he met, told stories of
fishing widows. The fisherman came home to find his wife
with a new lover, a new life. Saxon thought of coming
home to find Guadalupe gone and what he would do.
He couldn't think past the idea of an empty apartment,
expecting the next car pulling into the parking lot was her
coming back.

He wanted to tell her how he was learning to cook,
and he wanted to make her grilled salmon and vegetables
with rice pilaf. He wanted to buy a good bottle of wine. He
imagined their first meal once he got back home and how
surprised she'd be. He'd take his time with her for a couple
of days and not worry about anything but each other.

The clatter of aluminum cans from the bow startled
Saxon. Sometimes Drake took his sleeping bag and slept
on deck. The popping and the sound of a long drink
echoed down the side deck. Drake cleared his throat and
his tenor wrung a quiet song from the air in time with the
rhythm of the swells that held them both. Saxon stretched
and thought of cramming himself back into his rack. He
thought of how good the salmon had tasted. It would
hold him until the first set a few hours off. He made his
way below deck to sleep.

Late the next afternoon squall lines formed above
the Bering. The fish were making a big run. The crew had
been going for ten hours with only momentary breaks
for fluid or food. Drake put together thick sandwiches
and made sure plenty of water was available, but before
the morning was over Brandon had started to crap out.
He didn't pull as hard bringing the nets up and shuffled
listlessly when they pushed fish into the holds.

"Keep the fuck up." Saxon said. His fingers ached

from working against the monofilament.

"I'm going as fast as I can go," Brandon said. His movements were sluggish.

Saxon hated the way the kid flexed his muscles and talked about how tough he was when Drake wasn't around.

"Pull."

"Can't we take a break? We can fish here in an hour."

"There's no later. We got to fish while we have the chance."

Brandon slumped into the transom. He was done, exhausted. The net plugged. Sockeye hung from the gear between the stern and the ocean. Their bodies reflected and glistened in captured light. The weight of the fish started to drag the net into the sea. Swells of cold water splashed over the transom every time the boat's stern dipped into a trough.

Saxon spit water. His chapped lips burned. He planted his feet and leaned as the net crept through his grip. His hands cramped. His bones hurt at the end of every joint.

"Brandon," he yelled. "Don't let me hang."

"I'm burnt, man." Brandon's face was white. He turned his head over the side and threw up.

Drake pushed through the fish-filled cockpit. "Out of the way," he yelled. He grabbed the lead-line and pulled with Saxon. Within two minutes, the net squirmed with fish on deck.

Drake pointed at Brandon, "Useless fuckers like you are dangerous on deck. Don't sit there and snivel, get to work." His finger punched each syllable. "Do you hear me?"

Saxon stepped between them. "Let it go, Drake."

Drake looked at Saxon, "You keep to your job." He turned to Brandon. "You can't even stand up for yourself."

Sea foam splashed over the side and the fish slid in the cockpit in a gelatinous mass. They twitched and flopped, dying on the deck as their mouths opened and closed. Drake glared back at Saxon. Spit dripped down his beard. He turned and waded back to the wheelhouse.

Saxon opened the hatch covers and started picking fish out of the net and throwing them into the hold. Brandon sat stunned for a couple of minutes before moving to help. Saxon didn't know exactly how many more days they could fish, but each fish was money and if Brandon quit, Saxon didn't know if he'd break even on this trip. They finished clearing the deck in silence.

Drake called Saxon in to steer, then went to fix dinner. The surface of the sea mirrored and magnified the sun. Long swaths of quicksilver undulated around the boat. The land bobbed on the horizon as Saxon pressed his body into the seat and tried to quarter the boat into the low swells. Drake whistled, making Saxon at ease. Soon, the spicy smells filled the air.

"What's that?"

"You never smell curry before, Sax? I got the taste for it when I went to India," Drake said.

Saxon remembered when he was a kid and how he'd look at travel books and dreamed trips to exotic lands and adventures, but he couldn't remember when he quit believing he could actually do it.

"Think I'll go back to Prague this winter," Drake said. "My girlfriend wants to go to Thailand. I would like to go to Rome, too."

"Your girl," Saxon said. "Lucinda Lee?"

"Hell no, that was just the name on the boat when my dad bought her." Drake stirred vegetables as he wedged pans against the slide guard. "You can't rename a boat without incurring the wrath of the sea gods." Drake tapped the spoon on the edge of the skillet. "A friend of mine renamed a boat and it started leaking. The bilge pumps ran all the time. One of the pumps shorted out, and she burned to the water line." He moved three plates to the table.

Saxon smiled. "What's your girlfriend like?"

"Her eyes are nothing like the sun."

"Not yellow?"

Drake laughed. "Not blue."

Saxon rubbed his neck with one hand as the smells of curry drifted around his head. He thought how nice it was to pilot a boat, to feel the sea kick the wheel and the rise and fall of the swells with the sounds and smells of dinner coming and interesting talk. They anchored in the mouth of the Egegik River. When the food was ready, Drake called in Brandon from the deck where he sat against the wheelhouse. They all ate and drank some beer. Drake turned on the radio and they listened to a World Music show on Public Radio. The next opener was at 4:44 in the morning. When they finished, Saxon did the dishes and went to bed. He thought about the next morning and reminded himself to keep focused on the job, make some money and get back home to Guadalupe, get on with their lives.

At 4:10 AM Saxon set the coffee to boil and made oatmeal with milk and raisins. Drake came in with his hair wild and his eyes red. Brandon was still asleep. Drake stomped on the floor and yelled below, "Drag your ass up here and eat."

Saxon cringed at the rough voice as he dished out a bowlful and ate. He had hated oatmeal and raisins for as long as he could remember, but this morning it tasted good. He put his bowl in the sink. The deck shone from a light rain. The nets were laid out in the cockpit.

Drake jockeyed the boat in the tidal stream ripping out of the river's mouth. Seventy-some boats bounced their hulls off each other, vying for the best position. The buoys and old tires protected the vessels' hulls. The screeching of rubber, wood, fiberglass, and aluminum mixed with the driving diesel engines and the punching curses of skippers and deck hands shouting across the tide. Drake never stopped scanning the water.

"Sax, if anyone throws before I tell you, you throw and holler. I'll throttle up."

All the boats seemed to ripple with tension down to the waterline. A tarnished moon anchored in the sky, swung west on an invisible line. Fish rolled and jumped across the river entrance.

Drake plugged in a cassette and started singing the *Adagio Chorus*.

Brandon came out of the wheelhouse, still half asleep and was trying to put on his slickers when Sax heaved the buoy into a stream of moonlight and yelled, "Go."

The transom dug into the sea, and they surged forward. Brandon fell as he tried to get his bibs on. Boats all around gunned their motors, laying their nets before the running salmon. Corks bounced over the transom, beating a steady staccato.

Brandon got on his slickers and joined Sax, watching the net go over. The boat rocked hard, knocking them to the deck. Another boat had clipped the bow of the *Lucinda Lee*. Saxon pulled himself up and massaged his elbow. The music blared from the deck speakers, slow and eerie. The net raced out as the boat careened through the water. Brandon made a grab for the net. As he scrambled from the coils, his right boot slipped and caught in the mesh. The net ripped it from his foot and flung the brown, rubber boot into the ocean.

The end of net left the *Lucinda Lee*. The towline strung taut on the mast, caught between the net held in the sea and the boat's dead run. The pitch of the motor changed, straining against the weight of the net in the sea. Saxon looked as the mast creaked and saw Drake wasn't on the flying bridge. Saxon pulled his knife and cut the towline. The line popped. The boat launched forward with a shudder.

"What the *hell* you looking at?" Drake yelled as he

worked down the side and onto the deck. Before Brandon could answer, Drake climbed to the flying bridge and killed the motor. The other boats raced around them, and fish jumped all across the river and out to sea.

"Drop the hook and standby," Drake called. "The throttle's busted."

After Saxon went forward and set the anchor, he returned and lifted what was left of the towline. "That was spooky." He inspected the cut end.

Brandon looked at Saxon. He leaned against the side rail. "What a crazy asshole." He snorted. "Everyone out here's an asshole. Look at them, running into each other, cussing, and flipping each other off like a bunch of punks throwing fits."

"They're just trying to make money." Saxon secured the line against the mast.

"Who needs money that bad?"

Saxon pointed at his chest. "I do, that's who."

"Not after that hit. We'll have to put ashore and check for damage. Shit, we'll be lucky we're not sinking right now."

"We can still get work done."

Brandon crossed his arms and shook his head. "You'll do it without me. I'm out."

"You can't abandon us now. It's only a few weeks."

"I can and I will," Brandon said. "You all can keep this shit. I'm missing summer back home."

Saxon thought of the months on the sea, the muscle tearing hours pulling nets, and the sleepless nights, and before he came to Alaska, selling off his possessions and the overdue bills with the phone calls from collectors and their belittling words. He remembered how far he felt he had fallen going from skilled labor in a factory to delivering pizza with high school kids and being called pizza boy. He remembered the odd look of hope and fear on Guadalupe's face when she kissed him goodbye at the airport. His jaw tensed as he clenched his teeth.

"You spoiled son of a bitch," Saxon said.

"Fuck you."

Saxon doubled his fist. "Fuck you."

"I'm tired of all this crap. What are you going to do about it?" Brandon stood and held his arms out to his sides.

Saxon swung and slid. The punch hit Brandon in the chest as the boat pitched up and Brandon slid back. Brandon flailed, grabbing at the air, trying to stop his fall. He twisted in the air as his feet came off the deck. The weight of his muscled upper body dragged him down, and his head cracked on the rail with the sound of a bat on bone. His head lolled at a strange angle. He twitched and his mouth worked without sound.

The noise of the fishing boats faded as Saxon knelt by his side. He hesitated touching Brandon's body. Saxon took a couple of deep breaths and then slapped Brandon lightly on the cheek, "Come on now. Snap out of it." Saxon pulled his glove off with his teeth and felt for Brandon's pulse with a shaking hand. Saxon felt panic and sick. His heart thumped and bile rose into his mouth. He shook Brandon's shoulder, thumped his chest and felt and looked for a pulse again. Nothing. He pressed his fingers harder into the flesh. He repositioned and checked again and then put his head to Brandon's chest. Saxon thought, *it was an accident*, over and over, but he kept countering, an accident he caused. He sat up and looked to the flying bridge where Drake was working on the throttle. He didn't think Drake had seen anything. Saxon knew Drake would own up and turn him over to the Coast Guard. Jail— Saxon felt hollow and helpless.

Saxon's hands started to shake, and he breathed, trying to calm himself and then called Drake down.

He watched as Drake stood up and gazed down at the deck before climbing down.

"He slipped," Saxon said.

Drake shook his head and looked out to sea. He knelt down and held the boy's face in both of his hands. His beard, grizzled with water, dripped onto Brandon's face. He squinted his eyes and stared until Saxon wondered if he'd move again. Drake ran his fingers over Brandon's earrings and then stood. "Keep watch." He went below deck and came back up with a tarp.

Drake covered Brandon, working the edges under his body. "My father fished these waters. Never lost a man. I hadn't either until now." He turned his gaze to some of the fishing boats that had scattered out to sea, specks receding into the horizon. Drake tugged at his beard. "I believe I'm done with all this."

Saxon watched the vague forms of humpback whales sound and fold themselves into the dark sea beyond the river entrance. He wished his stomach would quit churning.

Drake called the Coast Guard over the radio. An hour later the cutter motored alongside the *Lucinda Lee*. The two vessels percussed as they tied off to each other. An officer climbed aboard. He was hurried and distracted because someone else had been killed south of there. Saxon told the officer that they'd been getting ready to haul the nets when the boat pitched. The kid had slipped and cracked his head.

As the Coast Guard zipped Brandon into a body bag, Saxon looked one last time at his face, rigid like sea ice. Saxon watched as four men lifted the bag up to the rail of the cutter where others pulled him onboard. He thought about helping, but felt shaggy, unclean, and in the way of the uniformed men. The Coast Guard motored away as the sun eroded the shore. Saxon traced the horizon. He couldn't remember if Guadalupe's scar was on the right or left side of her face.

Around the *Lucinda Lee*, boats kept fishing the river, motors roaring, crews yelling. Drake sang a mournful song from the flying bridge that Saxon recognized from Guadalupe's church. Saxon smelled the saltwater mixing with diesel smoke and bacon drifting on the wind. Gulls circled and dove into the sea as small planes flew over the fishing grounds. The breeze picked up. Waves broke on the rocks and the river's current rushed against the rising tide.

WHERE THE GRASS MEETS THE DIRT

Spring in the Sonoran Desert is hot. The grass of the diamond holds moisture and pushes up fragrant humidity making the air thick and its taste linger on the tongue. Quinn Belichick is in the outfield waiting for his father hit the last ball his direction. The mouth full of sunflower seeds has dried his tongue and gums. The sweat soaked glove makes it hard for him to keep his hand in the right position, and his hand is hot between the rough, split leather. He tries to scratch his palm without taking the glove off when the ball is hit. It is the kind of crack that carries the crowd to its feet and rattles the pitcher's nerves. The ball flies over the second baseman and drops in front of Quinn before he can move his hands back into position. He charges for the ball, but misjudges the speed and angle, and the ball bounces over his head. He spins and runs to get it as it rolls to a stop in the dirt warning-track against the fence.

Little League tryouts are wrapping up after a weekend of coaches looking over the prospects. They're watching for the kids with strong arms and a fast set of wheels. Quinn starts running from the outfield toward his father who is posting the team roster. The Blue Sox are sponsored by Bill's Bar and Bail Bonds. The roster tells all: who's going to start, and who are the second stringers. No one wants his name missing from the list.

Last year Quinn's father helped chopper the last

Marines out of Vietnam when the Fall of Saigon made it impossible for the embassy to remain open. He manned a machinegun in the door of the slick and bragged that he'd fired the last rounds over Vietnam. Quinn had prayed and wished his father would be home this year for the season and not off flying Marines. His mom always said if you prayed for something hard enough then you'd get it.

Quinn has waited for the tryouts; he would play for his father. Last Friday night, Quinn had oiled his Rawlings glove; the oil smelled sweet, and the slickness clung to his hands. His blue tee shirt looked like a map with oil stains for landmasses. His mother chastised him for using too much and getting more on himself than on the mitt. He cinched up the leather laces, double checked the knots, seated a baseball in the pocket, wrapped rubber-bands around it, and left it over night to mold it into just the right shape. He didn't wear cleats yet. Someday he'd work up to the cleats and the big league uniforms the older kids wear, and not just a colored tee shirt and cap with the sponsor's logo in yellow block letters. They still wear their own jeans.

Quinn wants to play second base like Joe Morgan on the Cincinnati Reds, but his father tells him that the outfield would be his best bet. It doesn't matter, his father will make him a better player, besides, George Foster played outfield, and *he* could hit homeruns. After he practices his grounders more, maybe his dad will move him up to second base.

Quinn's dad comes out into the yard, throws a few hard ones onto the grass, and yells at him, "get down on the ball." Most of the time the ball skips low. One catches a rock, bounces high and pops him in the mouth. His lips sting and his eyes water. The next ball whistles of the ground and he flinches. It skips between his legs. His father throws another, harder, and Quinn closes his eyes and turns his head. He can't help it. Every time the ball gets too close. He hears the voice like a loud speaker: "I told you to stay *down* on the ball." The sky reflects in his father's sunglasses, as Quinn punches his fist into his glove, nods, and crouches in the ready stance.

After about nine balls his father says, "You're no second baseman, Quinn. We'll put you in the outfield where the grounders aren't so rough." Then he heads back into the house to talk on his CB radio or watch *Hee Haw*.

Quinn's legs pump harder. Aphids swirl in the turbulence of his wake, and sparrows flee the sound of his panting. His father has posted the roster, and now stands by the Pontiac-convertible that is parked by the sno-cone stand behind the infield fence. Quinn wants to call out, but he's out of breath, and besides the sunflower seeds in his mouth make it hard to talk. Maybe they could get a milkshake or some fries. It doesn't matter. He'll look at the roster, see where in the outfield he's going to play, and if his friend Harlan made catcher. Harlan is already at the board with some other kids who point at it, laughing. Quinn hopes that Harlan is on the second-string because he's a Sox fan and bragged that Carlton Fisk made the last Series great with his homerun in the twelfth inning. Quinn thought it was stupid. The Reds came back and beat the Sox on their own field in the next game. So what about game six? Reds took the pennant.

Quinn stands behind some of the others. Harlan says he'll start second base. Quinn pictures himself in a big league uniform, back-peddling, eyes squinting skyward, the air quivering from the crowds collected breath, the grass giving way to the dirt smell of the warning-track, he coils for the jump against the wall, arm up, and his glove snapped open in the summer cheers. The impact knocks away his breath as his arm whips across the top of the wall, and it flings him down onto his back. Quinn studies the paper tacked to the faded board and all the names of the outfielders on first and second-string are written in his father's black penned scrawl, and Quinn's name is not among them.

He stands, still searching for his name. Quinn wonders at the next weeks when his father will spend afternoons coaching the other boys, wonders at what he will do during that time, and wonders if he had prayed too hard for his father to be home this year. Next year might've been different, Quinn thinks. He'd have had more time to practice, keep his head down, to keep his focus, his eye on the ball. He should've worked harder this last year. The snickers of the other kids drift off. His father calls after him. "Time to go. More than likely Mom's got some food on, and I'm hungry and want to watch a little TV before bed."

Quinn pulls himself away from the rosters. He walks past the sno-cone shack for his father's car with its top down, the heat from the late afternoon sun relentless in his face.

AN UNUSUAL SNOW

Thumb out, 232 miles of rain away from her, thinking
maybe I was too quick to walk out. The highway drops
from Mountain Pass, California into the dry lake,
stretching into Nevada. Fog rises out of the high desert
ravines and blends with sparse snow mottling the ridges.
Low-slung clouds meet ridge tops and shifts and blends—
ice, rock and water vapor. Wind gusts rain. Spray from
eighteen-wheelers forces me to look away. I can taste
the asphalt. The land and sky are smudged with grays
and dingy white. My last ride, an old cowboy with rein-
scarred hands, dropped me off at the Searchlight off-
ramp. His lever action rifle hung in the rack, and I knew
of all the people who'd rob or kill me along the highway,
it wouldn't be a man unafraid to show his gun. I walk in
the emergency lane. In my small pack are some clothes
and *The Portable Jung* with a photo of Carmen and me as a
bookmark. Cars and trucks accelerate by me as they rush
toward Vegas, believing hitchhikers are dangerous. From
a Trans Am a beer can flies out and clatters empty at my
feet. A '64 Mercedes, the color of a cold front, sputters,
dies, *Climb in*, the couple calls. Smoke rushes forward,
mixing diesel fumes with marijuana.

I'm alone in the backseat. I introduce myself as Bob,
but that's not my name. The Mercedes lurches onto the
highway. They wear matching blue sweaters and smiles,
and offer me trail mix and croissants, and a toke from a

mother of pearl pipe. Over the mountains, Danny and Barb have driven from Venice Beach, twenty miles from where I started, headed for a Vegas weekend. They have an apartment on the beach and like to say they live in the circus, "a freak show," she giggles as he pushes her shoulder, and spend some evenings rollerblading up and down the path, past Muscle Beach and stands selling sunglasses, tee shirts, and junk souvenirs, and love the bums playing music for beer money in the scales of imperfect tone. They eat at small bakeries and chic bistros, and ask if I've had the clam chowder at the Crab Cooker. I have. She teaches ballet and wonders if maybe she should try to get on a show in Vegas, but he laughs and reminds her that they plan to hike the Grand Canyon this summer, and she couldn't possibly commit to a show. I tell her to go to New York, why gamble in Vegas when you can risk the Big Apple, an international stage—Broadway, the Met, Radio City. When you're old, a continent won't seem so far to go. Sure, he says, they could hike the Appalachian Trail, before auditions, but he can't uproot his dreams of tenure. Besides, couldn't she dance *Lakme* in L.A.? "No," she says. "That's an opera."

We'll pass through Vegas's glittering moons offering a smaller façade of the mother planet: Prim, Jean, Sloan. The highway will rise over a small summit, the city's suburbs—a geography of gables and rain gutters of assembly line homes, a Great American Renaissance of fescue, stucco, and Spanish tile— offering an Americana buffer from the dystopia of red velvet wallpaper, brass, mirrors, and free drink coupons, idle gunmen, bag men and enforcers. The old "Welcome to Fabulous Las Vegas" sign hangs on amid the rubble of classical Vegas, replaced by the child friendly Vegas of up all night amusement parks, animal displays, and video arcades. The great cruise ship of the desert, spotted with an oasis of fountains, dropping more water in a day than rain in the Caribbean. The kind of place that if I crossed the wrong guy I could end up stabbed and bleed out in gutter or disappear— vanish.

I'll stay the night in an off-the-Strip motel, reeking of refuse and drugs and desperate sex caught in the throat like a last breath. I'll get a drink in a less glamorous casino, sit at a table with a margarita, fool myself into thinking I'm in a coastal town with rain fresh off the Pacific, which I already miss. It'll be a place from before I moved to Los Angeles, before Fremont Street turns into Boulder Highway, where I can see the street, the rain smeared lights. The sports book has banks of simulcast televisions with school desks that have cutouts for drinks and ashtrays, where gamblers forecast the future of lame horses and point spreads. Bookies offer better pay-offs and slimmer odds against crippling injuries for those who'll bet everything on superstition.

A local with foam curlers in her hair, wearing white shorts and a floral tank top overflowing with flesh, will hoard three machines. She'll fight an old man dragging an oxygen bottle and a Jack Daniels, who believes ruining himself is symbolic of independence and, by extension, make him a great patriot. Like colonial powers they'll argue over which machines are theirs and about to produce the payoff. A hooker in cut-offs and a soiled lace blouse, with a dent in her jaw, causing her to lisp after johns, will ask if I want to "parthy," her hazel eyes as dull as the iron bar that crushed her face. A man with shrunken cheeks and a rash on his arms eyes a girl's purse. His blond hair browned by too many hours standing in street corner exhaust and filthy hands forcing him down. We all believe we are in transition to better things. As I get drunk, I'll flirt with a black haired keno girl. I want to spend the night with someone and wonder if she knows the distance between animosity and reconciliation and how long the trip takes.

Barb looks back at me and says, "Put on your seat belt. We want you to stay safe." Her smile stifles my reaction to not put on my belt, a reaction of being bossed around for years with no particular smile. I click the buckle and adjust the strap. I can't help the habit.

East out of Vegas, the dam pushes away the Colorado River. It guts the Great American West. I'll be over a day away from Carmen and wonder if she misses me. Did she sleep the night before or did she pass out from drinking lemon vodka while watching cooking and redecorating shows?

I'll move through Arizona, land of the copper sun rising—through pine forests, over canyons opened out of flat earth, mesas layered like parfaits, and into the Navajo Nation colored with cayenne and cinnamon sand. The land of the Hopi, the Kachinas, where I imagine them bringing the news of the Anasazi with wordless mouths, using signs or whispering, the land so large that it swallows language and shouts are wastes of breath. A person could see me yelling long before I'm heard. I could look for a blessing and a sacred painting, waiting to be wiped away by wind or floods, but they wouldn't be mine; nothing there, but kids on ragged ponies and cattle. They do not know me, nor I them, except by how we look, and we'll both be wrong. I'll sleep in the sage and shiver in the desert cold, wait for scorpions and snakes, tremble at each brush of cloth against my flesh, feeling venom in each breeze, and wake with my scalp itching from my own dirt. Mammoths once walked this land of shot out highway signs, craft stands, and shards knapped from colored bottles littering the highway.

When the highway splits I'll climb the Divide and coast down to the plains. From the rarefied height I could fall miles to die, and I'll see both sides and wonder if Carmen has a hangover. I'll keep going, catch a ride in a '76 Ford long-box with a crucifix epoxied to the hood, Christ's wounds in red LEDs, and a pulpit mounted in the bed. The old man met the devil when he came and took his daddy's farm in North Carolina for taxes— Satan in a silk tie. The old man'll thump his Bible with a wooden index finger. He'll stand in the back of that truck at swap meets, at fairs, and rodeos, highway rest stops in the hinterland, and preach everything is a symbol of God's displeasure: usury and taxes. He seizes and shakes, pointing over crowds calling that people are not red ink. When God flips that table, the world will rattle. The Bible, indented from the constant thump of wood, is drawn like a snub-nose in a bar fight, God's gunslinger, riding like a lone outlaw across the frontier. He sees his sins in everyone and weeps every night for his wickedness. The two of us and bleeding Christ of the Hood will cross the wired and divided Great American Prairie where settlers converted the land with the plow, guns and disease, God's works.

I settle into the brown leather of the Mercedes, wipe sweat and moisture from my forehead. The smell of pot reminds of when Carmen and I stole her brother's stash, smoking it without regret. A state trooper flies by us as I put the pipe to my lips. I startle, he could haul us all in. They'd stick together, pointing me out as the loner off the highway. With my one phone call, I could only call Carmen.

On the Mississippi's west bank, the run-off waste of a nation will flow by me to the Gulf of Mexico. I'll get a bottle of bourbon and drink with a black guy who remembers the forced segregation I never understood, but see the voluntary isolation of people in the lunch rooms and schools. His face, cracked from sun and sorrow, keeps an easy smile. We share the bottle, Bull Durham, and poverty, and little else, but it is enough. He runs a trotline on the river, keeps the fish to eat, and panhandles for necessities. Figures, it's like bargaining for a deal on a car or a house, only in worse clothes—asking for money is asking for money. A bronze star hangs on his plaid shirt, and he sleeps under corrugated tin, rusting into the ground.

He'll row me across the river, south of Memphis in the Great American Bottom, and I might travel north to St. Louis, the belt buckle of the Mississippi. We'll make landfall on the eastern shore after bailing water with an old coffee can. The slup of wood on mud and the creak of rusty oarlocks will keep time with the geese of the central flyway. He'll tell me to take care and watch for the county sheriff. Loners and drifters upset his sense of propriety. People have disappeared. I'll leave the pouch of tobacco and what's left of the bottle, an offering for safe passage.

I'll forget about St. Louis when I see the road sign for Tupelo and can't help but draw out the ooooo. Tupeloooo. It'll glide out my throat like a last lover's name— Sorvinoooo. I won't know why I know the town, until I see the billboard advertising Elvis's birthplace. Town fathers trading on a name they tried to ban fifty years ago, hoping for economic prosperity. Fallow cotton fields and factories and failed mills collapsing from the inside, the numbers and predictors say it's all getting better. I'll think how much Carmen loved "Cold Kentucky Rain" and "Suspicious Minds," but I'm not going to Graceland. Instead, I'll pass the empty battlefields and abandoned plantations people can't let go of, where they worry the land like an itching scab, never letting it close.

Through naked hardwoods, a waxed, fast Prelude will streak me across the Great American Piedmont, down the tidewater, across land as flat as water, to the coast. A kid

with the outrageous arms of a football lineman, banded
with tattoos, talks about all the women he's had and how
his Ivy League business degree will insure an offshore
account and beach house away from prosecution because
the American dream is screwing people over for as much
as they got and hording it away. He'll drop me off at Kitty
Hawk, where man first flew, although the Indians have
been flying for centuries in the incantations of shaman
and dancers as Eagle and Raven, their wings spread around
millennia of fires. I'll have spent the continent. I'll sit
on the Outer Banks until dark, listening to shore break
and birds, and think of centuries of wrecks piled on the
ocean bottom. The Atlantic gray sky, with clouds backlit
by the moon, will look like a tornado, and I'll pause for
a moment, wonder if I should be running. In the past
I've run and the good it's done me. All I can show for
twenty-five years is a bag of clothes, a book with a photo
bookmark, sitting in the back of someone else's car headed
east, thinking some people are better off on their own.

Carmen will be on my mind with each of those
people I ride along with. The way she grinned like a new
forest morning, and how I erased it when I acted like an
ass the night before her finals. I didn't know until the last
fight. She shouted, "Why do you need to stress me out
before tests? Why?"

The Mercedes hesitates, and coughs, as it accelerates. Zero
to sixty in a minute. I consider asking to get out, turn
around and retreat to an apology. It's hard to weigh the
present against the future. I'll wait ten years, and while
looking through a box, I'll find a twelve year old photo,
now in my pack, of her and I, taken at Laguna Beach, on
a day we thought we were happy, watching the homeless
watch one of their own singing *Don't let the Sun go Down on
Me* like gulls dashing themselves against rocks they mistook

for schools of fish. We gave five bucks to the singer,
and he took our snapshot. The photo: a young couple
holds each other laughing; they lean against a waist-high
wall separating sand and asphalt, a sea-sky the color of
pomegranates and the flesh of plums risen behind them
before night. I'll come to know myself like the horizon,
wind blown in all directions, going everywhere—nowhere.

Snow starts falling on the desert floor, lowered from
the volcanic heights of the Providence Mountains. Late
winter wind falls off peaks, down arroyos, rustling brush
and damp grass like the relentless pursuit of a ruined life.
Dry rotted windshield wipers squeal and create grimy
rainbows from dust and pollution. Pungent smoke swirls
in the defroster, and Barb flips back and forth through a
CD case.

"How about *Swan Lake*," I say.

"I have the *Nutcracker*."

"No one wants x-mas music. Am I right, Bob?"

I wonder for a second who he's talking to, before
I remember my alias. Barb deflates into the seat at his
words. She won't gamble on dancing her dream show in
New York for the fear of being alone. Flakes swirl on the
highway, out of place—233 miles from Carmen. I love
her, and she can go to hell. We were never that couple
in the photograph. This impulse driving me forward and
getting lost in the country isn't the answer, but the only
option I can conceive. I have to put miles between us, no
matter what I can imagine or pretend she might want.

Barb looks back at me, and smiles a melancholy
smile as she holds up a CD. *Lakme*. I smile. She glances
at Danny before pushing the disc into the player, but
he keeps his eyes forward, tapping his fingers on the
steering wheel as he mouths an imagined song. I want
to lean forward, touch her shoulder and say, *I know it's
an opera, not a ballet.* When we get to Vegas I should say I

understand her need. We can go to New York together, build something from failure. But she's stuck on Danny, and I'm stuck with that photograph, marking page 266 in a book I'll never finish. But if she did, Danny wouldn't say a thing, he'd be stunned, mouth working like a ventriloquist dummy's, being left alone with all that he thinks he has to offer and a future sudden and blank, wondering why he stopped to pick up a loner along the highway when he should have driven past. I ask Barb to play "The Flower Duet," as I push my hands into the seat to steady my sensation of falling. Rain and snow pelt the car and the fog rolls down the mountains, engulfing us all.

DRINKING SANGRIA
IN THE COLD WAR

Diane knocks on the front door of the duplex. Her heavy hemp purse slips off her shoulder and clunks against the door. Flower-embroidered jeans disappear into calf-height moccasins, and she wears a fringed leather jacket against the cold. Lilith opens the door in jeans and a pink t-shirt with a black German Eagle spread below the word Munich across her chest. In the small space used for a dining area, an inexpensive glass table sets with two empty shot glasses next to an empty whiskey bottle, and a pitcher of sangria. Diane rolls her eyes at the college textbooks and notebooks spread around the feet of the chairs. Lilith holds a crystal goblet of sangria. Ed, Lilith's husband, lays face down on the couch.

Diane steps in and notices her reflection in sliding glass door on the other side of the apartment's living room/dining room. "What's the point of calling me over here?"

"I thought you might want to look for him. This may be Vegas, but February's still cold enough to kill a person."

Diane asks. "Was he drunk?"

Lilith points to the empty bottle. "Him and Ed hammered this bottle. I wanted to call you over earlier, but when I brought it up Jack was like 'no, don't want to bother her.' Then he stripped off his shirt, kicked his shoes off and was out the door at a run. Ed laughed and passed out. Drunk, oh yeah."

"Jack gets that way. Sometimes he doesn't even need
to be drunk. He'll be awake, get up, grab his motorcycle
helmet and be gone."

Lilith turns to the table. "So I called you over anyway.
Want a drink?"

"I thought they were supposed to be studying. A year
in college and every time it's the same." Diane shakes her
head. "You called me here for this? He'll be fine. I was
sleeping hard."

Lilith pours a glass and holds it out to Diane.

Diane's not sure about the grin on Lilith's face. "What?"

"Sangria means blood in Spanish you know."

"I'm a little tired for this."

The deep rumble of a muscle car roars down a street.
The long squealing of tires strips the night. Lilith sets the
goblet down and goes to look out the front window. She
looks up and down the street with her hand over her brow
to cut the reflection. She lets the curtain drop and returns
to the table, lifts the goblet and holds it out. "Don't you
want to wait for him? Your husband? Have some sangria.
It's a sweet blood."

Diane looks hesitant, but takes off her jacket. Her
dashiki flows around her torso like a guidon cut loose
from its staff as she takes the drink. "Okay, for a little
while. I have to work tomorrow." Diane sets her purse
down by the table and sits. Diane looks at the light
through the crystal goblet.

Lilith holds her goblet up. "Ed got these for our first
anniversary. In West Germany."

Diane examines the light cutting through the crystal.
"I always wanted to ask if you worried about the Russians
invading."

Lilith waves her hand as if brushing away dust from
a table. "Didn't think of it too much. It's always there in

the back of your mind, but you push it out and just live in the present and hope you don't explode in a ball of fire. Honestly, I was more afraid I'd die on the Autobahn." She looks at pictures spread on the wall above the couch where her husband snores. "There's some pictures of us at the Berlin Wall. Now that was scary, with all the guards, dogs, and guns. The barbed wire. Everything looked so fierce." She swirls her glass, the fruit like debris in a whirlpool and then drinks. "What are you guys doing over Spring Break?"

Diane takes three steps to the couch and examines the photos. The out of place American kids: Ed's obvious American military haircut and Lilith's hair feathered and blow dried back, the same as in her senior picture on the wall just above it. A long way from small town America, she thought. "He's got to work. Construction is booming you know, but I'm thinking about heading to the Nevada Test Site Protest. I missed last year."

A grin spreads on Diane's face. "Out there where them aliens are."

"No, Lilith, the aliens are a sham. The real business is nukes."

"Right, I forgot you were a peace protester."

Diane looks at the ceiling and sighs. "I don't protest peace. I protest the nukes."

"You and your flowered up jeans and dresses." Lilith points at Diane's embroidered pants. "And your husband used to be in the army and is all about war and martial arts. And you totally getting into it. Don't seem like you're committed to peace."

"I admit I haven't been much of an activist lately, but I used to lock arms and cross police lines singing. Now I carry a pistol in my purse. "What's crazy is I learn all this self-defense crap and I'm more paranoid now." Diane puckers her lips. "Feels like I've forgotten what it's like to sing peace songs.

"Peace songs. Jack and Ed," she thumbs to her husband, "get drunk and sing those military marching songs. Start head-butting and yelling in each others' faces." Lilith laughs. "Ed's a fucking clerk for God's sake." She motions her glass toward Ed's booted feet. "I mean the only time he puts on his combat boots is when Jack comes over."

Diane sings. "Give peace a chance. Mine eyes have seen the glory coming of the Lord."

"Don't make sense you two would've even met."

"It's weird. We were at a party, and a friend introduced us. At first it was all about the body, but then there was something else about him. Some strange attraction. I got swept away. We knew each other six weeks when we got married."

Lilith laughs. "I got married right out of high school to a guy I was dating to get the hell out of Wyoming and away from my lame family. Before the summer was done we were sitting at Ramstein Air Force Base."

"There's a culture shock for you."

"I had no idea." Lilith shakes her head. "I was a lame assed, small town girl who thought she knew the ins and outs of the world."

"What are you guys doing for break?"

"Nothing, but working extra hours. If it wasn't for my job we'd probably have to declare bankruptcy."

"The super power's military might on the backs of broke clerks," Diane says.

"Funny, I've never thought about it, if all the office guys didn't show up, the whole circus would come to a stop. Good thing for underpaid patriots."

The deep rumble of a muscle car roars down a street. Again the squealing tires cuts off their laughter. Some guys yell. A clattering of cans. Lilith gets up to look out the front window again. "It's that same car all the time. I thought maybe it could've been someone dropping your husband off. You never know."

"You never know," Diane says.

Lilith stares off at the pictures again. "Do you trust him?" Lilith moves back to the chair and sits down.

"What?"

"I mean he's so high strung. It just seems like if he got really mad or slipped—"

"I'm not afraid."

"I didn't mean to imply Jack abused you."
I didn't think you did."

"Just seems like he's got a fire." Lilith's eyes light up.

Diane looks into Lilith's face a moment. "He'd never hurt me. He's careful."

"Ed says he's thinking about reenlisting."

"He misses 'the big light show,' the tracers and the big explosions. Loves being out in the field. He says, 'It's like camping with machineguns and grenades.' You've seen the posters of all those Russian tanks and planes in our living room."

"My husband bitches if he has to stay in a barracks when he has to go for training." Lilith drinks, swishes the sangria around in her mouth. "How're you going to cope with all them army wives? I mean it's one thing for me. I'm the wife of an Air Force clerk, and I certainly don't dress like a hippie. You'd have to be around all those pro-war types. What are you going to do, forget protesting and join their choir?" She shakes her head and sips. "They don't promote guys whose wives make waves."

"I hadn't thought about that." Diane drains her glass.

Lilith sets her goblet down, picks up the matching pitcher and pours more sangria. "You know this crystal isn't even German. It's French."

As Lilith puts the pitcher down, she looks up and jumps, sucking air, her eyes widen, and Diane turns and sees Jack standing in the narrow backyard. He leans in the air against nothing and shivers, his boyish face serene. He squints as if seeing something bright and far away, blond hair combed to the side. His socks are gone, and he's not bleeding.

Lilith holds her pale hand to her chest. "Crap, he spooked me for a second."

"He has the quality."

"Your husband is gorgeous. I wish my husband worked out a little."

"The dangerous ones are the ones with charming smiles."

Lilith opens the sliding glass door. Jack's eyes focus on her. He smiles. He holds his palms up, away from the sides of his body, opening himself. Lilith takes his hand, whispers, and leads him out of the winter as Diane places her jacket over his shoulders. Lilith leads him to the couch where her husband sleeps. He leans into her, and she laughs as he tries to kiss he on the lips, but turns her face to take it on the cheek.

"Now you behave." Lilith looks over her shoulder with a grin at Diane. "I have a blanket in the hall closet."

Diane gets the blanket. Lilith guides Jack to the floor, and he lies down. Her husband remains motionless, face wedged between the couch's arm and cushions. Lilith kneels next to Jack, runs her hand over his hair then down his spine while she hums the lullaby, "Go to sleep, my baby." Diane returns from the hall and stops. Lilith looks to Diane. She pulls Diane's jacket off Jack and sets it on the couch arm and then covers him with the blanket. Diane turns to the table; she looks at her purse, but picks up a goblet and lifts it to her lips. Lilith pushes her hair back and stands.

Lilith starts to walk to the table. "How about putting on some music and finishing that pitcher?"

Diane sips, shakes her head. "I thought everything was over."

Lilith stops walking, looks at Diane. "Over?"

"Yes, over. It's obvious." Diane sets her jaw.

"Obvious?"

"Don't play games with me. I can see—"

Lilith cuts her off. "That maybe Jack couldn't just fuck me once."

Diane raises her voice. "We agreed—"

"To go on as if nothing had happened?"

"Let me finish." Diane's glare makes Lilith pause. "It was a one-time deal."

"Like that's what you wanted. Whatever. He called and met me at my office. Wanted to talk about it. At first he was like 'I just want to be friends and all.'"

Diane shakes her head. "I can't believe it."

"He said he couldn't believe you either."

"What?"

"Two mornings later, he showed up right after Ed left, before I went to work. I told him sometimes Ed comes back after something and Jack said, 'I like that idea.' He said it as he kissed me right there." She points to the couch where Ed is face down. "It was a great way to go to work."

"Every morning I just got ready like I always did with Ed. Jack'd show up about two minutes after. It was fun and exciting. Dangerous."

"I thought he was going to work."

Lilith smiles. "Jack started cutting it closer. Pushing it. The last time he was knocking on the door before Ed had turned out of the complex."

Diane turns away, shaking her head. "I don't want to hear anymore."

Lilith puts her fists on her cocked hips. "I can't believe you're acting all shocked."

"What? You can't believe I'm shocked?"

"Think about how shocked I was when I came out of

the other room and saw you shuffling my husband's boxers
down as he sat on the couch?"

Diane pivots. "You had your hands all over my Jack."

"He was showing me how to defend myself."

"You guys were in the other room for a while."

"Ten minutes. I wasn't sucking his dick. You even
looked at me and asked if we had frosting."

Diane stares at Lilith. "We were all drunk."

"Ed never even hesitated or even acted like it was
wrong. I thought about that every time Jack came over.
You are as committed to marriage as you are to being a
pacifist."

"We were wrapped up in a moment. Things just spun
out of control."

"When Jack took my hand and led me to the bedroom,
I just followed."

Diane smiles a cold smile. "I knew you wanted him."

Lilith sucks in a breath, but smiles back and looks at
Jack. "Sure I wanted him. Look at him. But, I'd have never
done anything."

"It's not like I planned to strike first…or strike at all.
We were drunk."

"It was Christmas Eve." Diane looks at the wall of
photographs. "I always thought of myself as a Christian
woman."

Diane turns and faces Lilith squarely. "It was, but—"

"You even started with the, 'Let's play strip poker.'"

"I did, but—"

"But what? Did you think you could keep it all
contained? Controlled after a casual night of husband
swapping? You think you can cross lines and all the old
boundaries are still in place? Please."

Diane clenches her fists. "But you didn't say anything."

"I was in shock. I didn't know what to say. What
could I say? It was like seeing a car running a red light with

me in the crosswalk. And you behind the wheel." She jabs her finger at Diane. "You."

"Yes, I—"

"Yes, you." Lilith punctuates each syllable with her finger and then drops her hand. "Everything was breaking apart. I couldn't go on with classes this year."

"I had nothing—"

"I was a good wife. Lilith points at Diane again. "Do you know what you've done to me?"

"I'm going to break your fucking arm if you keep pointing at me."

Lilith drops her hand. "Sure, that's easy when you have the advantage. Isn't it?" Lilith takes a step forward and pushes Diane's shoulder and she steps back. "Isn't it, bitch?"

Diane holds her ground. "I can break you, like this." She hurls a crystal goblet. Red wine and fruit spatter over the white wall, as glass explodes sending sparkling shrapnel through the air. Lilith lunges at Diane, her hands like claws at the other woman's face. Diane veronicas like a matador, traps Lilith's arm, locks her elbow and drives Lilith to the floor.

Lilith's breath pops like balloon. She looks around like a kid who tripped in gym class before pushing up onto her hands and knees and then sits up. "Some pacifist you are. You want to kick me while I'm down here?" She holds her arms out to her sides.

Diane's eyes widen. "You look like my friend at the picket line when the pigs came for her." Diane casts her face down and mutters, "I'm sorry. I can't believe it. What's happened to me?"

Lilith rests her hands in her lap. "So easy to lash out and forget yourself when you're not worried you can get your ass kicked. Guess that makes you the pig."

"This isn't me."

"We are married, Diane. I became frightened. I was

going to lose…." Lilith works her way to her feet, nods toward the to the couch. "Lose everything…."

"I'm sick. You're right. We are going to lose everything."

Lilith sighs. Her breath loose like the unsealing of a capsule door. "Are you going to tell Ed?"

"Somehow, I think Ed'll find out."

"Maybe."

"I'm getting out of all this." Diane waves her arm around. "All this."

"You're not getting out of it that easy. You can't just roll into someone's life wreck it and turn your back on the carnage."

Diane slips on her jacket. The fringe swaying like meadow grass in a breeze. "You might think you're trapped in this, but I'm sure as hell not." She grabs her purse and hefts it. She takes out the revolver. Glossy walnut grips shine in the light. The bluing gleams like a young girl's washed hair in the sun as Diane removes it from the nylon holster. Lilith's eyes widen. Diane cocks the hammer back. It clicks, metal locking metal from dropping on the primer that'd send a bullet flying. She holds it up in appraisal, then uncocks pistol, holsters it, and sets it on the table next to the pitcher of sangria. At the door, she adjusts the purse high onto her shoulder. "Tell Jack, I'm going to find my voice and sing again." The door shuts, no louder than the turning of the revolver's cylinder.

Lilith taps the crystal against her teeth the sound of bone against stone. She tips her glass straight up and drains it. Sangria streams down her cheeks. Red rivulets run the long furrows of her pale neck disappearing under her Munich shirt. Ed sits up. The couch creaks when he stands. He glares at Lilith, and then kicks Jack hard in the side. The cracking of ribs breaks the quiet. Jack tries to cover up and swings his fists at the same time, trapped in the blanket on the floor, but the kicks keep coming harder and faster, the hard soles of the combat boots not yielding against soft flesh or the delicate bones of Jack's face. Lilith grabs for the pistol, not knowing what else to do.

RED FLAG WARNING

El Pollo had left them before dawn, saying he'd be
back at nightfall to guide them the rest of the way. Over
these last mountains, El Pollo had said, to a spot on an
old ranch where a white woman took in migrants, feeding
them and letting them rest before continuing to the cities
of the United States or into the farmlands or the forests
for work. Armando looked over at his wife, Catalina,
and three children, Fidel, Soledad, and Pilar, as they
napped or tried to keep comfortable under the shotgun-
pattern shade. Pale dust clung to their skin like the lime
he had thrown on the dead. Soledad, his oldest daughter,
fourteen, coughed hard, her lungs phlegm filled. He
planned to go to Fort Bragg, North Carolina, where he'd
find old friends.

When dawn came he looked out from the foothills.
An archipelago of mountain ranges jutted off the desert
floor, separated by prehistoric lake bottoms. Rugged
and broken mountains rose to the north. Steep arroyos,
covered with slashing and stabbing grass, mesquite, yuccas,
junipers, and shattered rocks forced up from the tectonic
pulsing and pulling of the earth.

Their journey had begun in the jungle along the
Usumacinta River, flowing muddy past military outposts,
smugglers' crossing points, and the ancient Mayan cities of
Yaxchilán and Piedras Negras.

He knew the Guatemalan jungles and the paths and

led his family as if part of a combat patrol to the river's edge, floated across, and struck north past the oil fields in Tabasco until they climbed up the spine of the Sierra Madre Occidental, dropping down into the Chihuahuan Desert. In Agua Prieta they linked up with a man he had known in the Kaibiles, now working in human trafficking. He could get Armando and his family across the border, for a price, but a good price because of their friendship. The former soldier introduced them to a guide, who led them into the Guadalupe Mountains and along a trail that came out at Diablo Creek.

In the arid air Armando missed the jungle, the rich smell of decay, the close canopy, and the humid warmth sheltering him from sight. He kept thinking about the North Americans he had worked with in the army. Lean, muscular men who liked him and told him, "Hey, buddy, you get on up to Fort Bragg, stop in for a beer, my treat." "You get up Virginia way, stop by."

In 1987 he had traveled to Georgia to attend the School of the Americas. The North Americans taught him even more about counterinsurgency tactics and gave him the strategic world perspective on how insurgents from different regions were connected and how the Russian military sought influence through the guerrilla movements across the Western Hemisphere. It also taught him how the North Americans lived and what they believed. Their motto: Liberty, Peace, and Brotherhood. They considered him a brother, knew him as a man of honor and not a traitor to the drug cartel.

Armando's oldest son, only twenty, had been field executed after being caught assisting Mara Salvatrucha drug smugglers. The boy's mother went into mourning, kneeling in front of her altar, praying and lighting candles until the rings under her eyes were as black as the veil she donned. Catalina even lashed out at Armando, accusing him of putting his career before their boy. Then, official suspicion fell on Armando, and he was stripped of his medals and his rank, and his other children were asked to leave their private school, while the police started an investigation into his activities. The investigation was a formality that would have led to Armando being executed, so Armando and his family fled.

The southern breeze cooled Armando's skin. He figured about eight hours before El Pollo returned. With a small kitchen knife, he sliced an apple and handed the slivers to his family. On the trip he had seen many ignorant campesinos striking out with nothing more than a milk jug filled with water, a few cans of tuna, or beans and caffeine pills, not knowing how hard the land was, how it swallowed men without mercy. He got sick of hearing them as they moved north, talking about how they were going to strike it rich. He knew how to survive, to move, and the body's limits of endurance. For his special knowledge of covert operations, he would be welcomed, a combat leader, a major. The United States needed him. He would show them the way back into the Ixcán to crush the drug cartels. He knew names of those in Los Zetas operating in the south and knew of routes in the north like this one. A valuable man. The CIA would be happy to see him. They would buy him a beer.

His children chatted, wondering how far they had left to go. They looked forward to having a house and going back to school. Fidel's Mets cap was twisted off center in a hip, urban way, keeping his ungroomed hair contained. Armando smiled. Only a month ago, they'd talked about motorcycles and cars and television. Their greatest disappointment was Guatemala's failure to qualify for the World Cup.

Soledad coughed again. She looked pale. The mole on her cheek seemed darker. Everyone was worn from walking and riding in the backs of trucks and in freight cars. He was used to sleeping in the day, on the ground, and hiking for miles in rough country. But his family? They had lived a life of leisure in a grand colonial house in the capital city. It hurt him to see them struggle on the journey. They had proved tough—true to their conquistador lineage.

Armando sliced another apple and gave it to Pilar, who was nine. She wiped her hands on her pants, and took the slices, chewing them with deliberation. A toothy grin for such a skinny girl, Armando thought. He caressed her hair and regretted that during his years of service he had spent little time with his children. He rummaged in his pack and grabbed a bottle of cough syrup. He poured a dose. Soledad swallowed the medicine. He smiled, told her not to worry, soon they'd be in a place where there was a doctor. Catalina moved to comfort her. The older woman kept a bandanna tied over her head to keep off the sun. Armando loved her sharp nose and her dark fortune-teller eyes.

Armando looked over to where Fidel sat. In the dim light he looked like Armando's other son. The remembrance filled Armando's stomach with slag. Throughout the family's trek northward he coped with his son's execution. At first he denied his son's crime, believing his son incapable of treason, but as the miles passed he recognized the signs he had blinded himself to—the extra money, the jewelry worn by the women he took out, the Range Rover he had said was on loan from a friend. Armando felt foolish and soon forbade the family to speak the son's name. His embarrassment turned to anger and it smoldered, becoming so dense that he felt the weight of it in his chest and at times caught himself snapping at Fidel.

The morning shadows shortened. During their two-week flight, Armando thought of his former comrades in arms, of using his information, and exacting revenge on those who had destroyed his son and his family's life. Armando squinted his eyes north and saw a wisp of what he took to be campfire smoke drifting over a ridge. He looked forward to finishing their journey and to El Norte.

Armando hiked to a small knoll, after a helicopter had flown off, and crawled the last thirty feet like a sniper. The smoke he saw earlier grew to what he guessed to be a ten-acre fire. The helicopter circled the fire several times and landed out of sight behind a ridgeline. He recognized the helicopter. It was similar to the Kiowa, what the Americans called the little bird, except this one was painted red and white, not an army chopper. Armando realized he must be in the United States or very close to the border.

A couple miles distant he watched three people in yellow shirts, green pants, and red helmets wade through the brush in an arroyo and emerge along a trail. Although the trail snaked through a different drainage, he figured it was the same trail he and his family needed to take. He wondered how many other people would arrive for the fire. He saw the fire had burned along a hundred meters of the trail. Maybe they would wait it out or find a new way around, and either way it was a problem. Below he observed his family under the scant shade, wearing muted colors and conforming to the ground and vegetation.

Before starting back he heard a group of migrants a half mile north along the trail under a copse of trees. One larger tree had strips of fabric hanging from the limbs like prayer flags. Armando waited on the knoll a few more minutes, careful about stirring up the dust. Small flies glistened metallic green and crowded on his face, but he made no move to shoo them. Those campesinos made a lot of noise. He considered creeping down there before sundown, if they hadn't moved on.

Armando returned to his family in the shelter of the

shade. A semi truck followed the two-lane road on the playa to the south.

"I love you," he whispered to Catalina.

She kissed him on the cheek as he sat next to her. He told her about the campesinos over the hills and the three Anglo firefighters and said that the border must be just a little to the north.

Catalina shaded her eyes, looking at the curtain of smoke billowing up. "If they stop the fire, we'll be safe."

"The wind's blowing north. We'll be fine."

She shook her head. "Fire has its own ways."

The smoke rose like storm clouds.

"How will we get around it?"

Armando stroked her cheek. "Whatever it takes."

Their families had been close and they had grown up together, playing board games and soccer and swimming in the sea. Armando's friends took note as she reached adolescence and made comments about her beauty. He discovered jealousy and requested her father's permission to date her. He loved her dark eyes that seemed to read him and her unapologetic bluntness. Catalina's father was old-fashioned. They went on chaperoned dates with one of her aunts. At first she was shocked after the years of almost being siblings and resisted. When he arrived for the date, she laughed at his stiff correctness and chided him, "So formal." He persisted in his mannered way, and she rolled her eyes. She treated the courtship as a family obligation and expected him to lose interest, until one night as her old aunt haggled with a cabdriver, Armando leaned over and kissed Catalina's cheek. From that moment on they had been together.

Armando told Fidel to stay awake and keep watch. He moved some rocks and folded his jacket under his head. He closed his eyes and shifted his weight so that the points of his bones wouldn't grind into the rocks. He slept until

a falcon's shadow crossed his face. His son leaned against
a pile of rocks, keeping watch down canyon. Soledad's
breathing sounded ragged and moist. He feared it might
worsen. Pilar lay with her head on Catalina's stomach, her
head rising and falling with each of her mother's breaths.
Armando listened and then closed his eyes.

He slept less than an hour. The shade shifted and the
sun shone in his face. He rolled over, grazing his elbow
on a rock. He sat up. His son still leaned against the rocks
below him. The others slept. The spire of smoke twisted
straight up, thick and ropy like the smoke from a burning
village. Above him three deer clicked against stones,
moving south, moving away from the fire.

Downhill his son rolled over and curled into a ball,
asleep. Armando stood up and crept to his snoring son.
Armando nudged the sleeping boy with his booted toe and
knelt down.

The boy resisted and tried to wallow further into the
earth as if in his bed in Guatemala.

Armando reached down and squeezed the pressure
point on his son's forearm. The boy shot up, grabbed
at the sharp pain, and rubbed it. Armando stared. Fidel
averted his eyes.

"Look at me, Fidel." When his son lifted his face,
Armando backhanded him across the mouth. The boy's
cap flew into the rocks. Catalina sat up at the sound. Blood
trickled from Fidel's lips, and a red splotch swelled on his
face. Armando whispered, "Do not betray your family again."

Fidel nodded. He held back his tears. Behind
Armando, Catalina started for her son but hesitated when
Armando motioned her back without looking. She sat with
the girls and watched. Armando retrieved the boy's cap and
screwed it onto his son's head with the bill facing squarely
forward. He pointed to his eyes and then his son's eyes
and moved his hand in an arc across the desert, saying,

"Watch." He patted Fidel on the cheek. The campesinos over the hill were yelling and carrying on again.

The little flags in the tree were bras and women's underwear, flapping in the wind, mostly white, some black, blue, green, red, satin, nylon, silk, cotton. On the journey north, Armando had known of waypoints for water, food, a place to rest or meet with smugglers on the trip, marked with strips of clothing, tarps, cairns of rocks, signposts made from scrap wood, all of which looked like trash to the inexperienced. But this tree was not a marker for finding food or water or shade on a hot day.

He knelt in the shadow of an arroyo on the other side of the camp and adjusted his knife. Voices muttered over the rise. Someone laughed. Armando considered going back to his family but wanted to eliminate the problem.

He crawled up the rise and under a bush and waited. Two men were in the camp. Out on the playa a pickup truck drove east, sun glinting off the rear window like a signal mirror.

A small aircraft buzzed north up the spine of the mountains, over the fire, and winged out of sight. Armando rose and walked to the edge of the camp. The afternoon sun shone at his back and into the two men's faces as they turned. They were in their midtwenties. One had crooked teeth, and his hair was tied back in a ponytail. The other had mestizo skin.

"You're too loud," Armando said.

"No one cares."

"They can call others."

"You worry too much, old man."

"I worry just enough." Armando shifted his weight onto the balls of his feet. He heard the crying of a girl in the brush, then the crying was shushed by a voice that Armando recognized.

Ricky Baines emerged from the thicket. The sunlight

highlighted his blond dreadlocks. He wore a Zion National Park T-shirt, cargo shorts, and sandals. He'd been a Navy Seal in Guatemala. He had a disconcerting grin and glacial blue eyes.

"It is good to see you," Armando said. "Your discipline has slipped."

"Look who I have to work with, Major." Baines waved the other men away into the thicket.

"What are you doing out here?" Armando said.

"Operating."

"Operating what?"

"Transportation."

"No drugs?"

Baines waved his hand. "No drugs. Just people." His corded hair glinted in the filtered light.

Someone struck a match and inhaled from the brush. Armando didn't like any of it. There was no money in a few campesinos. Armando inclined his head in the direction of the smoker. "Your people are weak."

Baines shrugged. "It'll be dark in a few hours."

"How many people are you moving?"

"Three."

"Not much money in three."

"They're special."

"They must be," Armando said.

"A curse, purity." Baines grinned.

Armando didn't like the insinuation and shifted the subject. "How's Guden?"

"Blew himself up when he tripped an IED."

"That's too bad." Armando looked into the distance beyond Baines. "It was good to see you, but I need to keep moving." He put his hand out.

Baines shook it. "Be careful."

Armando left the camp and worked his way east until he entered the wash, and then he cut north. He knew

Baines would watch but wouldn't follow. From the base of the ridge he looked down on the smugglers' camp. The idea of Baines trafficking girls nagged at him.

As Armando considered his options, Baines left the thicket with a backpack, hiking south. Maybe it was a part of Baines's strategy, to wait a safe distance to keep his plausible deniability.

Baines's cohorts were arguing. Their voices rose, and there was a struggle. Armando slipped down into the wash, skirting the thicket's edge.

The laced branches and leaves obscured his view. He passed through a narrow passage that opened up under a low canopy of trees like a cave.

In the opening, the mestizo was masturbating in front of a girl with her top off and her pants around her knees. Tears and grime streaked her cheeks. The other man was sprawled out, face down. Armando crept out from the cover of the brush and picked up a whisky bottle. The mestizo glanced over his shoulder. Armando reached for a pistol on the ground.

It caught the man across the brow, fanning a cascade of shards. Birds flew out of the tree canopy. Armando swung again, slashing the broken bottle across the mestizo's throat. The girl pulled up her pants and ran. Armando picked up the pistol and backed into the brush. He held still and heard girls whispering.

Armando crept up to the sound. There were two of them, about thirteen or fourteen. They had fine features, slight upturned noses, and soft rounded jaws. Their eyes were wide, and they were dirty but unhurt, as far as he could tell. The smallest one's hair was pulled back in a ponytail. The older girl had bobbed hair with bangs cut straight above her eyebrows.

A third girl ran up from behind Armando. He moved toward her with the gun up, but pointed it down as soon as he saw her. The other girls grouped around her. She was between the other two in size, but finer boned and delicate. They were terrified. He was familiar with terror, knew its strategic value, knew how to use it to control people. But now he knelt down.

He extended his hand. "It's okay."

He set the pistol down. "Less than a mile," he said. "I have two daughters, one about your age, a son, and a wife."

The girls looked to each other.

Armando repeated, "It's okay."

The smugglers' backpacks were pushed into the underbrush nearby. He told the girls that he was going to see what he could take, and after he was done, he was going back to his camp.

They watched as he rummaged around, consolidating food and water into one pack and throwing drugs, cell phones, a pair of two-way radios, ammunition, a parachute cord, and night-vision goggles aside. He found a GPS device. He searched through their clothes and found driver's licenses and a money belt with pesos and several thousand dollars.

The girls murmured together. He couldn't make out what they were saying over the ringing in his ears.

Armando picked up the pistol and slid it into his belt.

The girls would be a burden, and he considered leaving them with some supplies and directions. Get them started toward the firefighters. The Border Patrol would pick them up, he reasoned, but many people disappeared in the desert.

"Ready now?" he said.

The oldest one nodded like a little bird.

He shouldered a pack and cinched the belt.

The girls all wore jeans and T-shirts, and they had identical green windbreakers tied around their waists. They each had a dark-colored, child's backpack. Armando figured Baines had made them carry water. They kept distance from Armando as they shuffled out of the brush. He didn't know what he was going to tell his wife.

He walked up the draw with the girls sixty yards behind him, and he saw the puzzled look on Catalina's face. She seemed to ask, What man goes into the desert and emerges with three children? Fidel sat higher on the ridge, obscured by a mesquite bush, watching. Pilar and Soledad wore the same expression as their mother.

Armando reached his wife and sat down as the three girls clattered up the slope. He slipped the backpack off.

"Pilar, Soledad, go help them." As his daughters scrambled down the hill, he whispered to Catalina. "They were being held captive, sex slaves."

Her brow scrunched, and her eyes darkened.

"I couldn't leave them. I told them they could come with me or stay."

"Not much of a choice."

Armando showed her the money he found, and her eyes widened.

Overhead a small airplane approached, and Armando called out, "Lie down." The girls rushed for cover. Fidel flattened himself against the lip of an outcropping.

Gradually the engine's whine faded.

The girls emerged from an ocotillo thicket, thorns in their hair and clothes. Soledad choked and spit, and Armando worried she was getting worse.

The sky was darkening with thunderclouds. Armando had the girls spread out and take cover under different bushes. The wind gusted, and the branches whisked the air.

Armando motioned for his son farther down the slope, and then he got out the GPS and sorted through the maps.

Catalina crept up. "The smugglers had this?"

"Yes."

"You can guide us out, then."

"I could, but I don't know the contacts."

She picked up one of the maps. "Are these from the army?"

"They're for backpackers."

He shuffled through the maps until he found the sectional he needed. He ran his finger up the edge, reading the latitude, and then located the longitude. "We're north of the border," he said.

"The United States?" Catalina said. "There aren't any towns on the whole map."

"There's a spring just over a mile from here."

"But how will we get rid of those girls?"

Armando sat back. He knew the edge in her voice.

"We've come so far," she said.

"When there's a chance."

She shook her head. "If you had left them alone, this wouldn't be a problem."

"It's not a problem."

"It is."

"They are with us now, and that's the end of it." A little ways off the girls were giggling.

Armando gestured to them. "You must be quiet."

"Yes, Papa," Pilar squirmed. "This is Abril."

"We're sorry," Abril said.

"And her cousin, Violeta," Pilar continued. Violeta sat motionless, gazing into the desert.

"We are in the North." Armando said. "You must be quiet."

"Yes, Papa."

Over the mountain thunder rumbled.

Pilar whispered after him, "Papa, I'm happy we're in the United States."

He smiled. "Me too, honey."

Soledad coughed and wheezed. Her skin looked

parched and brittle.

Catalina regarded him unhappily.

Armando gathered the maps and the GPS and put them away.

The wind gusted, picking up sand and dirt. Sparrows zipped like feathered rockets, beaks into the wind, wings rippling at the edges. The wind stalled, and the birds dipped and swerved downhill. Armando hunkered down and pulled his wife by the arm. The temperature was dropping. The wind came down the slope and struck them like a blow, and lightning flashed. Violeta shrieked. Another crack drowned her out. Pilar and Abril tried to calm her. The wind roared through the bushes. Lightning struck again.

Violeta put her hands over her ears and closed her eyes. She swayed back and forth. Pilar and Abril sat close and talked to her, but she clenched her eyes tighter.

Thunder boomed twice and the rain came. At first, carried on the driving wind, a few drops speckled the stones, and then fat drops pelted them.

Violeta went on screaming. Catalina winced. Fidel sat with his denim jacket shrugged over his head. Soledad and the third girl—Olivia—kept their backs to the wind and their heads down under a windbreaker. Rain swept the ground.

Gray sheets of water obscured the valley. It reminded Armando of tropical storms but the air was cool instead of muggy and hot. Pilar put her arm around Violeta. Thunder rumbled. Lightning crashed.

Violeta screamed. She wrenched free from the girls and ran down the mountainside.

"Papa," Pilar yelled and dashed after Violeta.

Fidel was up and sprinting over the broken rocks before his father stood. The wind pushed Armando. He struggled to keep his balance with each step. Rain lashed

him. Ahead of Armando, Fidel passed Pilar. Violeta's
jacket was caught in a mesquite. Armando caught Pilar.
She squirmed against his grip. Water ran out of her hair
and streaked her face.

"Cálmate," he said.

Another bolt crashed against the mountainside.
Violeta tumbled, skidding into a cholla.

Fidel reached her. She fought against him. Armando
caught up and held her.

Cactus thorns stuck into her face and down the length
of her arms. Her eyes were wild and rolling.

The wind switched and increased, but the rain
thinned. After a time they were able to calm Violeta and
walk her back up the hill.

Then, while Soledad and Olivia held Violeta, Catalina
pulled out the thorns with tweezers. Armando took Fidel
uphill to show him how to use the maps and GPS. The
thunderclouds had blown into an anvil shape and thinned
into mare's tails.

Catalina was applying alcohol to Violeta's wounds.

Later she pulled Armando aside. "Tonight," she said.
"We'll leave them with the firefighters."

They waited, soaking wet, in the dark. It was late, and
El Pollo had not arrived. Soledad had developed a fever,
and she shivered and coughed, while Violeta moaned.
She complained her knee was tightening against her jeans.
Armando cut away the denim, and purple flesh swelled.
The discoloration of it spread down her shin to her ankle.
He wrapped her knee with an elastic bandage.

Pilar and Abril huddled around Violeta trying to
comfort her, the three keeping each other warm and
talking about going to Disneyland, where they would
meet Cinderella and Pocahontas, where they'd ride roller
coasters, play carnival games, and eat cotton candy.

Olivia toweled Soledad's forehead and tipped the

water bottle to her mouth when she needed a drink. In the darkness, Armando listened. It had been a couple of hours since he had told them to be quiet and later to shut up. He listened to footfalls on the trail below. With each passing group he held the pistol and waited for the sound of people climbing up the slope. Wolves began to howl.

Pilar crept to her parents. "Will they bother us?"

"No," Armando said. "They have their own ways and things they do."

"Like what?" she asked.

"Well," Armando said, "they talk with the moon and hunt and get back to their dens before the vaqueros catch them out. The wolves don't want to get shot."

"Abril says wolves are evil spirits and their leaders are men by daylight who turn into werewolves at night."

Catalina chuffed. "Abril is a peasant. Men are men. Wolves are wolves."

"Abril says she was held captive by them. She saw them always take Violeta into the thickets and bring her back speechless and crying."

Armando thought about how he and Baines had rounded up the children in a village and how one mother yelled and pounded on him. Other women, emboldened, copied her and surged at the soldiers. Armando had pushed his pistol to the mother's head and squeezed the trigger. Her legs folded, and she crumpled.

"That's ridiculous," Catalina hissed.

A wolf howled, and Pilar cocked her head. "It sounds sad," she said. "If I were in a wolf body, it'd make me sad too."

Armando caressed her hair. "Those are just wolves. Don't worry about old folktales."

"When are we leaving?"

"Soon. Go rest. Care for Violeta."

When Pilar was gone, Catalina put her head in her hands. "El Pollo isn't coming back. Why didn't we go to a border town? You could've declared yourself. Those military officers you talk about would vouch for you."

"I can't claim political asylum," Armando said. "I can work covertly with the government, and you will all be cared for. If we'd tried to cross at a checkpoint we'd have been sent back to Guatemala."

"We'll die out here."

"No, we won't."

He hesitated before reaching out to run his hand down her back, fearing his touch might send her into tears. Armando had seen soldiers on long patrols break down right before the mission was finished. The last thing the girls needed to see was their mother losing hope.

Under his hand he felt the cold, damp cloth of her shirt, and her shivering. He slid closer and put his arm around her. He wished they had other clothes. The heavy rain had soaked everything. Armando remembered being wet in the jungle, but the heat and humidity made dehydration the problem, not hyperthermia. He pulled his wife closer and she nuzzled into his side. Pilar and Abril's voices broke the dark like a spring.

Catalina sat up and wiped her face. "Okay," she said. "It's in God's hands." She wrapped her arms around herself and stood and went to check on Soledad.

Armando thought of the last time he and Catalina had been able to lie side by side in a bed. Two weeks ago. They stood in the bedroom as he unbuttoned her blouse. The silk floated to the floor. She arched her shoulders forward and dropped her bra. He kissed both her breasts and wrapped his arms around her.

Two days later he was relieved of command, his oldest son was dead, and he saw the dark suspicion in everyone's eyes. He sent Catalina and the children to her sister's house in Flores, and two nights later just after sundown he stood in front of his house full of all their possessions. He lingered in front of the house longer than was wise, looking at the windows, remembering his children smiling and waving when he came home and how his daughters blew kisses as they jumped up and down. He had left on a light in the upstairs bedroom. The light was yellow through the curtains.

Soledad coughed. Her lungs sounded inflamed and broken. As he held her close, he felt the rattle in her throat. She was light and frail. She faded in and out of consciousness and muttered about the heat and how she didn't want the monkeys to ruin her quinceañera.

Catalina fretted cautiously.

"We'll take her to the firefighters," Armando said. "They'll take her to the hospital."

"We'll lose her."

"They'll send her to your sister in Guatemala. She'll help."

Catalina clicked her tongue. "We cannot give her to North Americans like that."

"If she stays with us she'll die. I'll send Fidel with her."

"Not Fidel. Tell Olivia. Give them the smugglers' money. They can pose as sisters."

"We can't trust those girls not to abandon Soledad."

"You didn't think about trusting them earlier."

Armando gritted his teeth. "This is not up for discussion. Fidel will take Soledad and those girls. You, Pilar, and I will continue."

"What if my sister can't help?"

"We must have faith she'll find a way," Armando said.

Catalina sighed. "I don't want to mourn any more children." She turned away, her back a closed gate.

Armando listened to the wolves howl in the dry air, thinking he might be making a mistake. But he had maps, GPS, and water. Soledad would get care. They'd run into other groups traveling north and in a city blend into a

Hispanic community and make their way east. Catalina believed they'd find sanctuary in the church. Armando had nodded, thinking about armed rebels he had chased from churches. He wanted to find a church, to confess, take communion, smell the familiar incense, walk into the embracing coolness, and kneel in prayer before the mystery of God. To the north the wildfire flared as it crested a ridge. Flames pulsed and roiled. Shadows of smoke and trees wavered in the burning light. Armando listened for noise along the trail but heard only the girls whispering secrets in their own darkness.

STILL LIFE: A NOVELLA

CHAPTER ONE

I have always looked good in black. Suit jacket, shirt, slacks, and silk tie. I wore it all the time when Jen Swallows and I split Vegas like an atom. Not because I was an artist or a biker or a hipster, but because she liked it. I tie on a double Windsor and smooth the tie down. On the counter my stainless Seiko watch ticks next to an old letter with an APO address from Todd after he rejoined Marines and felt the need to confess his sins. We'd been friends since high school and shared some hard times. His sense of loyalty was no better or worse than some I suppose, and even as he was doing wrong, thought he was doing right through some convoluted logic. But we all did. Odd how Todd sent the letter to my lawyer thinking attorney client privilege would keep his secrets safe from the law. They'd thrown his ass right out of the Corps. We like our heroes squeaky clean, unless they found the Lord, which Todd had not. I slip on the watch, and check the time. I still had a couple of hours before the funeral.

Accidents of time. Accidents of place and people. Accidents rippling in our guts like a hard punch, fucking us up for life. Like when the Berlin Wall fell. We should have seen it coming. Nothing's an accident. Some things happen beyond what we control, like the ass kicking Job got, but for the most part, we put ourselves in a position to get fucked over. My Uncle Allen used to love to talk about Job and suffering and how he had to endure what wasn't his fault. But I think if Job hadn't been so good, he wouldn't have caught the Devil's eye.

I thought a lot about those three days back in the 90s. Time has abstracted and twisted them a little, much like family is its own cosmic accident because you don't control that either. Atone for the sins of the father. But now it feels like I'm telling somebody else's story. In a way I am. Jen's story. Todd's story. Marla. The story of a dead kid. The story where I am a minor character, trying to avoid the devil's eye.

Just fuck.

*

In his mid-twenties, Hess fills a black suit with a muscular frame. He slugs Jen's boyfriend in the guts. He wears only and Iron Maiden t-shirt and boxer shorts. His breath bursts out like a runner legging the final yards, trying to overtake the leader.

Jen Swallows yells. "Hit him Hess!" Her Nikon F4 clicks and winds "Take that you faux white trash poseur."

Hess lets him drop to the concrete. He pushes his mirrored sunglasses up the bridge of his nose.

Jen wears a black mini-skirt, red silk blouse and red high heels. She snaps pictures of the man gasping for breath.

"Here take some of me." Jen hands Hess the camera and she hikes her skirt up, pulls her nylons down, and pisses on the man. "How do you like the abuse now, motherfucker?"

Hess looks around. "Hey, baby, that's enough. Let's scoot before the cops show."

Jen takes her camera from Hess and takes a couple of more shots.

"Kick him. Kick him."

Hess shakes his head. "He's had enough."

Hess turns and walks away. Jen kicks her ex, then follows. He whimpers, clutching at his guts.

*

And to think, when I was a kid I wanted to be an astronaut, heroic icon of the Cold War, and not a coke dealer, cultural icon of the eighties. Some story. I always imagined donning the bulky suit and taking the long ride up the elevator where a bunch of guys would strap me down into the seat. I heard the count down in my sleep and felt the rumble of a rocket roaring toward space. Like all kids I never imagined me as a man, but with the face of a boy peering from under the helmet visor. A kid's fantasy because for all the imaginative power a kid has I still couldn't imagine himself as an adult. My old man had been a decorated combat pilot, and after his last tour in Vietnam was going to be an astronaut before a gook missile said otherwise. He led raids in fighter jets, dropping bombs, firing missiles while going through enemy fire. One of the guys from his squadron said it clipped his wing and sent him spinning like one of those whirling fireworks that spin and whistle, throwing sparks over square miles of city. A guy from his fighter wing who visited me and Ma said he heard over the radio, "Eject! Eject! Eject!" and swears he saw my old man streaming into the night above the darkness the stars scattered above him. I wonder if the night quieted as the other aircraft flew off or did the ground fire remain intense tracing the dark, knowing men still drifted down far from home.

A silly dream.

I can't help but think of the millions of kids in America, who looked to the heavens after Armstrong's lunar jump. We were legion, but how many actually did? What concerns pulled us down to earth like gravity? Money? Wars? Who can tell about these things?

I could have loved anyone else, but had attachment issues.

Hess leans back in his seat, one hand on Jen's thigh, the other on the wheel as he races the BMW through traffic. Jen changes the film in her camera, looks through the eyepiece and sets it in her lap.

"Scoot. What the fuck kind of word is that. I don't scoot."

"Sure you do."

"Not in these heels."

"You too good to scoot?"

Her mom inherited old school war profiteer money and daddy presided over some high-end East Coast university where the students were either prepped out or pretending to be poverty-stricken by looking like a bunch of fucking sprout eaters. The kind of poseurs I used to short on a gram of coke. She liked to tell me about her experiences slumming from Brown to hang out with guys like me. I didn't even know what a guy like me was. A damaged loser perpetually high and alone?

Jen opens her compact and studies her reflection. She smooths out her glitter. "A girl has only so many good years to wear glitter. Besides, scoot is a crass word."

"You just pissed on your ex-boyfriend."

Back in New York, Jen got the silly idea of moving to Vegas with her boyfriend to be a fashion model. Vegas was going to be the new Paris. After a week in town, he slapped her around like he was some pimp trying to get dollars out of a girl. She packed her bag and slipped out into a studio apartment off Boulder Highway still thinking modeling would lift her up. When I met her she was dancing in Les Folies Bergere at the Tropicana. So much for modeling.

*

"Seriously, he was sitting around in his boxers before five. He had it coming. And what kind of douche-canoe opens the door in his boxers?"

"You're gorgeous enough. Cut a line on that mirror or put it up."

"All right. Light me a smoke."

Hess pulls a gold cigarette case and a butane lighter, from his inside jacket pocket and sparks a small jet engine flame, lighting the cigarettes. Jen pulls a folded piece of paper from her black and white leather handbag and taps out cocaine on to her compact mirror. She looks out the window.

"Feels like a two line afternoon. Where we going?"

"Todd's. He owes me money."

"Why do you let him slide when you goon the fuck out of everybody else?"

"Me and Todd go way back that's why. He's good for it and then some."

"Hey, stop. I need a picture of those ribbons."

She points to a light pole that has ragged yellow ribbons and a flier for a lost cat. People post their losses and devotions like playbills or the papers advertising high dollar hookers and strippers, littering the Vegas gutters.

An ambulance siren rips the air. Some cars start to pull over and a couple rev hard, trying to stay ahead.

Hess jolts. His gut swims up his throat into the pool of his mouth. A four-year-old girl stands on the sidewalk. She wears pink shorts and a red tank top. Her blonde hair is streaked with blood, and yellow ribbons ripple in a breeze that isn't there. She mouths words. All air and sirens. She lifts a hand, poised between stop and help. Hess squints his eyes, shakes his head, and when he reopens his eyes, the little girl is gone.

"I need to pull over anyway. Be a good citizen."

*

As a school kid, I dreamed the fantasy of emerging an
astronaut from a spacecraft. A butterfly from its metal
cocoon. The drifting weightless, I spun around the earth
so far and so close and even working on the hull like some
working class auto-shop guy expanded to the infinite. In
high school my dad was dead or MIA and math slipped
around folds of my brain and into nothingness, and the
small school I landed in didn't push too hard, instead
focusing on kids with the knack for numbers. Even though
I had little interest in cars, I ended up in shop as I'd
already taken Home Ec and began to wonder if somehow
I could tweak wrenches into orbit. Could shop guys go to
space? Only shop guys with engineering degrees, carrying
a fighter pilot's license in their hip pocket.

The first time I snorted coke, I hoped it'd get me laid, and
it did with Jen. I had gone to a party with a friend of hers
who I'd met at work. Gail, or some G name, who had
blown me in the back of the tire store for forty bucks worth
of used tires and invited me to party with some others
and, weird, it was at my high school friend Todd's. How
could I refuse? Todd's mom decked out the place with new
furniture, and the dining room table had a small pile of
coke and a lazy Susan mirror. Wine glasses and a couple of
wine bottles on the table reflected back the light from the
crystal chandelier that had one light burned out and cob
webs strung between the strands of crystals. His mom may
have decorated the joint to make him look like he had class,
but couldn't force him to keep up the appearance.
     The party full of twenty somethings rocked out to
a punk band belting out "Amazing Grace." I had on a
Clash t-shirt and blue jeans. Fresh from Los Angeles I still
staggered off kilter from the accident. I'd look and see
the dead girl's blue face, floating in a bowl of Fruit Loops.

See her flicker in the spaces between television shows and commercial breaks or in line at the liquor store. I drifted the world an observer, isolated and apart the way the moon orbits the Earth. I wasn't in the story unfolding. I was in a story past.

I saw Jen come in with a crowd. Jen's rippled blonde hair fell down to the middle of her back, tits in a tight black blouse, and hips sheathed in a black skirt kept my attention.

Todd ordered me to loosen up as if a squad leader in charge of R&R. "Private, I order you to get drunk and fuck."

I tore my eyes away from Jen. Smoking hot, but also she had that wild look in the way she walked and the way she carried herself. "I will."

"Cool, man." Todd wandered off with a slight list in his step.

I moved up next to her and we listened to the band. They were banging out all these old church hymns like my grandma got all drippy about when Elvis sang them except this band raged these songs like salvation was a curse. Jen backed into me, swaying her hips, smiling over her shoulder.

She motioned for me to follow her. We headed for a door leading into the backyard. She made all the black skirts sewn by kids in sweatshops worth it.

Just off the patio strung with white Christmas lights, she stopped and took out her compact and a small envelope and with a razor chopped a mound of coke in the moonlight. It glowed like plankton in the surf or lightning bugs catching summer breezes. She scooped it with her fingernail and offered it to me. I hesitated and she smiled. "Come on, a little stardust to send you zooming."

Her smile and the glint of light in her eyes from the moon and the lights looked what I imagined the magical Elvish world of Tolkien to be like. Some magic fairy world where I could be led to my doom, off into the night where forty years passed, and I'd be the same and all my friends dead or ancient relics. I'd always avoided coke or speed. I'd smoked weed like most of the dudes I went to high school with, but this was a big leap, and I didn't know where I'd come down. But she smiled at me again, and to me it was like a message saying, snort this shit and I will show you all you've been missing in life and fuck you into perfect oblivion. Slip out of time and slip back in and find this shitty life past and gone. Who said it had to be a tragedy to be Rip van Winkle?

I sniffed as hard as I could and in the dark winced at the sharp pain and the taste of acid down the back of my throat and then the tingle. The air charged. She dipped her nail again and snorted, and then wiped her fingertip across the mirror before rubbing it across my teeth. "A freeze," she said as the cold rush frosted my gums.

We moved into the large backyard behind a couple of trees and into a corner. A block wall surrounded the yard. Along the top of the wall broken bottles glittered like the edges of magic swords. Of shattered stars frozen mid explosion. The light. The light, I thought. Does it come from inside the glass? Jen led me to a darkened corner. Jen rolled up her skirt with her back to me. She leaned her forearms against the wall.

"What are you waiting for?"

My head surged wild and my skin tingled. Spark. Spark. Spark. I fell into orbit around her. The crowd-chatter, the band's hymns, and city traffic distorted and faded. It became one hum of blood in my ears. I slipped my fingers into her and felt her pulsing. I felt everything rushing and lights streaked with rainwater in the clear night. I undid my pants. I had never been so hard. We fit together, and I started moving back and forth. Her breathing deepened, and she mumbled, "Slower. Don't blow it so fast."

I asked if she was on birth control, and she chuckled, and it sounded deep into the night and far away. "Yes."

The shadows filled with the smells of roses and cigarette smoke, and I looked away from her back and out of the darkness and up into the canopy of light above the city, the dim pale scar of moon, and thought about being a kid, wanting nothing more than to kick lunar dust as I skipped weightless thousands of miles from home until high school ruined me. I remembered being a kid and seeing the moon's thin sliver and thought it like the oceanic tide, and the astronauts had to stay in the lighted part or be lost to the deeps of space.

I stepped outside my body. Watched the crazy kid with blond hair and a black t-shirt. Two white asses in the shadows. Music like a distant radio station fuzzed. Come in, can you hear me? Helpless in floating lights, trembling from a razor's edge of powder. The slimmest of spaces between a breath.

Gail's laugh broke the night, and I tried to focus between her and Jen pushing back against me. Gail's feathered hair bounced as she shook her head. "Figures. I meet a nice guy, and he fucks my best friend."

She disappeared into the racket of guitars and drums and the blur and smear of light, flooding from the otherworld of Todd's house. I never saw her again, like any one-day stand from the back of a tire store.

CHAPTER TWO

Marla peels her thumb with a razor blade. Her thumb sticking up on her pale hand looks like a hammer smashed a cartoon thumb. Her black lacquered nails reflect the light, and her deep red lips gleam against her white skin. A flowered sundress hangs loosely from her thin body.

Todd talks on the phone, wearing torn and greasy jeans, white t-shirt, and motorcycle boots. Tattoos wind around his biceps, and forearms. On his right forearm USMC is surrounded by Celtic knots and on his left a flaming dagger with Death Before Dishonor arcing above and below it. He'd left high school with below average grades and above average ambition to travel the world and fuck people up with high-speed weaponry like a true patriot.

"No, dude, I got him set up, not to worry.... Not to worry, man. We been pals since high school." Marla peeling her thumb catches his attention. "What the fuck, Marla? Knock that off. I don't want to snort your blood."

Marla giggles. "I'm just doing what Satan tells me."

"Tell the devil I'll kick his ass if he doesn't knock it the fuck off." Todd turns his attention back to the phone. "He won't know shit. It's a deal. We all go on like it's yesterday except you and I got more jingle in our pockets." Todd hangs up the phone. "Comeback time."

Marla pouts. She tosses the razor blade onto the lazy Susan.

Todd looks between the lazy Susan and her. "What?"

"You're stealing my high."

"I ain't stealing nothing, but a lickety fuck from you."

"Why didn't you say so?" She gives him I'm ready to fuck you look and starts to rise in a slinky way from her chair. "I like where this is headed."

Someone pounding on the door pauses her for a

second. "Just ignore it. Todd. It'll be in your best interest." She crosses to Todd and caresses his crotch. The pounding repeats.

Todd smiles at Marla. I would, but no sonofabitch is going to pound on my door like a cop and not get an ass chewing. He goes to the door and peers through the Judas hole. "It's that skinhead, Freddy. Jesus. I got to see Woo and thump his ass and this fuck shows up."

"Easy on Woo. He's cute."

Todd eyes Marla. "Yeah, okay, but now I have to deal with this."

Marla rolls her eyes and sits back down. "Don't let him in. He's a downer."

"Can't do that. It's rude. Besides," he smiles, I like to fuck with these cheese dicks. They are as easy to offend as telling an old church lady you want to hump her."

Todd unbolts and opens the door. Freddy's high gloss Doc Marten boots look like clown shoes on his skinny legs in his cuffed jeans. A tattoo of an iron cross below his throat shows above the top of his black tee shirt. The shirt is stretched so tight over his skinny body that it looks like a child's size.

Todd grins at him. "What's up, nigger?"

Freddy eyes widen. "Fuck you."

"Your head is pink. You need to put on sunscreen."

"What the fuck?"

"Why you coming over here, Freddy?"

Freddy pulls a snub-nosed .38 revolver from behind his back. Light shines on its mirrored surface. "To take you down, man. You and your Jew girlfriend."

Todd looks over his shoulder at Marla. She shrugs. "No shit."

"You want to run any business you need to pay."

"Pretty sure she's Lutheran."

"We know." The gun shakes in Freddy hands. "If you

want to stay safe you'll have to pay us. We want your bike."

"Whoa, now. I don't think I'm going to live to see a piece of shit like you ride my bike."

Freddy holds the gun up and points it at Todd's forehead. Freddy can't keep his hand steady. He stutters. "Shshshshe's a Jew whwhwhore."

"Ouch." At the table Marla cuts a line of coke. "A whore, Freddy? I thought you liked me."

"You want to kill me, Freddy, that's fine, but you leave her out of it."

"I...I...I'm serious."

Todd takes a step forward. "Go ahead. Shoot me."

"Maa maaa man, I will man."

Todd takes another step closer. "You got a case of the trembles, Freddy."

Marla snorts the line. "I don't like the spinning mirror. Makes me feel like I'm in a circus and not real life."

"Go ahead, nigger. Shoot me."

"It doesn't have to go rough on you, Todd."

"I said to shoot me." Todd takes another step.

Freddy takes a deep breath. "I will, man. Jew lover." Freddy takes a step back. His skin flushes, and his lips tremble.

Todd yells. "What the fuck does that even fucking mean? Kill me!" His eyes set hard. Todd steps forward until the gun barrel is pressed against his forehead, and he continues forward as Freddy backpedals and smacks the door.

Todd grins. His face lights. "What's your problem, big man?"

Todd slaps Freddy in the forehead. "What's a matter?"

Freddy struggles with the doorknob. Marla snorts another line. A parrot screeches from a back room.

Freddy's voice trembles. "You fucker."

Todd slaps him as he struggles with the door. "Piss yourself or shoot me."

Freddy fumbles with the doorknob. The jiggling sounds like a kid fiddling with a toilet handle. "I'll fu fu fucking shoot you, man. I sw sw swear."

"Then fucking shoot me."

Freddy finally pulls the door open and stumbles out into the bright sun. Freddy falls. He scrambles to his feet, scuffing his Doc Martens. Blood streams from the torn right knee of his jeans. He stumbles by a pale blue chopper in the driveway. He runs for a dusty black Cadillac with an iron bumper mounted on the front, parked on the street.

Todd walks into the driveway with a measured pace as if marching back in the Corps. "Kill me!" His voice echoes in the neighborhood. Some people glance out of windows of houses, and the sound of an ice cream truck laces the air with its child-luring tinkle.

Hess's BMW pulls up behind Freddy's Caddy. Todd stops by his chopper for a second. Freddy trips over his feet and scuffs his boots again. He struggles to his feet and runs. Todd bears down on him. Freddy makes it to his Caddy.

Hess and Jen get out of the BMW.

Todd continues down the driveway and kicks a dent in the door of the Caddy. "What's your problem bad ass? Kill me!"

The Caddy jerks and speeds away, tires squealing.

Hess watches the smoke of the burned rubber curl and drift. "What's up, Todd?"

Todd laughs and coughs until he hacks up phlegm and spits. "Not much."

Jen waves away the smoke from her face. "That guy had a cute gun."

Todd laughs again. "He did at that." He pats Hess on the back. "Hey, Hess, You know Johnny Woo?"

"Can't say that I do."

"That slope owes me money."

"Funny, you owe me money, fucker."

"True, but Woo has an ass-kicking coming. Help me lean on him a little."

Jen smiles at Todd. "Such a badass. Is Marla around?"

Todd laughs. "Yeah. She's in there making a sacrifice to the devil."

"Don't we all?" Jen kisses Hess on the lips. "Take your time and try not to get arrested again." Jen walks to the front door and enters as Hess watches her walk.

"Let's hit it." Todd thumps Hess on the shoulder knocking him out of his trance.

CHAPTER THREE

Todd and Hess sit in the truck behind a pizza joint. The
faded red paint on the truck has been powdered from
the sun. Hess leans back in the passenger seat. No clouds
blemished the bleached sky. No breeze stirs papers
scattered on the ground. Two bums rummage in a dumpster
dropping napkins and empty pizza boxes on the ground.
One in a grimy blue shirt pulls out a half eaten pizza slice.
The second bum snatches it before the other even can look
up and begins to run. The man in the grimy shirt pulls a
paring knife and slashes the back of the other and chases
after him.

Todd watches them with a smile. "See, I fronted Woo
the coke on a promise he was going to get back double the
price."

"You mean you fronted him coke that I fronted you."

"Shit, man, let's not get into fractions and shit, "You
know what I mean."

"The money is in the fractions." Hess pulls at his
collar a little. "Man I hate this heat. This beater needs
better air flow."

Hess kicks the door open.

"You're the fool in the suit."

*

My earliest memories involved high heat, the roar of
fighter planes and the smell of jet fuel, rolling across the
desert and all the hope and power it conveyed. Those
blended away to smog and traffic honking and then to the
heavy dust and blast sirens of a mining town. Somehow,
my whole life I'd been trapped between Vegas and L.A.
along Interstate 15. The highway rises up out of the Los
Angeles basin, over Cajon Pass to stretch its wicked neck
across the high desert past Death Valley and back up

the mountains and the mines and the myths of mines scattered like a fortune tellers cards by an unpredictable wind, until dropping down into Vegas that great breaker of dreams.

I had always hated the desert, and kept thinking why don't I move. Go somewhere cooler. But then I didn't know how. Sometimes when Jen talked about Manhattan I thought about going there with her. Get out of town and start over. As I grew older I recognized those early sensations divided my life from what was possible to what would be withheld. After my father got shot down I had the inescapable feeling my life had gone into free fall, and it was just like my father's, only longer.

*

"Don't start acting like you're above your raising. You might be some Miami Vice coke dealer to Vegas, but you still a mining town bitch to me."

"Fuck that noise. It's fucking hot."

"This ain't shit, man. Try being loaded down with all your war gear in the back of a one-one-three at Twenty-Nine Palms. When I was in the Corps, water was not a necessity. It was a luxury."

"This ain't the Marines."

"No shit." Todd looks wistful. "If I knew we were going to go after that camel fucker, I'd stayed in. I figured after the Wall fell, nothing was worth fighting any more." Todd had always dreamed of being the first kid from the mine with a confirmed kill. "Fuck. I should've known we'd fucking kill over oil."

"Like two bums over a crust of bread."

"I don't care. Honor and glory to the Corps. I'd stayed in to shoot me some... There's Woo." Todd tilts his head toward the back of the pizza place.

Woo shuts the door behind him. He wears a red flowered Hawaiian shirt khaki pants and deck shoes. He walks past the dumpster and stops to put the garbage back in. He continues past a delivery truck. He stops short when he sees Hess and Todd walking across the lot and turns back to the door.

"If you run, I will fucking break your legs when I catch you. You know I hate to run."

Woo stops. Todd slaps him in the head after he walks up to him.

"That's for thinking about running."

Hess musses Woo's hair. "What's up, Woo? You look like you got caught trying to feel up your cousin at a family reunion."

"Fuck, man. I wasn't running. I forgot to punch my timecard."

Todd slaps him again. "Don't worry about the card. If your punk assed manager has a problem give him my name."

Hess grabs Woo by the shoulders and smooths his hair down. "Can't having you look askew."

Woo stares at Hess. "Askew? What are you good cop bad cop?"

Todd slaps him in the back of the head. "No, we're guy in a t-shirt and guy in a suit who are going to kick the ever loving shit out of you."

Woo holds up his hands. "Okay, I know I owe you."

Todd grins at him. "No you owe us, dumb ass. This is the guy who fronted me the coke and because you are dumping on me, he is going to dump on me. Do you see how may times me is getting dumped on?"

"Dude, I..."

"No one forgets three fronted keys of coke."

Hess says with a straight face. "I could say the same."

Woo's voice becomes shrill. "I told that dude that the coke—"

Todd cuts him off. "My coke."

"My coke." Hess cuts in.

Todd says to Hess, "Seriously, man, I am shaking this slope down and you are killing my play."

"I just want to be straight on who owes who."

Todd sighs a rough breath. "Fine his coke. So you're ruining my good name with him, and I can't have that."

"Look, man. I don't have it. The dude that was supposed to hook me up took off to L.A."

"Boo-the-fuck-hoo, Woo." Todd shakes Woo. "Me and my boy here don't give a fuck."

Woo hangs onto Todd's forearms. "Man, I ain't cheating you. That dude is."

Todd shakes him again. "You mean to say I got to forget you owe me because you gave the shit to a loser who won't return your calls?"

Hess laughs and thumbs at Todd. "At least he returns my calls."

Woo looks like he just came up with an idea. "You should go after him."

Todd shakes his head. "I got you right here. Why do I need to drive all the way to L.A.?"

Woo says, "I gave him the shit. He was going to trade it for guns to some guerillas from Central America. Man he's a big player. I was going to triple my take. Get fat on the CIA dole, bro."

Todd says, "You believed that bullshit. He's probably got his ass arrested or killed with that many lowlifes scrounging around. Or he's suckering you."

Woo talks fast. "He's still got it. He owes you."

Todd pushes Woo back. "No, little man, you owe me." Todd cracks his knuckles. "Me and Hess are going to fuck you up. You'll have a week to come up with what you owe me."

Woo puts his hands up. Todd grabs his right wrist and pulls him into his fist. Woo's feet come off the ground and when he touches down he collapses into a heap.

"Kick him," Todd says to Hess.

"I'm not going to kick him."

Really?

"Really, Reilly. He needs to be a little more loathsome for me to kick when he's on the ground. I got standards."

"You shitting me?"

"No. This is twice today."

Todd laughs. Woo rolls on the ground like a sack caught in a swirling breeze trying to catch his breath. "When did this happen?"

Hess shrugs. "It's always been that way."

"No shit?"

"No shit."

"Didn't you kick Cochrane when he was down?"

"He was a scumbag."

Todd nods as he considers what Hess said. "True. Fucking high school pedophile."

Woo pulls a knife out of his pocket, flicks it open and tries to swipe at Todd's leg. Todd jumps back. Hess stomps Woo's hand into the asphalt and kicks him in the ribs. Woo curls into a ball wheezing. Hess picks up the knife a cheap, loose-bladed folder.

Todd says, "Glad to see he became loathsome enough for you."

"Don't mention it." Hess examines the blade of the knife. "You couldn't cut string with this piece of shit. You get this at a truck stop?"

Todd squats down and turns Woo's face up by his hair. "Listen up, Johnny, me and Hess are going to find you next week. But you know we have to break your fucking arm."

Todd drops Woo's head.

"Wait, man. Wait what. Don't break my arm."

"Why not? You going to shit the money you owe me?"

"I'll tell you where he's going to meet those guys. You can get the guns and the coke. Day after tomorrow."

"Why should I go through all that trouble when I can just get my money from you?"

Woo pleads. "Just the guns are worth more than triple what I owe you."

Todd looks to Hess. "Believe this shit? Like he thinks he's on some fucking cop show on TV."

"I'm serious. Just don't break my arm. I can't afford it."

Todd slaps Woo's face." You can't afford to owe me either, bitch."

Hess looks around. The bums are back at the dumpster picking through pizza boxes as if their earlier fight never happened. "We got to scoot before the cops roll up."

Todd smiles. "Yeah. Where is this meeting supposed to take place?"

"You can't be serious," Hess says.

"In Venice Beach. Not too far from the pier."

Todd looks contemplative. "Uhh huh. I tell you what, I'm taking your slope ass with me, and we'll all three get it done. If it's a set up, I'll kill you."

Woo nods, "Okay, yeah, I'll go in with you.'

Todd wipes his forehead. He stares a Woo. "In the back of the truck, Johnny."

Woo looks at the pick-up and back at Todd. "What?"

"You heard me. Get your skinny gook ass in the back of the truck."

Hess pulls out a cigarette and lights it. "Fuck, this is bullshit. I should have your ass in the trunk. Todd, let's get out of here. Leave Johnny."

"No can do. I swear to God, get in the truck, Woo, or I will beat the ever loving, commie loving shit out of you and you're going to wish we'd have napalmed your daddy over in Nam."

Todd grabs the back of Woo's shirt and the waistband

of his pants. "Let me help you, Johnny. You should be glad you're riding in the bed of a truck and not at the end of a chain."

Woo gets to his feet and cradles his hand. As he climbs over the tailgate, Todd pushes him in. Woo loses his balance and falls into a heap.

"Stay down, Johnny, if I see you up looking around like a dog I'm going beat you."

Hess looks for cops. "This is useless. Let's get out of here."

They climb in the truck and slam the heavy doors closed.

Todd fires the engine and revs it a couple of times.

Hess turns down the radio. "Woo is Chinese."

"Why do I care?"

"You said he was going to wish we napalmed his daddy."

"So?"

"We fought the Vietnamese not the Chinese."

"Don't tell me some of those Commie Chinese bastards weren't snooping around. The problem with you, Hess, is you got a narrow scope of vision."

*

The problem was that I didn't have narrow scope of vision. I'd read every book on that war and wars I could find, trying to understand how a place could swallow so many fathers for nothing. As I grew up the subject of pointless deaths became taboo. No one wanted to admit they had fought in a war that meant nothing and had sacrificed for nothing and friends, fathers, mothers, brothers, and sisters died or had limbs blown off. I read and read. My father's old friends told me stories of glory and heroism, but left out the nationalistic reasons and all the moral ambiguity so I became confused. Was the purpose of the war for them to seek honor and glory? Because it seemed so. All that mattered was to fight well. Duty? To show courage? How all their words began to fall like a bunch of tin plates. My father had died and, as far as I could tell, democracy was not better off for it. Narrow scope? Maybe my problem was just the opposite. To see too many possibilities. Left with all the questions of what might have been. Dear Dad: What is dying for duty like when duty means dying and leaving a fatherless son? Did your death make the country freer?

*

Todd says, "You and I got to go to L.A. We score the coke and guns to sweeten the deal."

"I don't want any fucking guns. Too bulky for too little pay back. Fucking guns are a hassle."

"Man, you could turn them easy."

Hess chuffs. "What? To people who might use them against me?"

"No, man, to that crazy survivalist uncle of yours and his whacked out friends."

"Uncle Allen won't want no part of that."

"All survivalists want firepower. That skinny fucker got more illegal guns." He brakes at a stoplight. "If not I got some bros from the Corps who are all hooked up in South Africa. I'll still split the money even though you're being a bitch."

"I don't have to go to L.A. You do."

"You'll get your coke back."

"No, you'll get the coke back you still owe me for. I don't move shit twice. That's just a bad policy."

"Man, we been bros since shitting high school."

"Which is why I don't fuck you up."

"Hey, man, I gave you a place to crash when you fell a fucking part in Los Angeles and came dragging your ass here."

Todd gets a cigarette and lights it. He blows smoke. He looks both hurt and angry. "Who was there for you, man? Me. That's fucking who. Now this is my chance to comeback. Woo fucked me, and now I'm going to get that and extra back. You got to help me. You owe me."

Hess looks out the truck window. He sighs and shakes his head, exasperated. "Fuck you, man."

"I thought so."

Todd bangs on the steering wheel, acting like he has just come up with a great plan. "What?"

"Dude, you should bring a couple extra keys so we look like major players and instead of dumping on them, work with them. We could go big. A major guns and drugs racket."

Hess continues to look out the window. "You can. I'm not. I'll help set you up with your own racket. I don't want nothing to do with guns. This one time I help, and we are square. Fact is I might get out of this shit for good."

Todd looks in the rearview mirror, speeds up and slams on the brakes, causing Woo to slide into the front of the truck box with a crash. Todd yells as he looks in the review mirror. "I hope that hurt!" He looks back at the road. "Tell you what. I'll drop you off at the house, and I'm going to drive out to Blue Diamond Road to drop him off so he'll have a long walk to think about his sins."

Hess shrugs. They drive a little further. Todd throws his cigarette out the window. "You know why I joined the Marine Corps?"

Hess looks over at him tilts his head down to look over his sunglasses. "Either to one: get the fuck out of that shitty mining town or two: you were too stupid to do anything else?"

"No, man. Reagan said, 'Some people wonder all their lives if they've made a difference. The Marines don't have that problem.'" Todd looks over to Hess and back to the road. "I wanted to make a difference, man."

Hess shrugs. "Yeah, blowing the shit out some kids' village is definitely making a difference."

Todd slugs Hess in the shoulder. "Fuck you, man. I just wanted to go off like your old man."

"For all I know if he didn't die out there, he's still working a gook chain-gang. Shot down while blowing up some kids' village."

"You're a fucking piece of work. You're old man was a bona-fucking-fide hero and you act like he's a low life criminal."

Hess stares out the window. His voice a monotone. "Just saying making a difference can be spreading bread or spreading napalm. Peace Corps, Marine Corps. Just saying."

In front of his house, Todd pulls the right tires up onto the sidewalk. Hess gets out, slams the heavy door, and walks around to the driver's side. Todd leans out. "Without the Marine Corps, there'd be no Peace Corps. Just saying."

Todd speeds away with a loud rumble before Hess can speak. The truck backfires, echoing down the block and Hess flinches. He stands as the desert and concrete heat swirls over him so thick he feels as if it might carry him off in rip curl updrafts.

CHAPTER FOUR

Jen opens the door to a cool rush of air conditioning like a splash of water. Marla sits at the table examining her thumb. "What have you done?"

Marla smiles up at her as if she just woke up. "So good to see you, love. When did you get here?"

"Just walked in."

"Silly, sneaking up on me like that."

"The boys are off running errands."

"My thumb kind of stings."

"We should bandage it."

Marla shakes her head. "What brings you over?"

"Hess had business with Todd."

"Todd has business with Hess too. Or is that about Hess?"

Jen takes out her camera and clicks a picture of Marla. Marla smiles and tilts her head.

"Get my good side."

"All your sides are good." Jen winks at her.

Jen takes close-ups, from across the room, different light, and different angles.

"You want me to get up or anything?"

"Nope, just stay as you are and let me do the moving around."

Marla kisses at the camera. "How about take my top off?"

"Nice."

Marla pulls her shoulder straps down. "You want to make out?"

"Not right now."

Marla pouts to the camera. "Pictures can wait. I have a surprise for you." Marla gets up and approaches Jen, runs her hand through her hair.

Jen is caught in a moment of desire and weakness. "Not now. Hess will be back soon."

"Don't worry about him."

Marla kisses Jen softly on the lips as Jen closes her eyes. Marla runs her hands down Jen's body and backs away. Jen sighs and opens her eyes. "Later."

"It'll be worth the wait."

Jen smiles at Marla. "Will you come to New York with me?"

"I'd love to, but I'm working on a deal. Afterward when it pans out."

"I have plenty of money."

"I know, babe, but I don't want to be a kept bitch. I have to have my own dollars to spend."

Jen takes another picture as Marla keeps her breasts covered. "Sure you don't want to give these a taste?"

Marla slips the top of her dress down to her waist. Jen's camera clicks and winds as she takes several photographs.

"We can do this tonight."

"Come on. We can now and later. You know you want to."

Jen sets her camera on the table and kisses Marla's breasts and works down and under her dress. Jen pushes her down onto the couch. Marla squirms, and her breath deepens until she climaxes.

Jen emerges after Marla's orgasm.

"I knew you wanted to."

Jen gets two cigarettes, lights them and gives one to Marla.

A truck rumbles by outside. It backfires.

"Come to New York"

"I will, love, I will. Wait a second. I almost forgot. Too much dope." Marla smiles over her shoulder as she goes down the hall. When she emerges she holds out a gold chain with a charm. "A swallow!"

"Does this mean you'll fly to me?"

Marla unclasps the chain and puts it on Jen. "Hell yes it does."

The door opens. Sunlight streams in as Hess walks in, shutting the door behind him.

Hess fans his face, relieved at the cool air washing around him. "A/C, best invention since fire."

Jen shakes her head at him. "Fire was a discovery."

Hess shrugs. "Whatever. What are you ladies up to?"

Marla giggles. "Just girl talk. Check out my thumb."

CHAPTER FIVE

Todd pulls up close to the delivery truck, stays behind the wheel with his truck idling. The two bums from earlier have moved on, leaving garbage around the dumpster behind the pizza joint. Woo sticks his head up. Todd leans his head out of the window. "Get the fuck out." Woo climbs over the tailgate to the bumper and when he is perched between the two, Todd pops the clutch, and Woo falls to the asphalt. Woo gets up and walks around to the driver's side.

Woo stops just out of arm's reach. "Fucker. You didn't have to hit me so hard."

"Fuck you. Had to make it look real. What about that fucking knife stunt."

"Wanted to make it realistic."

"You're just lucky Hess doesn't like to pack a gun. He'd blown your fucking brains out."

"Where's my money?"

"You're even luckier he didn't stomp your teeth and brains out."

"The money?"

"Did you forget you're working on a commission? Hess is all in. Two more days and you'll get yours, unless you fuck it up."

"You need to quit acting like I'm yo—"

Todd flips him the middle finger as he revs his engine. He shouts as deep combustion roars, "I cunt hear you." Todd waves, pops the clutch, squealing the tires. Smoke from the burning rubber rolls in a thick cloud as the truck lurches forward, fishtailing before catching traction.

Woo coughs and begins to walk.

Freddy's Caddy pulls up with Freddy at the wheel and three other skinheads in black t-shirts with racist slogans.

Freddy waves at Woo. "What's up, chink?"

Woo shakes his head.

Freddy motions to the back of the car with his thumb. "Get in."

Woo reaches for the front door handle.

Freddy grins. "Not up here. Back there."

Woo reaches for the back door.

"Will someone help this chink?"

A skinhead the size of a football lineman gets out and pops the trunk.

Freddy hollers as he looks in the side-view mirror. "Get in."

Woo's shoulders slump as he walks over and climbs in. The skinhead slams the trunk lid with a grin.

CHAPTER SIX

The evening spreads out on the horizon like a reflection
of the casino's neon lights. Hess's BMW rolls into the
parking lot. A punk version of "Swing Low Sweet
Chariot" blasts, as he finds a space.

The music dies as he shuts off the motor and gets out.

He walks through the parking lot, ignoring bums,
hooker come ons, and trash in the street.

Some light bulbs flicker in the marquee and several
are burned out.

An average white guy, middle aged, wearing a red
polo shirt with collar popped, Bermuda shorts and sandals
hassles a skinny, white hooker. Scars ripple her face. She
wears frayed cut off jeans, a dirty white tank top, and flip-
flops. The white guy grabs at her tits.

Hess stops within arm's distance. "You should move on."

"What's it to you?"

Hess steps forward slugs the guy in the stomach,
crumpling him to the pavement.

The white guy sucks and heaves air.

*

Uncle Allen always said, when a man says, "What's it
to you," punch him hard and punch him fast as he's
expecting to get lip back from you and not a fist. Before
he got saved, Uncle A could clear a bar with a look. He
even beat a man with a bowling pin once in a dispute over
who's old lady had the nicest tits. He used to drink a lot
before he got saved.

*

Hess says, "It ain't a thing to me, but everything to you."
Hess flicks open a Bali-song banana knife, rolls the guy on
his back, and holds the tip just over his eye. "How about
I make you a one-eyed wise man? Now why do you want

to make her life harder?" Hess presses the knife onto his lower eyelid.

The hooker laughs a strung out laugh. Her skin like old sheets fallen from the clothesline. Hess looks at her. "You want to kick him?"

She puts her hands on her hips. "Why don't you?"

"Not my deal."

She laughs again, her eyes dart around. "That's mighty Christ like of you. I'll take what he's got, though."

Hess keeps the knife pressed to the guy's eye.

The hooker takes the guy's money, his watch, gold chain, and his wedding band. She hurls his car keys out into the night and walks away, her flip-flops thwacking as she goes.

"You should've stayed home, asshole." Hess stands, flicks the knife closed with a click, and walks to the casino doors.

The guy gets up and rushes in the direction of his car keys.

Hess walks through the casino. Welfare and low economic gamblers crowd nickel machines and the one-dollar blackjack tables—the ruptured and desperate. People who always believed they could parley loose change into a fortune and make an empire born out of *Life Styles of the Rich and Famous*. Each coin holding the dream of walking up to the boss and say, take this job and shove it. Get the hell out of the rat race. Or at least pay the rent as it's behind a couple of months. Stupid bill collectors. Fuck 'em. Cling Clang. At least free drinks and a buzz.

Hess walks up to where Jen sits at a table with a couple of drinks.

Jen is looking at her compact mirror. Her camera sits on the table.

A one-man band is setting up his drum machine, keyboard, speakers, electronics, and stringing electrical cords. He has an electric and an acoustic guitar on racks.

His silk turquoise shirt shines, and his black slacks shimmer in the stage lights.

"This place looks like an old woman who puts on good make-up over bad." Hess looks at Jen spreading around her make up as he sits. "Stop it already. You're a gorgeous woman already."

Jen looks at him. "Fuck you, a girl's—"

"I know. Only so many good years to wear glitter or she looks like an aging fairy stripper."

Jen shuts her compact, looks to the man on stage. "Hey, music man."

The music man looks around.

"Here." Jen leans forward to get his attention.

He smiles as he sees her. "What can I do for you?"

Jen smiles back her model smile. "You play, 'Amazing Grace'?"

The music man looks around at the broken down gamblers and faded decor. "What, are we in church?"

She rubs Hess's shoulder. "It's our song."

He shakes his head, still smiling. "Sorry, I don't know that one."

Jen sighs disappointed. "How about 'Thunder Road'?" She takes a drink and swirls the ice. "If you can't play 'Thunder Road' you should think about blackjack-dealer school."

Music Man's smile widens. "You buy me a drink, and I'll show you 'Thunder Road,' lady." Jen leans back, crosses her long legs. Music man's eyes follow the hem of her short skirt.

People gave her respect, which is why she insisted Hess dress in a suit about to foreclose on some sap's life. Cops look at some biker trash and him, and that other guy will be the one draped over a prowl car's hood.

Jen reaches into her purse and pulls out a few bills and waves to the bartender. "Whatever he's having."

Hess says, "I always loved that leaving this loser-town, screen-door-slamming song."

"Me too. I couldn't wait to leave my loser town."

"You grew up on Manhattan. You don't know loser towns until you see the mine sell the houses and crack them in half so they can load them onto flatcars. Ever see a train hauling a bunch of sawed in half houses?"

Jen looks him up and down. "Don't give me that hierarchy of poverty crap. If you knew Manhattan like I do, you'd know what I mean. Even as much as I miss it now, then it was a prison of manners."

Hess waves his hand like he's waving away flies. "Yeah, yeah, yeah. So hard to be the socialite in the big city."

Jen flips him off. "Fuck off asshole. We have our own hierarchy of cruelty you'd never fathom."

Hess laughs. Jen reaches into his jacket pocket and takes his cigarette case and lighter and lights a couple of cigarettes.

"I'll fuck off. I got to go to L.A. Todd needs some help."

Jen sits a little straighter. "I want to go."

"Hard for me to fuck off if you go with." Hess grins and drinks.

"I can get some photos of Hollywood Boulevard to go with my Glitter Gulch photos and take some of the highway memorials."

"Memorials?"

Jen rolls her eyes. "I've been fucking telling you about death shrines as a public display of loss and as a way of grieving, acting as a coping mechanism so survivors can go on with their lives—not stuck in that moment of tragedy. I'm exploring in images the roadside displays and what it says about us as a culture. I also want to show how the car was both destroyer and healer by being both the cause of tragedy and the enabler of closure."

Bells ring and coins clatter as someone hits a jackpot in the casino. People hoot and holler

Hess looks completely lost. "Whatever you say, darling."

"Come on. It might be my last chance to go for a while."

"What?"

"I've been telling you that I've been thinking about going back to New York."

"Oh, right."

"Come on. I'll blow you in the car on the way."

"Why didn't you say so? It's a quick trip though. We leave tomorrow and back the next day. I got court day after tomorrow."

"That's what I love about you. Impetuous."

Jen grabs his arm and squeezes. Drops her cigarette and picks it up. "Five-second rule."

"I'll remember that when I'm on the floor." Hess gives a wink.

"Hello? Hello?" The music man thumps on his guitar. "What did you think of that?"

Hess and Jen look to the stage. They look at each other perplexed. Hess shrugs and then back to the stage. They had zoned out.

Jen smiles. "You were breathy in the end. Work on it, and I'll buy you another drink when I get back."

*

Hess the astronaut drifts tethered to the spacecraft. Some people will tell you no kid plans on being a drug dealer, but they come from neighborhoods that didn't foster the illusion of possibility. This is your America, fucko. Get over it. Some kids grew up in such shitty places they were thugs and petty criminals the way prep school kids became bankers. Instead of learning math in school they learned to do math by the dime-bag. Me, I was sure I was going to fly in other ways. The stars, man. My old man guaranteed we'd be on Mars twenty years after hitting the moon, but instead we were lining up to spend billions to get bogged down in a sandbox. When did we lose dreaming as a national trait? Maybe we'd grown out of it like teenagers suddenly worried about looking tough.

CHAPTER SEVEN

Hess walks through the crowd of people playing slots and video poker. This place had higher end losers, mostly from out of town. Hess makes his way to the tables. Only a few gamblers and tourists mill about the casino floor. A long line stretches from the buffet. A woman in a red pantsuit fights with a woman in a gold evening gown over a slot machine, ringing and buzzing. Two security guards show up with a floor manager, who starts handing out free steak dinner coupons. Hess shrugs thinking about the last casino he was in. Security would have thumped them and dumped them in the street.

*

I used to hit that place pretty hard, but got asked to leave one night after I got caught balling Jen down by the pool. Some nights you just can't get away with living the dream. Security guard said kids might've come in. No shit? Kids shouldn't be allowed in Vegas. Besides if some kids are drifting around the pool at two in the morning they got bigger problems than seeing two people fucking. Losers talk about cutting loose and being free and then tell others how to act. Figures. Those who shit talk the most about freedom are the first to try and take it away. They should've stayed in L.A. or Wichita or Salt Lake or whatever uptight town they came from and die or go to Reno.

My mom had been dealing cards and spinning roulette for losers since the 70s after Daddy disappeared over Southeast Asia. About the time I got thrown out of her casino I quit gambling anyway. Uncle A used to say casinos were just like life. A few people controlled all the money and made sure enough got down to the losers to make them think they were getting ahead, while slowly raking it all in. Not only that. The bigwigs cultivated the myth of the winner, giving away free rooms and cheap meals and free drinks and the cool guy image of the gambler to keep them faked out. Living the Dream where it was rigged so a person could never realize the dream. Uncle A would say in a low voice. "See, if we didn't give our money to the banks they'd have no power. Usury's a sin anyways, but greed will drive them all to hell." Of course Uncle A was a cash and carry man.

*

Hess walks up to a blackjack table. Hess's mom deals cards to a cowboy sporting a straw cowboy hat and a denim suit with a scorpion bolo tie. A sizable stack of gambling chips sits in front of him.

"Ma, when you go on break?"

"Hello, Son. I'm due, Chrissy's late coming back."

Hess looks around, then takes a cigarette out and lights it.

The cowboy doubles down and loses after Mom draws two cards to get twenty. Mom deals again.

Chrissy rushes up, her long hair frizzed and flying. Mom fans the cards on the table and shows her palms and backs of her hands to the cowboy. He tosses her a chip.

Mom takes the chip on the table. "Thank you."

The cowboy nods.

Mom walks away. Hess follows her back through the casino.

*

Not all the vets who visited us were whacked out. A bunch of guys from his fighter wing at Nellis would roll by with presents for me and her. There was this one black guy who came back with a Vietnamese bargirl wife and Buddhist's ways. Brother Weed and Sister Speed. All those years training and he up and got out and founded a church. More like a spiritual retreat without all the fire, brimstone, and judgmental assholes. Even guys who never

served with him because they named a building after
him, and he was like a decorated legend for flying wicked
combat missions. After a few years, Mom shacked up with
some professional gambler, Cal, and after the visits by the
Air Force guys, he'd get all jealous and worked up, and
we'd get a little slapping around. Must be hard to have a
bunch of guys come over and talk about what stud your
predecessor was, not even knowing if he was dead or
going to show back up with years of pent up Hanoi prison
rage. Plus those boys treated me especially good. Kept the
dream of flight alive in me for a little while. Must've been
double hard on old Cal with me right there, knowing what
a douche bag he was. One day he up and disappeared.
Not packed up and left, but straight up disappeared as he
never came for his clothes and trinkets, and his car stayed
in a parking space at a cheap dive bar for a week. Just
gone. I figured he crossed the wrong bookie and ended up
anchored to the bottom of Lake Mead. Some men have
the swagger, but not the guts.

*

"How's wasting your life these days?"

"Come on, Ma."

"You don't think I read the paper, watch the news?"

"It's just a misunderstanding."

"Does it have something to do with that Todd?"

Hess follows his mom into the break room. Several
tables and chairs are empty. On the wall hangs a corkboard
with notices and fliers and a Workers' Rights poster. Mom
gets a cup of coffee from one of the two pots on Bunn
coffee maker and sits at a table. Hess sits next to her. A
television runs news footage of Desert Shield and the
masses of aircraft, soldiers and vehicles in the sand.

"What does Todd have to do with anything?"

"He's trash. He'll bring you down."

"Ma, I'm not..."

"You shush."

"I can't live up to that. I'm not a hero."

"You could be. You need to give yourself another chance. You just quit, gave up."

"Ma, the girl died."

"People die all the time, but you can save a life, even so."

"I can't live up to that."

"You could. You just quit college and dropped out of the ROTC. Then you quit working on the ambulance. You need to stick with it, work at it like your father did."

"Dad's dead, Ma."

"He could be still alive. Bo Gritz came over..."

"Let me guess. He's got photos and needs money to go back to Southeast Asia..."

"You shush. He's a good man, looking after us."

"He's whacked out, living in the desert, training those Afghan fighters. Dad's dead, and everyone has to let that war go and move on."

*

After a bunch of MIA movies in the 80s, some
traumatized vets looked my mom up, trying to get her
to chip in money so they could go search for my dad.
Bo Gritz made headlines chasing after MIA rumors
in Southeast Asia with a bunch of faded photos and a
reputation for being a decorated Green Beret. All during
the 80s he trained future Taliban in Nevada to fight
the Russians in Afghanistan. Last I heard he ended up
founding some apocalyptic church compound up in Idaho
where he and his followers await for the world to collapse.
Funny how much you can sell people with loss. Not all had
his prestige and some even asked if I'd be interested in
going with them. What the shit do I know about tromping
around the jungle? Those fools took movies way too
seriously. But that's a problem with a lost war. How does
one gain closure when one had to retreat, leave behind the

missing and the dead like so many Jeeps and trucks? It is a powerful emptiness that drives a man to obsess over who he thinks he let down. To chase ghosts.

*

"Just never mind. Did you come over just to make me feel bad?"

Hess stands. "I wanted to let you know I'm going to L.A. and if you'd feed Whiskers for me tomorrow evening."

"Yes, of course. All I have in the way of grandkids."

"I'll see you, Ma."

Mom stands and Hess kisses her on the cheek and begins to walk away.

Mom calls after him. "You be careful and don't let those friends of yours get you into more trouble. They are all bad news. And be sure to stop and say hi to your grandmother and Uncle Allen."

Hess walks out of the room. She sits down and lights a cigarette as she watches the television with footage of the build-up for the first Gulf War.

CHAPTER EIGHT

Jen drives her white 1988 VW Cabriolet into a parking space in a high-rise garage. She gets out heads for the elevator.

Jen makes her way through the crowd of gamblers and cocktail waitresses. She stops at the front desk. A well-groomed desk clerk stands, looking through a folio file. She places her driver's license on the counter top. "I should have a key waiting for me. Jen Swallows, 206."

"Yes, here we are. Miss Kline left a message to meet her in the Jacuzzi."

"Thanks." Jen slides a five-dollar tip across the counter and then takes the key from him. She heads for the elevators at a quick pace.

Jen walks across the pool area in her black with gold dots bikini and slides into the water next to Marla in a red bikini.

Two kids swim and splash water in the pool, jumping and shouting.

Three middle-aged pudgy men stare at Jen as she gets in.

Jen smiles at Marla. "Miss Kline, I presume?"

"You are correct, Miss Swallows. I have a Cape Cod for you."

Jen slides close to Marla. "Expecting me, I see."

"Those guys have been staring at me for the last thirty minutes."

Jen eyes them. "Oh, really."

Jen slips her arm around Marla's neck and pulls her mouth to hers. When Jen lets go she smiles at them. "That should give them something to think about when they're beating off in the shower."

One of the men works his way off the lounge chair. He wears a Speedo and rubber shower shoes. Hair cream glistens on his hair plugs, sticking out like rows of corn. A mixed drink sweats in his hand.

"Excuse me ladies."

Jen and Marla kiss again and then look at him.

"We'd appreciate it if you'd refrain from making out. We have kids here."

Jen kisses Marla's cheek. "So sorry. I thought this was Vegas, and I was at a casino after ten at night."

Marla giggles. "A week night."

"I can call security."

Marla wrinkles her nose. "What a drag. You're killing my high."

Jen looks around his pasty legs, hair worn off his calves. "Why don't we ask the others?"

"That's not necessary."

She rises out of the water. "Hey! You men don't mind if we make out do you?"

Smiles spread across their faces.

Jen smiles at him. "Maybe you should find your wife before the cabana boy does. If she already hasn't found him."

He clenches his jaw, and his face reddens. He storms off, his flip-flops scuffing against the concrete.

Marla splashes some water. "Now where were we?"

Jen picks up her drink and sips. "Drinks and a kiss so far."

"Excellent. I feel my high coming back."

They lean into the Jacuzzi jets, sinking a little further into the water. Jen caresses Marla's shoulder.

Jen says, "How long before you can come to New York?"

"You're not leaving that soon are you?"

"Less than a month, maybe."

"I'll have to see how my deal goes."

Jen looks away. "Tell me, what's the deal."

"Just one of my foster brothers got some connections, and I act as a go between. Might be a month before I see any dollars from it."

"That sounds dangerous."

Marla smiles slyly. "Nah, he was a Green Beret, and he's been with the CIA down in Nicaragua. I got full protection. Once in high school, I was having problems with a couple of boys and he rolled in with a couple of his army pals and made them hurt."

Jen asks, "And this is going to be a lot of money?"

"More dollars than I've seen. I just want to be my own keeper. Even if it's only for a little while." Marla drinks and sighs clinking the ice. "You don't know what it's like to be a guest in another's house and spend your whole life trying to be cute and adorable enough not to get thrown out. All the boys thinking it's okay to fuck you because you're not blood and they figure you got no parents, so you must be a slut brought in for their entertainment. Thanks for the slut, Dad! Like some hooker called to a party. Trying to act like the girl you think they want crushes your soul. Pretty soon you're second-guessing yourself and how you should be. Who are you?"

Marla looks at her peeled thumb. "I should go to New York and try acting. Bet I'd kill 'em on Broadway. Get on stage and pretend to be somebody I'm not to get people to love me." Marla empties her drink. Fumbles with the cigarette pack and lights one with a slim lighter. "Man, I'm killing my own high."

Jen caresses Marla's cheek. "Oh sweetheart. I love you for who you are."

"I don't even know who I am."

A clamor of keys and the scuff of shoes and thwack of flip-flops from the casino entrance across the cement.

The pudgy man shuffles up to the Jacuzzi. "Right there. There. Those two women." He points like he's in court.

A young security guard walks behind him, pulling his belt up. "These two?"

"Yes. I want them removed."

The Security Guard looks from the Jacuzzi to the man and shakes his head. "For kissing? The way you talked it was a couple of sea donkeys out here getting it on."

"In front of the kids!"

The security guard scans the pool area. "What kids?"

The man looks at an empty pool. He creeps to the edge and scans the bottom. He rushes about the chaise lounges as the other men smile and drink.

He yells "Fran! Ollie! Where are you two! Come out now!" He storms back to the security guard and yells. "Don't just stand there gawking at those girls, get some help!"

The security guard smiles, tips his head to Jen and Marla. "Ladies."

CHAPTER NINE

Todd's truck speeds down the highway through the night.
Woo rides shotgun. Vegas behind them pulses and flinches
against the horizon like a mechanical sunrise. The heat still
holds in the air like a big-block engine after a race.

They pass a sign that giving the mileage to Los
Angeles. The faint glow of the old dashboard lights cast a
greenish-blue haze. Smoke fills the interior. The tires hum
on the asphalt.

Woo has his hand between his legs. "Why doesn't that
guy carry?"

"Doesn't want to that's all."

"Fucking going around in his business without a gun
is insane."

"He always said if someone was going to pop him
they'd do it gangster style and he wouldn't even get a round
off and if he did it wouldn't make him live any longer."

"That's insane."

"But he's a major bad ass. His Uncle A trained him to
fight in the Apocalypse. Huge End of Days fanatics. I ran
with them a while, but Uncle A tossed me out. Thought I
wasn't serious enough." Todd flicks cigarette ash onto the
floorboard. "Once I saw a dude pull a gun on Hess and he
pulled out his clickity knife and cut the stupid fucker's wrist
to the bone before he could blink. Can't pull the trigger if
you're bleeding from the wrist like a teenaged girl."

"Insane, man."

"Fucking-A insane. But most people with guns not
going to shoot you anyway. They wave it around try to
scare you a little so they can get their way." Hess smiles.
"Sometimes all you need to do is yell at the fucker. They
piss themselves to get away."

"I don't believe that."

Todd shakes his head. "That Hess, man. One tough motherfucker. A good dude to know."

Woo looks Todd up and down and then back out into the night. "What the fuck you backstabbing him for if he's such a great dude to know?"

Todd flicks his cigarette at Woo. It bounces of his head. "Fuck you, man. I'm not double-crossing nobody. Get that straight, slope."

Todd jerks the wheel and slams on the brakes. Woo bounces off the door. The truck fishtails. The tires screech. They come to a stop in the emergency lane. Dust rolls into the headlights. Todd jumps out and storms around to the passenger side. He jerks Woo from the truck, throws him against the front fender, grabs his throat with his left hand, and slaps him in the head.

Woo covers his head with his arms. "Fuck man! Stop you crazy bastard!"

Todd slaps Woo hard on the crown of his head. "You ever say anything like that to me or if I hear of you saying that to anyone else I will ass fuck you with a shotgun."

"Okay, man. I fucking swear."

Todd releases Woo's neck. Still breathing hard. Calms in a second and gains control. "He just doesn't know the full extent of the deal. Get it? Nobody's going to get hurt, but I need Hess. I knew he wouldn't do this unless I made it a favor for an old pal."

Traffic goes by on the highway. A tanker truck flashes by like a quicksilver streaking the night.

"Cool, man I got it. I'm all in, bro."

"Get in the truck, slope. You ain't my bro."

Woo climbs in.

Todd walks around to the front of the truck. He unzips his fly and pisses in the halo of headlights. Dust, steam, and stars.

CHAPTER TEN

Hess and Jen drive out of Vegas into the desert toward Los Angeles. Jazz plays on the car stereo. The early sun shines slanted rays through the rear window. Hess's mirrored sunglasses reflect desert and asphalt.

Jen wears a vivid blue, short dress, knee high black boots, and her swallow charm on the gold chain. She looks through her camera viewfinder at the passing landscape.

They pass a sign for Sloan, Nevada in one mile. Jen points at it. "Pull off here."

"We just got out of town."

"There's a shot I need for the show I'm thinking about for a gallery in Soho."

"Soho, some ho." Hess chuckles.

Jen rolls her eyes. "Just pull over."

Hess pulls off.

Jen says, "Go left and take a right at the stop sign."

They merge onto the old highway, drive past a few older buildings that hadn't caught up to the Vegas boom. Someone has zip-tied a sun-faded and wind-ragged teddy bear to a cross that had been pounded into the ground at the asphalt's edge.

Hess says, "Is that a warning to all the other teddy bears?" He laughs. She does not.

"A kid was killed here. A pickup lost control and flipped him out."

"How in the hell do you know that?"

She rolls her eyes. "Research."

"You don't have to say it like that."

"I've told you before about how I track things down."

"I must've been high. You don't need to act like I missed Christmas."

"Whatever."

Hess stares out at the bear and the cross. "The parents should swap out that bear. You think maybe that particular bear belonged to the kid and no other bear would do?"

She flips her hair back. "You are such a flippant moron."

Jen gets out and walks around and takes pictures, while Hess watches. She gets back in the car. Hess stares out the window. Cars and trucks stream by on the highway.

"Research. Did your research tell you what it's like to watch one of these kids die? You ever even seen one of these accidents? I mean up close and not in some fucking picture."

Hess grips and un-grips the steering wheel. Jazz continues to play on the car stereo.

"I was a paramedic. Once I watched a little girl die after her mom backed over her. When I pushed on the little girl's abdomen she screamed, yelling about how much I hurt her. The mom freaked out, grabbed me. My partner wrestled with her. It took only a minute, maybe less. I can't remember, but when, you know . . . when you get off track how you can't remember exactly where you're at. You get fixed on that one thing. You clear her airway, start mouth-to-mouth because that's the obvious problem, but that's no help because she's bleeding into her guts. When you realize you just felt her last breath in your mouth, it kind of fucks with you. I'd seen adults die, but not a kid. Not like that."

Jen reaches and touches his shoulder. Hess clears his throat and wipes at the corner of his eye.

"I'll never forget how angry I was. That mom, she's yelling and screaming, and I'm thinking she was yelling at me and there's this crowd of fucking suburbanites standing around."

Hess pounds the steering wheel, causing Jen to flinch. "And I'm thinking this is just a spectacle for them, like this little girl is a beached whale." He breathes in deeply. "All I could think was I had just sucked in her last breath."

Hess takes a cigarette from his case, lights it, hands it to her, then lights one for himself. "You know what I did then?"

Hess waits, but Jen doesn't answer.

"I lost my temper, like it seems I do. I hit some dad wearing Dockers who was mouthing some crap. The cops arrested me. The ambulance company fired me. Good luck getting another job with that kind of recommendation, so I went to see an old high school pal in Vegas."

Hess put his hand on her leg.

Jen puts her hand on his. "Todd."

Hess nods.

Jen turns her head away, but Hess keeps looking ahead.

He removes his hand from Jen's leg and shifts the Beemer into drive. Hess wheels the car around, heading for the on-ramp. The BMW gains speed and hits the highway, the light rippling across the waxed paint.

*

I hadn't planned on telling her the story, but sitting there like a shithead, it came out. I just didn't tell her I had fucked up and killed the girl. I was going to, but as I formed the words in my head, the other story I had told to myself and others came out like rehearsed testimony in court. I'd gotten to where I believed it myself sometimes. The truth or some version of truth. If I was the only witness who is to say it's not true? Memory is tricky and unreliable anyway. This happened, and fuck you who says different.

As an EMT I had trained until I could work on autopilot, and so I could keep operating under high stress. I heard the legends of my father and how he never panicked. He flew hot, raining steel and fire on the enemy no matter what they threw at him. Uncle A told

us stories about men freezing in fear and how they all
did until they got used to it and moved in fear instead of
seizing up, but there were always a few who never made
the switch. They remained paralyzed. I refused to believe
I was one of them. Who was to say I panicked and froze?
All the commotion, the screaming and people and that
little girl whose skin turned blue, and no one could finger
me except me, and if I had only kept my temper, I'd still
be a paramedic. I came to realize later, Todd's strength
was he could control his anger, but could slip it on like a
mask, and he had a strange propensity for doing bad and
not getting caught. Luck or karma or some force in the
universe seemed to keep him off the cellblock.

CHAPTER ELEVEN

In the coastal sunshine a white panel van drives along the coast, leaving San Diego. It drives past the I-5 North sign. Frank, a Caucasian man in his mid-thirties, close cropped hair, muscular military bearing, drives. An El Salvadoran, Angel, in his twenties, serious and tough looking lounges in the passenger seat. Marla leans forward in between the seats from the darkness behind.

Frank and Angel look at her briefly and then back to the road. "There's a great place to get fish tacos close to where we're staying."

Frank says, "I thought you didn't want your boyfriend to know."

"What's he got to do with tacos?"

Angel says, "Dumb ass. If he sees you he's going to wonder why you around." He looks at Frank. "What the fuck, Frank?"

"She's family. Sort of."

Marla says, "Right. But they are really good fish tacos." The two men stare straight ahead. She shakes her head at them. "You can't get as good in Vegas.

Frank laughs. "You can't get as good in prison either. Keep it straight, little sister."

Angel stares at her hard. "Or the bottom of the bay."

Marla slumps back into the rear seat. "Fine. You two are stealing my high. We can order in, whatever."

CHAPTER TWELVE

The BMW drops out of the mountains and crosses the
edge of a playa into California before climbing into a
mountain range. Hess steers onto the off-ramp at the
summit toward a dilapidated mining town with a rundown
bowling alley, gas station/store.

Just past the bowling alley stretches a semi-abandoned
trailer park with rundown trailers, empty spots with
cracked trailer pads and dead weeds waving in the wind.
It sprawls up the rise to the north of town where the half
operational mining buildings and the mountains of tailings
blown and hauled out of the earth blot the horizon.

*

Mom came up here to stay with Uncle A so I'd have a
man influence in my life after Cal went missing. Imagine
moving from an airbase full of hot-shit fighter pilots to
a place scrubbed out of the side of a mountain. Uncle
A had been to the Farm three times where the mine sent
its employees with drug and alcohol problems. The last
time Uncle A came back it was with a bible, sporting a
new pair of combat boots, preaching the end of days was
drawing nigh, and we good Christians had to bunker-up
to be ready to fight the godless Communists who at that
very moment were going to nuke and invade what was
left. I never did figure why anyone would want to invade
a wasteland, but at the time I was swept up like dust into
a dustpan. We were to rise out of the ruins of the old
order, chase them to Mexico or Canada, and establish a
new temple ruled by God's Law. He wasn't one of your
Rapture type Born Again Christians who thought all they
needed to do was wait around until God plucked their self-
righteous asses off the Earth where they would then mock
us poor sinners. No, he was an Old Testament, heaven

bent warrior against Satan for God on Earth. Most of the family thought he was working through some shit from Vietnam and the holy warrior shit would wear off, but he had been saved.

*

Hess wheels the Beemer in front of Uncle Allen's old and dingy trailer, and parks. A '72 International Scout II is parked out front next to a '69 Ford Fairlane. Tufts of desert grass litter the dirt yard.

Hess gets out and motions for Jen to follow him. They climb the creaky steps.

Hess knocks on the door and two dogs bark. A terrier mutt and a mottled shepherd.

Uncle Allen yells, "Shut up!"

The door opens. Uncle Allen kicks the dogs back. His work boots are dirty and cracked. He steps onto the rickety wooden steps. Dirt coats his jeans, plaid shirt, and his clean-shaven face. Blond/gray hair hangs to his shoulders, and a tattered cap keeps it corralled.

"Well, look who it is. The prodigal nephew."

Hess smiles and hugs him "I didn't squander a fortune."

"Yeah you did. Just not one you can spend. Good to see you."

"Good to see you too."

"Just got off work, so I's got nothing ready for visiting."

"Not a problem. I can't stay long anyway."

"Figures. I bet you needing a piece."

Hess nods. "Got some business in L.A. and even though I hate it, I'd better have me a little something."

Uncle Allen looks over Hess's head. "Who's the little filly?"

Jen's jaw drops. "I am not a little filly."

Uncle Allen rubs his chin, smiles. "And a spirited one at that."

"When you're done here you can come find me. I'm sure you won't have too much trouble." Jen storms to the car, takes out her camera bag, and walks off. Her heels click on the gravelly asphalt.

Hess calls after her. "All right."

Jen yells without turning around. "Look at this place. A memorial for American industry."

A 1976 white GMC pickup without a bed on it honks and the young men hoot as they rattle by Jen. She flips them off.

Uncle Allen smiles as he watches Jen walk away. "Why haven't you brought her by before?"

"I knew you'd just piss her off."

Uncle Allen shrugs. "Well, come on in."

Hess follows Uncle Allen into the living room. It is clean and neat, but the furniture shows wear and age. An old recliner in front of a television has been patched with duct tape. Family pictures adorn the walls. A bible sets on the light stand next to the recliner.

The dogs sniff and wag their tails at Hess. Hess pets them, and they go into the kitchen claws scratching against the linoleum.

"How's your mom?"

"Good. Still dealing cards to losers."

"You going to visit your grandma?"

Hess looks at the family photos on the wall.

*

I didn't like visiting as her as a kid. Grandma sitting in that hot trailer with foil covering all the windows, the swamp cooler ticking, dark with only one shrouded bulb on an end table filtering the hanging smoke from Pall Mall after Pall Mall. I'd come in, and she'd grind that electric easy chair forward, shoot out her arms, hissing almost, "Come to grandmother my miracle baby, my miracle baby." When I got close enough, nudged forward by mother, the old woman would grab me by the shoulders and suck me into that dank cotton dress reeking of sweat, bitter smoke, beauty powder and jalapeños. The wind always rattled the sun faded siding. I tried to hold my breath, but she squeezed me so hard and long her sweat soaked my shirt. It was like I was a fly being sucked into the Venus flytrap she kept on her table next to the lamp. Once she started coughing and hacking as she kept a tight grip on me. I swear I heard shit breaking loose in her chest, but trembled to say anything, and trembled when she released me with a dry kiss on the cheek. I stood there as she pushed a button on a panel at the end of a heavy cord. The chair would grind back to a normal, non-ejection looking seat.

"Miracle baby" because grandpa had cancer and when I was born he got better. I heard all the time from that smoking crone how I gave them all the will to carry on, "To live, my boy, to live, you saved us," and she told me that if I ever quit loving them they'd die. Got to be I believed it. It's a heady thing to be hero-worshipped as a boy. What kid wouldn't buy into it when all the adults told you so? I could even will my father safely back to the States if I wanted. The old woman creaking out words like breaking the spine of a book. "You wouldn't want grandmother and grandfather to die? Would you?" Fuck me. I was ten when my miraculous powers ran out.

*

Uncle Allen says, "She's your grandma and it's right you go see her. She talks about you all the time. You have to respect that."

Hess suppresses a chuckle. "Like all the respect they gave me."

"You still messing with the drugs?"

Hess snaps out of his trance of memory. "Just a business like banking or the stock market. Supply and demand and investing."

Uncle Allen chuffs. "Those two worse than slinging dope. Legal thieves. People forget they bible."

Uncle Allen starts down a narrow, paneled hallway and enters a room. Hess follows. Along the walls squat four gun-safes. Uncle Allen goes to one and twists the dial.

"Just one?"

"Yeah."

Uncle Allen opens the safe. Takes out a semi-auto handgun in a holster, hands it to Hess, then two empty magazines, and a box of bullets.

"You going to say hi to your grandma?"

Hess clips the holster onto his belt. "On the way back if I have time." Hess begins loading the magazines.

"You should make time now."

"This is a shit lot of bullets."

"Yeah, you can pack a lot of killing into a small space."

"I'll come back to visit."

"That so?"

*

Some glitch in my love system let Grandpa die, and it all got laid at my feet. My dad had already been gone a year. It's a bitch to have your whole world looking at you to save them. The whole clan raising you up like a faith healer, except you're so powerful and full of goodness you don't even have to lay hands on folks. No. All you need to do is direct your love at them, and they live for as long as you can love them, and you're only a little boy. A wonder-kid. What great things will you do when you get all growed up they mused with faraway eyes.

*

"Granny talks about you all the time."

"Yeah, she can keep talking. I'll be back." Hess finishes loading the magazines and puts them in his pockets.

Hess follows Uncle Allen as he walks into the kitchen and opens the fridge door.

"Want a soda or some tea?"

Hess shakes his head. "I need to get going."

Uncle Allen pulls a gallon jar out of the fridge and pours himself a glass of tea.

"You think you can pull the trigger now?"

Hess shrugs and looks at the family photos on the wall. One with Uncle A in Vietnam with a cigarette dangling out of his mouth, helmet shifted back on his head as he straddles a water buffalo with a Vietnamese kid in front of him like they're at a carnival pony ride. Hess smiles out of several as a teen in camouflage and armed with guns, shooting at human silhouette targets with Uncle Allen and others in camouflage and military gear.

*

We got all wrapped up in the militia movement. We trained like an infantry platoon, and learned martial arts from some guy who worked with Uncle A like an infantry platoon. I recovered some sense of my power after losing my hero status. I also became arrogant, believing I knew something others didn't, and they would have to depend on me to survive. We'd have guns and food and carve out a city-state. The guys spent a lot of time sitting around talking about how they were going to rise up from the ashes to make a new community, and all the others would be dead or starving because they were unprepared. They said no room for compassion in the Apocalypse. I was slowly withdrawing from them as they ranted, but when Brother Weed and Sister Speed swung in for visits, I began to see the world in a different way. He wore some African robe and she an ao dai of beautiful blue. She shimmered in the light like a jewel cut from the fabric of the universe fallen to earth. I was wearing a Kill Commies t-shirt and camo pants. He just shook his head at me. "You all primed up to be a killer."

"A survivor."

"You don't look like you ready to survive shit.

Where's your hammer and a saw?"

I didn't know what to say.

He continued. "Surviving means being a builder, not a destroyer. Let me guess, you and all your pals training like you in the infantry, but not like carpenters?"

"We train to defend and fend off marauders." My voice cracked.

"Sure you do, son. Sure you do. Why don't you train to save people instead? Help and build. If an apocalypse does happen, which I doubt, any silly ass can shoot a gun, but who will rebuild and who will minister the sick?" His big smile spread across his face like a light. "Hell, I killed motherfuckers by the truckload, but Sister Speed saved hundreds."

At the next meeting I looked around me. Brother Weed's words ringing in my head. These men and boys looked desperate in a way I hadn't noticed before. Many of them misfits and outcasts even in a place of misfits and outcasts. They wanted to be relevant and they wanted people to depend on them and this was the only way they knew how. I began to feel ridiculous dressed in my cammies, cradling a rifle like a puppy.

Plus, something key happened when Sister Speed hugged me goodbye. At first I wasn't aware she had said anything her whisper like the breath of a baby sleeping. Now the guys who hung out with Uncle A would say she was full of shit, and in their false bravado insult her world vision, but she grew up in the war. She'd seen darkness and fire fall from the sky. "Restraint of power is the greatest power." "Once you kill someone you can't take it back." Such an obvious statement. No shit, I thought. That's the point, shoot to kill so he couldn't come back to get you. In my youthful belief that my kin and their friends were always right, I kept shooting up the targets, but I started to swing the other way. I'd been reading a lot and discovered every age has its lunatics who holed-up believing the end was near and adopted a bunker mentality. I looked at the broken and ruptured men: the skinny wielder who only shot 22 caliber, the obese truck driver who couldn't walk a hundred yards much less hump his ass all over the mountains, a guy with long blond hair and boots that reached above his knees, a short stocky man with dragon tattoos on his forearms like Cain in the television show Kung-Fu. They loved their guns more than women and some of their women had drifted off to other men. Fuck that.

But Sister Speed also planted an image in my head. We'd imagined killing enemy soldiers, thugs, and gangbangers and not running Vietnamese girls dripping with napalm and tears.

*

Uncle A sits down in his recliner. "I suppose you'll figure it out."

"I suppose so. I don't know. I don't know exactly what Todd's got going on."

"Todd's a douche bag. You need to cut him loose."

"After this I am. We'll be even."

Uncle Allen shakes his head and takes a drink of tea.

Hess keeps talking. "Anyway. I just want a little fool-insurance. If it goes south, I can draw it to back people up."

Uncle Allen laughs. "What backs people up is shooting them. Keep that in mind."

*

I could shoot with the best, but Uncle Allen always said, "If you pull a gun you got to be ready to drop the hammer on a guy." Before Sister Speed, I had made myself believe it was as simple as squeezing a trigger, but after her whisper, her words wove a net of doubt, and I realized I was never sure I could kill someone. That was my real reason for not carrying a pistol. I made up the other stuff because if people thought I was scared to kill, they'd come after me.

CHAPTER THIRTEEN

The pick-up truck without the bed speeds up after passing Jen, scattering dust and pea-gravel. She lets up on her quick walk as she distances herself from Uncle A's place.

She takes photographs as she continues: Some dead grass, a new Ford pick-up truck with a roll bar and off road lights in front of ancient trailer with water stains down its sides, a small mutt chained to an engine block, a lightning struck tree by a trailer with a plywood room built on to it.

A four-year-old little girl plays in a yard patched with brown grass. A swing set sags in back, a bicycle lay on its side, and a small wooden fort built of scrap wood leans by the road.

Jen calls out. "Hey, little girl."

The little girl pauses and looks at her. Dirt smudges her face and snot crusts her nostrils. Her dark hair is pulled back in a tight ponytail with a scrunchie that has plastic flowers dangling from it.

"Don't be afraid sweetheart. Can I take your picture?" Jen holds her camera out to show her.

The little girl looks to the trailer and back to Jen and shakes her head.

"Come on now. It'll be a nice picture. Why you're so cute."

The little girl shakes her head again. Jen puts the camera to her eye and starts clicking. "See it's not bad."

The little girl smiles. Jen steps into the yard. "You're a cutie."

The trailer door bursts open like a rattle of beer cans. A fat young woman with dirty hair and a baby on her hip rushes onto the steps of the trailer. She wears a oversized t-shirt with a picture of Garth Brooks and cut-off jean shorts. The sound of daytime television applause comes from behind her.

She yells, "What in the hell do you think you're doing?"

Startled Jen pauses, but swings her camera and snaps a quick shot. "Just taking some photos. You have a cute little girl."

The woman looks down to the little girl. "Lucinda, get your ass in here now. What have I told you about strangers?" She fixes her stare on Jen. "Especially ones looking like whores."

The little girl runs into the house.

"You get on back to where you come from." The woman slams the trailer door behind her.

"At least I'm not trash," Jen yells back. Jen takes a picture and turns away.

Jen walks to the gas station and stops at a phone booth. Cars on the freeway rush by like flights of birds in a jet stream. She picks up the receiver missing the earpiece. "Figures," she says. She walks into the station. At the desk a high school boy sits, reading a dirt bike magazine.

Jen clears her throat. "Got a phone I can use?"

The boy looks her up and down smiling. "Ahhh, yeah, but nothing's local from here."

Jen puts her hand and on her hip, looking down at the kid.

"Even to get your mom on the line?"

"Yeah, she dumped dad for some well driller passing through."

"Sorry to hear about your loss. The phone?"

"Oh sure this one here or you can use the one in the garage."

Jen walks past him into the garage area.

She squeezes by an old Rambler on jack-stands, a tire mounting machine, an empty bay with the lift to a workbench with greasy phone.

She takes a phone card out of her purse and picks up the handset. She dials. Phone rings and Marla's answering machine picks up. "Hey, this is Marla. I'm out tripping or just tripping, so leave some wisdom." After the tone, Jen cups the receiver as if somebody might be listening. "Hey, babe, just checking on you. Thought you'd be home. I'll call before I come back from L.A."

Jen hangs up and leaves and walks back toward the mining camp, past the bowling alley where the pick-up truck from earlier is parked next to an orange muscle car. Rock and Roll blasts from the car.

Hess's BMW turns on to the road and heads toward her. She stops, and he pulls up next to her.

"We're done here."

Jen sighs. "Thank God."

"You want to see a local highway memorial?"

Jen perks up. "Yeah."

She gets in and they drive to the highway on-ramp and the BMW pulls over and Hess gets out.

She gets out with her camera and stands on the asphalt as he rummages around in the brush.

Hess stands and surveys the area. "It's got to still be here. Maybe a little further."

He walks parallel to the on-ramp. Jen walks, her heels clicking.

Hess stops. "Here it is." He picks up a small wired together cross. The weathered wood has a rusting dog collar hanging from it.

Jen snaps a few photos. "Let me guess, your best friend."

"Brandy got off the chain and dashed down here and got squashed by a Celica."

Jen takes his picture as he poses, holding the cross. "I bet you cried."

"You know I did. Like a kid who had let his dad's best friend get killed."

Jen lowers the camera a moment and raises to take another picture. "Shoot me some tears now to make the photo more dramatic."

"Nah, I gave up on crying. It don't make a shit of difference to the dead."

He tosses the cross off into the brush, and they get back in the BMW and pull onto the highway.

*

Funny how we take trips expecting one thing and discover something unexpected. How a moment of action or inaction doesn't change the course of our lives, but redefines who we were, even when those people from our past always see us as we used to be. Almost like no one expects any change.

CHAPTER FOURTEEN

Yellow hash marks slip by. The air-conditioning blows cold, and the radio plays more jazz. Jen leans back into her seat, hand up in front of the a/c vent as she looks out the window.

"Thank God for tinted windows and sunglasses. Second and third best inventions ever."

Jen leans forward. "Pull over there."

Hess clicks on the blinker. "The mile markers look like little grave markers. Every quarter-mile a sign for the dead."

Hess pulls over. Jen gets out and walks to where someone had stuck a cross in the ground and planted at its base plastic flowers and a cardboard four-leaf clover painted metallic green. Along the highway trucks and cars whip by, rumbling the air. One big rig honks its air horn.

Jen squats down, and points the camera as level as she can, as her skirt climbs up to her hips. She moves around and takes shots from different angles. The wind blows her hair across her face and a strand gets caught in her mouth. She draws it away with a finger and Hess loves the small moment as she looks out of another world. A kid on a summer day with a camera and all the wonder a blue-sky day could hold.

Jen gets back in the car. She changes the film in her camera. She marks the used roll and records the number in a small Steno pad.

Hess shifts the BMW into drive. "I wonder if there's a highway marker for everyone killed on the highway." He accelerates onto the highway. "Then there'd be a constant memorial."

"That last one had a picture. Those are my favorite."

"A picture within a picture. What's that for?"

Jen sighs long and loud. "I told you. That gallery in Soho. I'm thinking about making a collage from the photos from accident sites. I think it'd be cool to combine these photos with some from burial sites along the old emigrant wagon trails. The marking of the grief inflicted by those journeys mirror each other in an American way."

"Whatever. Once they're gone, they're gone, and all the plastic flowers out of China don't make a shit of difference to them, mirrored or not."

"You're so pale. I should put some plastic flowers on you."

"I wonder how come I never see any of those Jewish stars."

"Don't be a moron."

They drive off. Jen looks through her camera.

Hess sticks his tongue out at her when she points the camera at him. "What do you want to do when we get back? We could get some food at the Chinese place in Commercial Square."

"It's Japanese." Jen turns back to the front. "I think I just want to go home."

"My place? I guess we could order out."

Jen shakes her head. "No, New York." She stares out her window, camera up to her eye.

I'll get tickets. Be nice to get out of Vegas.

The BMW speeds down an off-ramp and onto a two-lane road leading out into the desert. Heat waves flow over the road, blurring a building with cottonwood trees, trembling in the distance. The apparitions of Joshua trees flicker as they punch through the heat. The road opens up and Hess wheels up in front of a wooden church freshly painted so white it glows and shimmers in the sunlight. The roof and steeple pulse blood red.

Jen leans forward and looks out the windshield. "Are you kidding me? Church?"

"Chill the fuck out." He smiles at her. "You can stay

in the car if you don't want your skanky soul saved."

"Ha ha ha." She stresses each ha.

Hess gets out, and Jen follows him.

Hess strides up the steps and pauses at the door. A plaque to the right of the door reads: Church of Celestial Light. Cleansing Doors of Perception Since 1973.

Hess put his hand on the door. "Brace yourself."

Jen looks at him with her "what the fuck" look.

Hess opens the door and walks in followed by Jen.

Green, yellow and red light streams through a giant stained glass peace sign. Instead of pews, cushions and pillows lie strewn on the wood floor. Incense burns in potted palms in the corners.

A lean woman in her late fifties, wearing dancer tights, ballet dances on the stage with a pulpit to slow tempo Arabic music.

Hess whispers. "That's Abby. Her husband disappeared with my dad."

Jen nods.

A curtain of beads and pooka shells rattles and clinks from a side doorway. Brother Weed, a tall black man in his fifties, enters the main room. Sister Speed, a petite Asian woman, follows him. He wears a yellow and brown dashiki and jeans and she wears a turquoise ao dai.

Brother Weed sees Hess and smiles and walks quickly to him. Sister Speed's face lights up as she moves.

They embrace.

"This is my girlfriend Jen Swallows. Jen this is Brother Weed and Sister Speed. He was in my Dad's squadron in Nam."

Jen sticks her hand out, but Brother Weed hugs her, as does Sister Speed.

Sister Speed smiles. "Have you eaten?"

Hess says, "No, but we don't have a lot of time."

Sister Speed touches Hess's forearm. "Nonsense.

Come on. You eat or I shoot out your tires."

They follow her through the curtain.

A wok simmers on the stove. The air hangs with the smells of turmeric, curry, and garlic.

Sister Speed stirs the vegetables. "We were just cooking when we heard the door open." The big metal spoon rasps against the wok.

Jen smiles at her. "This smells delicious."

"And good for your blood," Sister Speed says.

Hess puts his hand on Brother Weed's shoulder. "I need some help tomorrow. Can you get loose?"

"You bet. Fill me in."

CHAPTER FIFTEEN

The evening light smudges the smog and the sunset burns the sky. Traffic slips along. Streetlights light up. Hess fidgets behind the wheel. Jen shoots some photos. She sets her camera in her lap. "Let's go tear it up."

"Let's get a room first."

*

Funny thing about being coked up, the trip compresses and flexes. You're in Vegas. You're in L.A. I didn't even remember passing the Gateway to Death Valley. But crazy enough, time blew itself out and my brain and body started this slow motion crash like running a car off an embankment and hanging in the air forever, so long I thought I might actually be flying, marveling at all the shades of smog and sky.

We rode the carousel at the Santa Monica Pier with hand-carved horses making frozen leaps and the Ferris wheel on Balboa Island and we sat in a bar off Melrose with funky blue lights, making everyone's skin look dead as if they were dragging their sorry asses through a zombie movie.

Drinkers lean against the horseshoe shaped bar. The bartender, a hipster with eyeliner, died black hair like a Goth and face piercings glint blue light on his face, ignores people until they ask for a drink. Twangy country music plays low on the jukebox. A woman with ragged white hair in a blue paisley housedress walks up to Jen. "Lady you can really fly."

An old man who drank next to the ragged hair woman wears a Tirol and bright red suspenders hold up red and gold surf shorts. He wanders over to Hess. "Are you German? I'm German. Fought the Russians. Those bastards deserved to lose everything."

"No, man. I'm not."

He says, "Ah, Norwegian then." He stumbles away
to sit next to the woman with ragged hair, and they sing a
German song together.

"Let's go to the Improv and then go for a walk on the
beach."

Hess shrugs. "Sure."

Jen takes her camera out. "Can I photograph you two?"

The crazy couple whoops and starts dramatically posing
for Jen as Hess flags down the bartender to pay the tab.

Driving down Hollywood Boulevard, jazz plays on the
radio. Jen scans the side streets as if looking for a lost dog.
"Pull over, quick. Toward the back."

Hess pulls into a mini-mart. She jumps out and walks
around back. Between a dumpster and the building, she
hikes her skirt around her waist, pulls nylons and panties
around her knees and squats. She pisses with a vengeance.

The night air thickens with the low clouds, and the
streetlights' rays break through her hair, giving her head
a blonde halo. Traffic moves in spurts. The BMW's radio
plays some jazz. Her piss hits the ground, spreading away
from her boots like surf receding out to sea. The lights
buzz and pop and horns honk as people drive in and
out of the mini-mart, pulling away from the fuel pumps.
No one notices her. I snatch her camera and click a few
snapshots of her. Let's see her put those in a gallery. She
could call an exploration into the failed manners of an
upper class woman. Salt air, smog and sweat coat Hess's
skin. Jen wipes herself with a tissue and pulls down her
skirt. She smiles, skipping into the parking lot—and with
all of her modeling school grace, climbs into the Beemer.
She smiles, said, "I just peed on L.A."

"Sure."

*

I knew it was Hollywood.

I had seen Los Angeles at night from the darkness of San Gabriel Mountains. All the lights spreading so far out they became a haze. Some high school pals and me used to hike up there to watch the city and lay back and stare at the stars. All was a stew of lights. A cemetery sprawled over acres of darkened ridge, and highways dotted with vehicles speeding in a one a.m. rush hour to beat closing last call traffic. Beyond the light-mottled skyscrapers— the Hollywood Hills and the sign, the Griffith Park Observatory and the constant hum of industry. I liked to watch aircraft dropping for LAX or launching into the dark, and listen to the noise under a dome of lights that blotted out the night sky. The electric city thrummed and popped. I believed I was untouchable, suspended above it all in the dark.

*

Hess noses out of the parking lot in between a pick-up truck and a piece of shit Toyota when an ambulance shrieks, trying to work its way through the clogged street. Horns honk. On the sidewalk across from Hess a homeless couple play a guitar and a tambourine next to a suitcase with a giant yellow cat sitting on it. The blonde girl with bloody ribbons streaming from her hair pets the cat. Hess stares at the blood vivid against her blue skin. A shimmer, a faint glint in the eyes like a distant wink of a star through high thin clouds. The bums strum and shake as people drop coins in a cup, but jazz fills Hess's head. A piano, a trumpet, drum kit. Can he hear the cat purring? He wonders at the sound, rising from the back of his head. Something both content and nervous. Hess waits for the girl to look at him. To raise her hand. To beckon him for help. To beseech him to stop. But she pets the cat as the homeless play on.

Jen slaps Hess on the shoulder. "Quit zoning-out and let's go." Cars honk.

"All right, don't get your panties all twisted and shouted up."

Hess pulls the BMW out, merging with traffic, leaving the blonde girl behind him.

*

We went to a club, and I faded in and out of consciousness. I laughed out of reflex not knowing what the comedian said. I ordered a drink and all I could make out about the waitress was the flat black of velvet, the gold trim on the hem and chest of her strapless dress. The vague image of Jen dancing at a different club, spinning and spinning, her hair like a blonde cape. "I love dancing," she yelled over the loud music. We danced and sometimes I just stood back as the crowd churned around us. It dizzied me. The dark and flash of strobe lights—there and gone in fractions of moments and ghost images in my darkened brain of her between the light pulses. The crowd cheered as some new disco song flooded the place.

I hated Disco more than Jazz. I blamed the Cold War for Disco. People had just given up on the future with the threat of nuclear annihilation; just dance and snort coke and fuck random strangers. But without the Cold War we wouldn't have Punk Rock, so you have to take the good with the bad.

*

They swirl and dance and head for the bar and get drinks. The night whirled in and out as time clocked on. Jen leans close to Hess's ear. "You want to head back to the room? You got a busy day tomorrow. Business in the morning and the drive to Vegas."

Hess stares at her, then looks at his watch. "After another drink. It's only ten."

Jen tugs at Hess's arm. "You know I been thinking. Why do Central American guerillas want to trade guns for cocaine? I would think it would be the other way around."

"You'd think. But Todd's got it figured."

Hess looks across the dance floor at all the people dancing and grinding as his vision fades to black.

*

I didn't really think about her slurred words. I became cut loose and blacked out. It amused me to think of my unconscious body functioning loose in the city. I might as well have been dead. I could have been on the dark side of the moon. I imagined myself as Hess the astronaut, drifting outside the ship with my shop-guy wrench, working on something. But because I am a fuck up without an engineering degree I lose my grip on the tool, and it floats away. I grab after it. Because I am incapable of planning ahead or considering the real weight of consequences, I jump free of the spacecraft. I grasp after the wrench, floating above the earth. I wonder if I'd have enough air to last until gravity skipped me off the atmosphere like a sorry meteor.

CHAPTER SIXTEEN

Hess wakes, twisted in the hotel sheets. CNN blasts with footage of Desert Shield. He looks around puzzled at first. Through the open curtains the city lights still wait for dawn.

Jen had taken a shower, and Hess watches as she starts to dry her hair in the nude. "You're better than CNN."

The acne on her cheeks stands out. The light makes the water on her fake-baked skin shimmer, and Hess gets up and runs his tongue along her shoulder. His cottony mouth sucks up the water, but the chemical taste leaves him thirstier.

She flips her hair as she bends over. The blow dryer whirs, drowning out the news. Jen backs against Hess and starts grinding.

"You'd better hurry."

Hess's brain hurts, but he gets an erection anyway. As they have sex, he stops to call room service for a couple of bloody Marys.

*

Hess starts the BMW. Jen fiddles with her camera. She wears a black mini-skirt and a sheer black blouse over a gold lame bra. "Hold on." She produces her compact, flips it open. She grins. "A little toot before breakfast."

"Sounds good to me. Keep you from slumping over in your eggs. That wouldn't be a pretty sight."

"Everything I do is pretty."

"Even pissing in the street."

Hess takes a baggie of coke out of his jacket pocket and dishes out a little onto the compact mirror. Jen chops it with a razor into two fine rows.

She hands him the compact and he holds it in his lap. She takes a cut down drinking straw and leans into his lap and snorts one line. She massages his crotch before sitting up.

She takes the compact from him and holds it in her lap.

"My turn." Hess leans into her lap and as he inhales, works his fingers into her.

Jen moans. She cocks her hips and opens her eyes. "Hey. We aren't alone."

She points with her chin and Hess looks.

A homeless guy in a filthy jean jacket and surf shorts stands next to a garbage can eating an apple core, staring at them through the windshield. Hess rolls down the window.

Hess yells, "Move along if you don't want an ass beating."

He grins a wretched grin of nasty teeth and wanders off. Jen squints and rubs her red-rimmed nose. "You looking to get arrested? Cool out."

"That bum ain't going to do shit."

"Yeah, but he might." She points at a well-dressed businessman a couple cars down, loading a large suitcase into the trunk of a Mercedes.

"Whatever. He won't do shit over a bum. Get his shoes dirty or have to pony up a fiver."

Hess rolls the baggy with a couple of grams left and puts it in his jacket pocket.

"You're such a moron."

He smiles. "Yes, but I'm your moron. You ready? I want to be earliest birdiest."

"How ready does one need to be to sit and be beautiful in a diner? You're the one who'd better be careful."

Hess slips the BMW into gear. "Don't get all 'I can't fuck this up' on me. If I'm not back by nine, shit's gone wrong. Cover your ass, get a cab, and light out for the John Wayne. I'll page you in the American terminal."

Jen rolls her eyes. "Don't worry. I'm smarter than you look."

Hess laughs.

"You know, you really shouldn't go. We should just hit the highway back to Vegas. Still weird they'd come up here for dope."

"Can't do it. I owe Todd."

"The whole thing is flaky. If you go you should tell him to back off. Just let it go."

"Look, things are in motion. I got to follow through."

"Even if it's stupid and will get you killed or arrested? What the fuck did he do to make you even risk being late for court tomorrow?"

Hess backs the BMW out. "You let me worry about that."

Jen turns up the jazz.

CHAPTER SEVENTEEN

Jen sits at the coffee shop counter. Her camera sets next to a cup of coffee and a half eaten pastry. A waitress wipes down the counter in front of Jen with a dishtowel.

An old timer wearing a fedora and an almost black purple velvet suit sips coffee a couple of stools down. A walking stick with a pearl top leans against the counter. Others eat breakfast in booths.

Jen toys with her swallow charms, gazing off.

The waitress stops in front of Jen. "Now that's pretty."

Jen blinks and for a second doesn't realize the waitress is talking to her, but then smiles. "I'm kind of bummed that I never made it down to San Juan Capistrano."

"To see the swallows?"

"Yeah. For centuries they've come back to nest where they hatched."

"That's something all right."

The old timer shifts in his seat to angle himself toward Jen. "When I first came here during W W-Two there were a lot more swallows."

Jen smiled at him. "That a fact."

"Sure enough," he said. The chair squeaks when he turns back to his coffee.

Jen spins the saucer with the pastry. She picks a flake of frosting off and puts it on her tongue, savoring it. "My last name is Swallows. I've always had an affinity for them. You know they fly continents to make it back home."

The old timer coughs.

Jen continues. "But they don't do it alone. As a flock, a family. The males build their nests from mud in the spring. They always come back. Jen realizes it's the right time to go back Manhattan, those soaring cliffs of skyscrapers that stifled her as a girl.

Jen stirs her coffee and the spoon clacks. She blows across the liquid surface before sipping from her coffee cup. The old-timer and waitress watch her.

Jen sets the cup on the counter. "True hope is swift, and flies with swallow's wings .... What good's a life without hope?"

The old timer taps his cane. "Indeed. What good?"

The bell on the door rings. Hess walks in. Blood streams down the side of his face. All conversations and eating stops. Only the sound of canned music, traffic, and a helicopter fill the emptiness.

Jen gasps. "What's wrong?"

Hess surveys the coffee shop in a second. "We got to bail."

"All right. Let me pay up."

Hess throws a few bills on the counter. "Now."

Before Jen can gather her things Hess pushes out the door, the bell ringing behind him.

CHAPTER EIGHTEEN

On the street in front of the diner, Jen gets out and pauses. "You sure?"

"Yeah." Jen shuts the car door and steps away. Hess ejects the jazz CD and tosses it in the backseat. He pulls out a CD case from the band that played the night he and Jen met. *Songs to Save the Soulless*, with the band's name, Napalm Cocktail, written in fire, framing Death with a martini shaker, serving burning people at a bar.

He slips the CD out and slides it into the player. The speakers blare the punk band's version of "Onward Christian Soldiers" Hess head-bangs to it as he drives and air plays instruments.

He passes the parking lot not seeing Todd's pick up. He drives several blocks away and parks and walks to the parking lot and notices the van with Frank and Angel. He checks his watch. Two hours before show time. Hess stops and lights a cigarette and gets an L.A. Weekly out of newspaper rack. Hess walks past the parking lot, across the bike path and over to the beach. He sits on a bench. He pretends to read. Joggers and bicyclists go by. Seagull cries punctuate the rolling surf.

The two in the van look half asleep. They chat and lean back in their seats, drink coffee, and eat some pastries. Hess gets up and moves to another bench just out of sight of the van. If it left he'd see, but now they couldn't see him. He smokes and waits.

An hour and forty-five minutes later, Todd pulls his pick-up into the lot and parks, backing into a space.

Hess folds his paper and waits a few minutes before getting up. The surf crashes against the beach as a helicopter flies just off the coast. Hess watches to see if it's a cop chopper.

Todd and Woo talk, oblivious as stones.

*

I first moved to L.A. out of high school. I didn't have
the typical Hollywood reason for coming here. I drove
from that shitty mining town because some guys who'd
graduated the year before me had a big house and needed
a tenant. I followed my impulse into emergency medicine
and found it cool to work. I'd go out to see Brother Weed
and Sister Speed every month or so and hang out. I drifted
away from the gun culture of my family and the guys at
the house. They had guns, but shit, it was like mounting a
major expedition to go shooting from the city. Not like at
home where in five minutes you could be blasting the shit
out of the desert. I wondered if the urge to arm myself
would come back. The strange eroticism of forged steel in
recoil, smoke filled sinuses as sharp as sex, and the sublime
joy of a bullet splintering steel, glass, wood, or bone. For
a time I walked in Sister Speed's philosophy, but the other
thing was deep inside me, installed by family, society, and
life to rise up like some dark sea monster. Would Uncle A
win out over Sister Speed?

*

Hess crosses the bike path and begins to walk toward the
Todd's pick-up.

Hess reaches the pick-up and leans on the driver side
door. The window is down. Todd smiles. "Hey, man, good
to see you."

"Yeah. How's the hand, Woo?"

Woo flexes his hand. "Fucking hurts."

"Good. You deserved it."

Todd slugs Hess on the shoulder. "You ready, man?
Where's the shit?"

Hess looks at his watch. "Another fifteen minutes?

Todd "Yeah. Woo says they're going to meet that
other guy right over there."

Todd points to a bench where a homeless guy plays a guitar with only three strings on it.

"You guys walk around at all?" Hess watches the homeless guy to see if he wasn't a cop.

"Nah, got here and parked."

Woo adds, "To see if they got here early."

"So, you two vacationers didn't see the van parked behind that motel over there?" Hess points across the street. Todd twists around to see. Woo leans forward.

Todd leans back into his seat. "Just a van, man."

Hess shakes his head. "A van with a mean looking white guy sporting a crew cut and a guy that might pass for a Central American guerilla."

Todd looks back at the van again. "Nah way, man."

"Yah way, man. They been sitting like that for the last two hours."

"Two hours?" Woo says, "They must be the contact."

"Hey Woo," Hess says, "that the guy you fronted the coke to?

He licks his lips and he looks down. "No."

Hess leans back from the truck and looks around. "Really? Where the fuck is that guy?"

Woo avoids Hess's stare. "I don't know man."

"What the fuck, Woo." Hess points at Todd. "So we got the gun guys over there, but not Woo's fuck-up. This stinks of a set up. I'm out."

Todd sits up straight. "No way. Woo's guy is solid."

Hess steps away. "No, Woo's guy's not solid. And why would a Central American guerilla group want to trade guns for coke?"

"How do I know, man? They want to make a deal, I want to make some money... Are you backing out on me? You owe me—"

"I don't owe you arrested or killed. Your stupid ass is being set up, and I'm out. The only reason I came was to get you gone before you do something they can actually arrest you for. Consider this a favor. Drive off. Now."

The van creeps out a little bit.

Todd pounds the steering wheel. "It might be them. Where's the shit, Hess?"

"Close. I'm not carrying that much coke around until I know they're not cops or thieves."

"That's bullshit man. This could backfire. You fucker."

Hess nods toward the van. "Here they come. Early I might add. I'll post up behind the truck to keep an eye out. You two assholes try not to fuck it up."

Hess walks around behind the truck.

The van crosses the street and into the parking lot and stops perpendicular in front of Todd's truck.

The driver's side cargo door slides open. Angel points an AK-47 at Todd and Woo. Frank hangs his arm out the window and taps a Beretta 9mm semi-auto against the door.

Frank smiles big. "Good morning, bitches. Hand over the dope."

On the street parked about half a block away as the van pulls up to Todd's truck, Freddy sits in the passenger seat of his Caddy scanning the parking lot with a set of binoculars. The NFL lineman sized skinhead sits behind the wheel. The other two are in the back.

Freddy yells, "Go! Go! Go!"

Freddy grabs a Molotov cocktail from the floorboard.

The Caddy lurches forward. The engine roars and the tires smoke and squeal. They cut off traffic. Horns blare.

Freddy yells over the engine. "Clip the corner of the van with the bumper."

They jump the curb into the parking lot, careening in a semi-circle before accelerating toward the van.

Hess draws his pistol. The revving Caddy causes the others to look. Hess levels his pistol as the Caddy crunches the van's rear right corner, launching it into a spin. The AK-47 blasts. Hess drops to the asphalt.

The Caddy screeches to a stop. Freddy jumps out and lights the Molotov cocktail.

Frank face plants the steering wheel and slumps in the seat.

Freddy holds the flaming bottle like a side-armed pitcher. "I warned you, Todd."

Hess gets back to his feet.

Todd kicks the door of his truck open and leaps out. "Fuck you." Todd jerks his revolver from his waistband and fires. The bullet hits the Molotov cocktail, tearing away part of Freddy's hand.

The gas and flame splash up Freddy's arm. He screams. "Fuck oh! Fuck! Oh fuck!"

The other skinheads stop. Angel jumps from the van. The AK-47 rips as he sprays them with bullets.

Hess levels his pistol at him, but hesitates. He stares down the slide. The guy turns toward Todd.

Todd stops. "Let's get the fuck out of here!"

Woo gets out of the truck, reaching behind his back. The AK-47 pops, stitching Woo's chest with bullets. As he falls a small semiautomatic pistol clatters on the asphalt. Hess drops steps and kneels at Woo's side. He thinks, too many holes in too many important places. Woo's mouth works, the air rasping and gurgling. Blood and more blood.

Todd squeezes the trigger twice, hitting Angel twice in the chest. "Fuck you."

Woo's mouth quits moving, and he stares into the sky. Hess takes off running. At the street Brother Weed picks him up in an old blue Subaru wagon. They drive away and merge into traffic.

Todd gets in his truck and speeds off.

Hess turns to see if anyone noticed him getting into the Subaru. In the parking lot Freddy runs as if he's

holding the Olympic torch and smoke hangs around the
cars like a marine fog.

Brother Weed glances glassy eyed at Hess's ear. "Your
ear is bleeding."

Hess touches his ear and looks at his bloody fingers.
"Now ain't that the shit."

Brother Weed rolls to a stop at a light. "By the
slimmest of spaces we live."

*

Later I'd think of a bump. Of Woo full of chest wounds.
Of me dropping, of kneeling, of living. For every action
there is a reaction. Woo reaches for a gun and gets killed.
My gun was already out, but the guy didn't notice me.
I could've popped him clean. A body at rest I suppose.
But the reaction. Not to shoot, but to kneel and see if
I might save a life. Many times I dreamed floating away
from a spacecraft to chase a tool I'd let fly. Adrift above
the Earth. In space only the fabric of the suit lets you live.
The seam in the suit with a slow leak, and below me all the
air in the world, if I can only get back. Time to get back.

CHAPTER NINETEEN

Marla sits in one of the beds in a cheap motel, smoking. The television blares a morning game show's cheers and whoops of the audience and contestants.

The door flies open, slamming against the doorstop, startling Marla. Frank stumbles in. He kicks the door closed behind him.

Marla pulls the sheet up around her neck.

Blood streams from a knot on Frank's forehead. "We got to get the fuck out. We have to hide. Fucking set up. Your friend killed Angel." He grabs a daypack and stuffs his clothes and shaving kit into it. "Get your skinny ass up. Fucking van's wrecked. We wait here and we're fucking dead."

Marla shakes her head. "Todd was in on it. He wouldn't have shot."

Frank keeps moving.

Marla watches him. "No fucking way. Okay, no worries. No one knows where we are. We can ride this out. Besides we didn't kill him. We can—"

Frank stomps toward Marla and jerks her up by the shoulders. Her red panties like warning light against her pale skin. "Angel has some very bad friends and family who don't know the meaning of 'we didn't kill him.' They just need somebody's blood to make it even."

Frank drops her on the bed. "You've always been a stupid slut. I don't know why I let you talk me into this."

CHAPTER TWENTY

Hess drives on surface streets headed for the highway. His hands on the wheel at ten and two. Jen stares out the passenger window. "You've got to be fucking kidding me."

"Fucking believe it. Todd fucked the dog on this."

"We just got to get back." She gets the cigarette case from Hess's jacket pocket.

"I am going to visit some Old Testament retribution on Todd. Hell and fire and damnation."

She lights the cigarettes, hands one to Hess. Puffs and blows smoke, fidgets.

"No way. I don't believe Marla's involved. Just don't."

Hess looks her up and down. "What the fuck does that mean? That little fairy girl say something I should know about?"

Jen blows smoke. Her lips tight for a moment. "No, not like that. Okay, whatever. I'll see when we get back." She throws the cigarette out the window. "Let me clean up your ear."

*

I still dream of being an astronaut, skipping across the surface of the moon. It wasn't until I was wearing county orange watching the news in the common room that I found out that little fairy girl had tried to double cross Todd. Whoever she threw in with ran her up on angel dust and dumped her into Mission Bay. I saw them in my sleep. Marla drifting through space, dead, in a sundress, her face blue and her lips black, past. Her eyes stare, wide and blue like burning gas lit by the flaming sun. Jen cries, sweeping a table clear of magazines and a vase. She shatters dishes against the wall, collapses on the couch, as she clasps the swallow pendant Marla gave her. In the dream I swim in space, trying to get to Jen, but we are too far apart. No matter how hard I flail in a vacuum, I went nowhere. Only the gravity of the earth to pull me back home.

*

The BMW speeds east down the highway, through Baker, CA. Jen looks through her camera viewfinder and snaps pictures of the sign Gateway to Death Valley.

"They bused me from that mine down here to go to school here."

Jen looks around at the smattering of restaurants and gas stations and motels surround by desert. "That must've sucked."

"It did. That was after we went to live with Uncle A. Felt like I was being exiled."

"You were. Exiled by a grateful nation."

"It's how I met Todd. Total fucking accident. He was a pretty good second baseman."

I'd never see Todd again. The marines got hard up enough to take him back and away he went. During his first tour, he sent a letter to my attorney, figuring the attorney-client privilege would protect him. For some reason he confessed about his plan and how he and Woo staged the whole thing to get into business. None of that deal ever got tied back to me. To the cops it was open and shut. Skinheads fucked a deal up with guerillas and everybody died. While I drove toward Vegas, the cops were busy shaking down Nazis. If you're going to have a scapegoat and someone take a fall for you, I couldn't think of a better bunch of assholes to do it.

CHAPTER TWENTY-ONE

The door from my apartment slams closed. In this rundown neighborhood I lock it up. Criminals are everywhere. I walk to my '88 Trooper II and get in. The heat swelters inside, and I think about Woo and when Todd and I thumped on him. It's not just because of today, but I am always reminded it was then that my life broke from one way to another. I drive through Vegas, and the heat has most people hunkered down inside. A few people stroll about, but damn few. I don't go past any of the casinos or the touristy part of town. I could be in any town America among the houses and apartment complexes I motor by.

I never made it to see Grandma. Prison made sure she died before I could visit. No miracle to keep her hanging on. Reconcile the past with the present I guess that's one reason I decided to go to Todd's funeral. And to make sure the bastard was dead.

The funeral home hung with yellow ribbons and American flags. Bikers lounge around on Harley-Davidsons. A few have the MIA/POW flag flying on whip antennae. A little bit away there are some war protestors and the Westboro Baptist Church with God Hates Fags signs and other inflammatory slogans.

I shake my head and walk into the funeral home.

*

In a way, Todd's story became what he dreamed about when he thought about my father. Making a difference in people's lives. I heard the story and imagined an older Todd, wearing full battle-rattle, with other marines riding in a Humvee. They drive down a street in Fallujah with another Humvee ahead of them. They turn a corner and a crowd has gathered along the sidewalk. A man throws a little girl into the street in front of the speeding Humvee, but the driver cannot brake fast enough and hits her.

Marines pile out and the insurgents spring the ambush. Bullets pop and whizz. Todd scoops up the little girl.

Todd yells over the noise of gunfire. "She's alive. Let's get to an aid station."

The other marines continue firing. The turret gun pounds out bullets.

"Fucking now!" The marines pile into the Humvee and speed off to an aid station. Todd runs in.

Todd has the girl in his arms, his M-4 slung on his side. There are marines being operated on. A lance corporal approaches Todd with hands up as if to slow Todd. "Whoa now, Marine. Where do you think you're going?"

"This girl needs help."

"Okay, we can't help civilians here. You have—"

Todd switches the girl to one arm and brings his rifle to bear on the corporal. The corporal stops. "Who do I start killing to get her help? You first?"

The corporal backpedals.

A major in doctor's scrubs cuts in. "We can do this. Take it easy, Marine. Stand down."

A woman takes the little girl from Todd. "Don't worry. We'll take care of her."

Todd lowers rifle. "Okay."

Todd emerges from the aid station. A single gunshot rings out. A sniper on a rooftop scrambles to get away. Marines return fire. Todd drops dead, not even a little alive.

*

Like when my father disappeared in the early seventies, no one outside the family and his unit cared. It was the end of a war when the shininess of it had worn off, and the only people who cared were merchants selling patriotic wares. We had made it an honor to fight in pointless wars and somehow connect it to that basic American impulse of freedom. My dad disappeared and America shrugged its huge shoulders — so fucking what. What's on TV?

*

In the funeral home, I make my way to the casket. Mourners whisper. Three marines sit in the front row in dress blues.

Older Todd lies in a coffin, his uniform is immaculate with ribbons and medals and an NCO sword reflects light.

Some people mill about. An old woman in a black polyester dress walks up. "A true American hero."

I smile at her. "Yeah, he was a true American all right."

The old woman sniffs. "A shame."

She has the look of someone I may know, but I can't place her. I knew a lot of people in Todd's family and she didn't strike me. I saw his mom and step-dad #10 in the front row and assorted others. "How are you related to Todd?" I ask the old woman.

"I'm not. I just go to funerals for our heroes to show my respects."

Her face had real grief etched into it, and I wondered what ghosts drove her to funerals. Does she fear losing the country and her home? Does she wake in the darkness at night when she lies in bed? Does she go from some past loss, a father, husband, brother, sister, mother, or is it a calling for her to be there for the country? One stranger without an agenda just to mourn the dead? She daubs her eyes again. Does she go because so many don't?

I tied on the black tie for more than the mourner of the dead. It is a combination of all the colors, but an absence of light. It is everything and nothing at the same time. This is what the soul is. Uncle Allen suggested they write in Todd's obit in the Baker paper: local douche bag dies a valiant, but pointless death. The editor wanted nothing to do with it.

I look over the body. "You still owe me money." I

put the letter in the coffin. His confession will go into the ground when he does. If the ancients are right and what we have in our caskets makes it into to the afterlife with us then he can reread it and show it around. He'll be a funny figure with his uniform and sword and evidence he was a back stabbing asshole. Who am I kidding? This life is the only shot you got. He died and now he is nothing. Maybe we'd be less inclined to blow each other up if we knew the wages were a black void. I fucking doubt it, but a boy can wonder.

The minister moves in front of the coffin. "Let everyone please take their seats."

I continue down the aisle. The old woman follows me and pauses before taking a seat in the last row. Her dress rumples like crumpling papers. "Aren't you staying?"

I soften. "No ma'am. I'm afraid I just don't see the point." I tip my head. As I start to leave an old man in a kilt and the full outfit blows "Amazing Grace" through a set of bagpipes. His bluish skin sucked up the candlelight as his cheeks puffed, and blew air and his short inhalations were the gasps of a man already dead.

I am dizzy.

I am in the desert.

CHAPTER TWENTY-TWO

My fucking ear stung. I slouched in the seat as the desert swiped by in panoramic brown. Jazz played, weaving notes with the air-conditioning. Jen took some pictures at a passing memorial.

"Sorry we don't have enough time to stop."

Jen rolled down the window, leaned out and took another photograph. Her skirt climbed high and I caressed the backs of her thighs and run a hand up to her crotch. "I think I found the Promised Land."

She eased back into her seat. She reached into my jacket pocket and got the cigarette case. She lit two between moans. She leaned back and cocked her hips toward my hand. "We fly by with no time memorialize."

Jen and I came up over a rise before Cima Road as the highway started climbing into some mountains. A VW Beetle was upside down about fifty feet off the black top. A guy staggered by the car. We pulled into the emergency lane. I clicked the hazards, and we got out. I had a déjà vu moment of exiting the ambulance.

The man by the car was fuzzy and out of focus like a ghost, floating in the heat waves. He reached us and was yammering Spanish. A Mexican. Blood dripped down his forehead.

"He says his wife is dead, but his daughter is hurt, knocked out," Jen said.

I stopped and stared at her, said, "You speak Spanish?"

"Spanish, yeah, and Russian, Japanese and French."

"No shit, I never knew that."

"You public school kids think you're so fucking smart."

The Mexican guy was frantic, pulling at my sleeve, so I had to brush him off as I walked. Steam rose off the back of the car, and one of the tires still spun. It smelled like antifreeze, oil, and dirt.

A woman's legs stuck out from under the car, and I thought about the Wizard of Oz—couldn't help it—red shoes. I stopped and thought, What the fuck am I doing? I have to get out of here. I shivered. Instead of turning back I walked on. The teenaged daughter lay knocked out on her back, breathing raspy breaths. Pink blood stained her white blouse in the middle of her rib cage. A fucking sucking chest wound. I couldn't believe it. I could fix this with some plastic and tape and she would live a motherless daughter, but live.

"Ask Paco if he's got any tape." I knelt next to the girl. Her cheeks were smooth, and her forehead had a couple of pimples, but her skin was brown and alive. I heard the Mexican guy ratchet up his voice. He stood behind me by the car. I yelled, "Jen, does he have any tape?" I reached to unbutton her blouse.

The Mexican guy yelled and Jen said, "He says keep your hands off his daughter."

"What?" I couldn't believe it. What did this fuck know about saving lives? I reached into my jacket pocket pulled out the baggy. It'd fit right over the hole and seal it. A little tape to hold the plastic to her skin—she'd breathe. "Tell him I'm saving her life."

The pearl button was awkward, like the hole was too small. My fingers fumbled with it as it slipped in my grip.

I dumped the coke on the ground, wanting the plastic to be flat and get a perfect seal. With my other hand I tore her blouse open, tired of messing it. Buttons popped away, glinting like shooting stars.

Sweat dripped into my eyes, and I wiped my forehead. Jen quit talking to Paco, her feet apart, and handbag dangling from her hand, gorgeous in the sun. "What the fuck do you think you're fucking doing?" Jen asked.

Paco really started going off behind me.

I smoothed blood the color of cotton candy away from the puncture. "Tell Paco get some tape and quit shouting that gibberish at me."

"You moron. I can't fucking believe you. The cops will be coming," she said.

"Jesus," I said as I took a shot to the back of the head. It was weak—my Ray Bans never even came loose. The guy had never hit another man in his life. I stood up and clocked him. The Mexican sprawled out into a bush like he was trying to get out of a net. A screeching black bird pecked at the woman's legs. I jumped at it, flapped my arms and hollered, "Get out, you fucker." It hopped away a couple of feet. I scooped up a rock as I ran, hurled it. The bird flapped into the air.

An eighteen-wheeler came over the rise of highway and its brakes came on, squealing and smoking. Huge rolls of steel lined its trailer like mirrors exploding silver rays. I walked back to where the girl lay. I couldn't make out a thing Jen said.

My shadow fell over the girl, and I couldn't hear her breathe. Her bra shone in the sun. I knelt down. She had a gold chain with a gold Virgin Mary that I moved out of the way to check her pulse. My fingers found her carotid artery. I kept my fingers there and nothing. I held my fingers there longer waiting for the soft beating. It was faint, fuck, so faint.

Jen started yelling that we needed to get in the car before it was too late. "Cops, drugs and you have court in a couple of hours." It was all a buzz and clatter around me. I tried to focus.

The pink froth of bubbles oozed out of her chest. With my hand, I smoothed the blood away, again, and fitted the bag over it. Her flesh was warm and soft. Her broken ribs flexed and crinkled under the pressure of my palm. I winced. Jen talked Spanish again, and as I looked I saw Paco coming back at me.

"He says get your drugs and filthy hands away from his daughter," Jen said. She pointed to the baggy in my hand.

I stood and knocked him back down with a palm to his chest. That's when I saw an explosion of lights as the truck driver hit me from behind. He had hit someone before. I'd been so focused on the girl, I'd forgotten about him. I tumbled forward. I came up, feeling blood and heat and the tingling of crushed nerves. Son of a bitch broke my sunglasses.

He yelled, "What do you think you're doing to that little girl?"

I scrambled to my feet and pointed at the truck driver and said, "You fucker, I'm trying to save this girl's fucking life, that's what."

His white tee shirt was dingy in the sun. He backed away and his eyes widened like he'd been given a bad fortune. Jen moved behind him. My eyes hurt a lot, and I squinted.

Paco jumped on my back, and I flipped him off. Fucker. I turned and kicked Paco in the ribs to keep him sucking air awhile.

"Jesus if these people would leave me alone I could get this done."

"What do you expect? You look like a zombie in a suit molesting a little girl. Let's go."

A couple of birds were back pecking on the woman. "Not till I patch this girl up," I said. "I can save her." The highway patrol blazed up over the rise, screeching to a halt, roller lights flashing. I looked at Jen. "Just get me some tape. I can do this. The cops will know what I'm doing. They'll see and if they don't I'll show them my old card from my ambulance days. We're a lock."

I limped after the plastic bag where it had blown into a bush. I retrieved it, went and knelt next to the girl. My foot hurt. I brushed the dirt off the plastic bag, shook it, and placed it over the girl's puncture wound. I felt the plastic suck against her body and held it as steady as I could, though my hands were shaking and my knees ached. My whole body started to feel like one giant broken tooth. It began in my stomach, and rippled out. I looked up at Jen. The cops were getting out of their car behind her.

She stared at me. Her hip cocked, with her hand on it, she stood in her heels. The wind blew her hair around and it looked like rays of light were shooting out of her head. She wasn't even sweating. I said, "After you get the tape, you could get your camera. These could be some cool pictures for your collage. The pre cross and flower scene."

"You're a fucking moron," she said.

The cops came up and after a quick glance around, drew their pistols what with the trucker shouting and Paco pointing and shouting, "Drogas." Even I could interpret that. Fuckers. I tried to tell the cops what I was doing, but it was all shouting and gun pointing.

The cops yelled at me to get away from the girl. I kept my hand on her wound. "No, I need tape."

"Get the fuck back. I will shoot you." He stressed will as if to say he's put holes in something besides paper targets.

"Kill me and kill her, assholes."

The cops looked back and forth at each other.

"She's got a sucking chest wound," I said.

One holstered his gun and knelt opposite of me. "I'll hold it and you back away."

He slid his hand next to mine, and I thought about how soft his fingers were. I put my hands in the air, my job done.

"Tape her," I said.

The other cop pushed me face down, cuffed and frisked me. "You have the right to remain silent, use it."

Sand stuck to my face. My suit was trashed—stickers, dirt, pea gravel, and blood. I was glad I wasn't wearing a tie. Cactus stickers pricked my chest, and my Bruno Magli shoes were scuffed to shit. A county cop showed up and was looking at the girl. Jen took pictures of me. I told them check my wallet for my EMT license. One of them got it and said, "You can't be fucking serious. This thing's been expired for years." They rolled me over. The sky was a stark blue. A rock poked into the small of my back.

The cops sat me up and walked over to talk to the county cop. One walked back over to inform me that there was a warrant out for my arrest from Nevada for assault on Jen's ex to put on top of violating the conditions of my bail. The trucker walked back to his rig. Paco stood by the car, dazed, while Jen ghosted her way through the bushes around the accident, taking photo after photo. Kneeling, standing, from different angles and directions—the car, birds, the mother's legs, Paco, the cops, me. And the girl. Jen lingered over her. No one seemed to care. After picking her way through the desert, she knelt next to me. She reached into my jacket and pulled out my cigarette case, and got two out. She lit them and wedged one between my lips. She coughed, smoked and smiled. "Listen," she said, "I'm leaving." Her voice sounded rough.

I blinked through the smoke.

"I'll get your bail, but afterwards I'm headed to New York."

"I won't be able to go until all the court stuff is settled."

"I don't want you to go."

I shrugged as best I could.

"I been talking about it awhile now, but you don't pay attention. I want more."

"We have a good thing here."

"Vegas is killing me. The drugs, drinking. The night and day living. There's more things I need to do." She smiled. The glitter on her face sparkled, but her eyes were shaded and flat. "You were fun, but I've got to go."

"What are you going to do?"

She gave me the look like I was stupid for asking.

"Give modeling another shot?"

She shook her head. "I'm not a model."

I nodded. "That jazz, you know? I still don't like it."

She smiled. She stood, her long legs arcing above me, and tugged her skirt down. I wished I could reach my hand up it.

What else could I have said? A party always broke up. But as she walked away I called her back. She turned. "Sure we can't go to New York together? The change might do us good. Like 'Thunder Road,' blow this town full of losers."

She shook her head. "'Thunder Road's' about high school kids. Besides, you and I can't exist without Vegas."

She left. My high was wearing off. I wanted to sleep. I thought about calling her back and telling her about the girl I killed in L.A., but that would have been a poseur thing to do, some pathetic effort to keep her. When I was in the joint I read this poet and he said, "There are more mysterious things than the human heart, but I don't know what they are." The past was one big wreck anyway and useless to worry about.

I didn't blame her for the assault rap I had to beat. I didn't have to go over and punch that guy, but I did.

All I needed to worry about was staying out of jail and figure what next after that. Jen'd go on to that art dealer.

I saw a profile in an art mag I started to subscribe to and imagined being there. In a black evening gown, Jen moves amongst people, drinking wine, talking with others. Along the walls hang Jen's Memorial Photographs. Some of the accident photographs hang interspersed. It made me laugh that she used the one of her pissing behind

the mini-mart and hung it over the reception book. My
name was inscribed on a gold plate next to it. It'd take
her sixteen years, but Jen made it to Capistrano and shot
photos of the swallows at the old mission. She had quit
wearing glitter and used very light make-up. Her skin
cleared up when she got off coke and away from me.
Around her neck always hung the swallow charm Marla
gave her. When I found out about her and Marla it was
like one of those ah-ha moments, of course they were
lovers. No matter. She found her way home.

I spit the cigarette out. My mouth felt like I'd sucked
a battery dry. I wanted a drink and a little coke. Dead
looking mountains stuck out of the eastern horizon. In
front of me Jen chatted to the cops, the light glinting off
all their metal surfaces. Paco kept shooing the screeching
black birds away from his wife and those fucking glittering
red shoes. I smelled sweat, blood and dust. The Mexican
girl I saved looked like she was sleeping. Her skin, smooth
and brown, the texture of an ironed silk shirt. Pretty.
Everything was going to be o-fucking-kay. Closing my eyes
against the sun, I nodded off under the paling sky, there in
the desert and dreamed of flight.

ACKNOWLEDGEMENTS

I want to extend my gratitude to Kimberly Verhines at the SFASU Press who saw enough value in my fiction to invest time and effort into to the production of this book. Also thanks to those others involved with the production, Shaina Hawkins and Andre Fleuette for their great work on the cover layout. You both are awesome. I need to thank Claire Davis, Kim Barnes, Mary Clearman Blew, Luke Whisnant, Daniel Orozco, Ben Fountain, Lan Samantha Chang, and all of the living and dead writers whose words inspired and taught me from the page. I appreciate my fellow students of writing and impromptu writing groups over the years: Ida, Dean, Ryan A., AnnE, Lucas, Kelly, Andrea, Matt, Lisa, Kim, Annie, Mike, Ryan F., Linda, and the others. I want to give Heather Moe special thanks for reading the manuscript several times, helping with my blindness to typos. I must also mention the Jack Kent Cooke Foundation and my deep appreciation for the scholarship they saw fit to award me. Graduate school at the University of Idaho would have been insurmountable without their support. Thanks.